Also by the author:

Gone West
Defending Infinity

A CEREBRAL OFFER

Ken Janjigian

Livingston Press
University of West Alabama

Library of Congress Control Number 2020940008
Printed on acid-free paper
Printed in the United States of America by
Publishers Graphics

Hardcover binding by: HF Group
Typesetting and page layout: Sarah Coffey
Proofreading: Maddie Owen, Tricia Taylor, Jada Baxter,
Hilary Nelson, Mike Faulkner

Cover Design: Joe Taylor

Cover Art: Mark Ashkenazi

For Sharmistha
In memory of my father

A CEREBRAL OFFER

"It seemed like a matter of minutes when we began rolling in the foothills before Oakland and suddenly reached a height and saw stretched out ahead of us the fabulous white city of San Francisco on her eleven mystic hills with the blue Pacific and its advancing wall of potato-patch fog beyond, and smoke and goldenness in the late afternoon time."

—Jack Kerouac

1 — Mutiny at the Cabrillo

Dana and I co-owned the Cabrillo, a small independent theatre on the outskirts of San Francisco in the Richmond District, an area few tourists ever visited, save for some intrepid surfers and swimmers who braved the frigid and sometimes shark inhabited waters of nearby Ocean Beach. Richmond's most frequent visitor was actually the fog. It rolled in early and daily all white and pristine over the Marin County hills from the north, majestically crossing the bay as if it were on a mission before it grayed and slowed to a shrouded pause right above the Cabrillo. Richmondites would often get fog fever and flee across the Golden Gate just to get a desperate dose of sunshine. I, too, would occasionally join the solar seekers, but after a few sunny hours in Marin, I was more than ready to return to my foggy home.

Forgive my romanticism but let me confess this right up front: I had a profound, almost ethereal love of San Francisco. It was my adopted home during those liberating escape years of the early twenties, and I had no desire to ever live anywhere else. In fact, I had no intention of ever leaving our little Richmond enclave. Dana diagnosed the love as obsessive, perhaps even pathological. She had some new evidence too that reasonably supported her hypothesis.

I had recently developed gephyrophobia, a fear of bridges. I'd had a panic attack crossing the long and mighty Bay Bridge last year and ever since I refused to cross any bridge. I had to admit it was an odd and sudden psychic eruption at my age and made leaving peninsular San Francisco more complicated. Dana thought this was a cupcake of an analysis. My fear was simply a neurosis manifested from the confrontation of her desire to leave the city and my need to stay.

Maybe she had a point. But maybe something else was brewing...

Contrarily, Dana was very ready to leave San Francisco and move on from our movie theatre life. We lived above the Cabrillo in a small two-bedroom apartment. We could often hear sounds from late movies sneaking through the crevices in our floor or the white noise of crowd chatter as moviegoers lined up at the old-fashioned ticket kiosk on the street just below our bedroom. I loved those sounds, but Dana's initial intrigue with it all was fading fast into fatigue.

"It's like we have 500 roommates every night," she'd say.

We discussed compromises like moving to Marin, but the commute would be torture for a gephyrophobe. The same was true with going the other way to East Bay, its villainous and endless bridge mocking my commute. I agreed to go to therapy to address my new enemy but stopped after a few sessions that I deemed useless. We considered moving to another part of the city, but it was so expensive, and money was getting tight. The theatre was not doing well lately.

"Harry, the Cabrillo is going under. It's unsustain-

8   *Ken Janjigian*

able. I spoke to Mariana and she gave me all the gory fiscal details. We are basically surviving on my job now." Dana worked as a graphic designer downtown and she was right. Her salary was carrying us.

"It'll turn around," I promised many times. "The new changes need some time to take root. I'm optimistic."

"New changes? A bookstore and gallery for local writers and artists? Readings? Doubling down on bohemia is not exactly entrepreneurial ingenuity. It's delusional."

"The bar is doing very well," I countered. "That's factual, not delusional."

"It's only eight seats. Even if every seat is filled all day with big spender drunks, it's not enough."

"Give it a little time," I said, not really believing it myself. "I could always expand the bar."

Dana was shaking her head slowly in frustration. "Harry, it's a movie theatre, not a pub."

"It's more than a movie theatre."

"Look, Harry, I know you don't want to do this, but we need to sell the theatre before it cripples us, financially and otherwise."

That last word resonated, but I chose to ignore it. One battle at a time. "I'm not ready to give up."

"I get it and I admire the determination, but we won't have a choice soon. You lived your dream for a while. Who gets to do that for even a day?"

"What the hell would I do with myself without the Cabrillo?"

"Use your real talent like you were doing when we met. That's how you made it before."

And to the past we went. I was once a filmmaker. The key word being *once* because I only made one movie. My MFA thesis at San Francisco State was a biopic short on Jack Kerouac. One of the side projects with the thesis was to develop marketing materials to promote the film that all of us would soon be shopping to producers after graduation. The graphic design and film departments at State collaborated for this and that's how Dana and I met. She was also a second-year MA student and was assigned to create the poster for *Kerouac*. She dove into the project by carefully reading my screenplay, and even some of the Kerouac and Beat oeuvre for research. She came up with a great abstract collage that captured the heart and soul of the movie. The heart and soul of Jack.

We started dating soon after.

Not long after graduation a small indie production company bought the rights to the film, paying me to expand the short into a full-length version. I negotiated to direct as well, and Dana used her design talents on the set and in promotion. It was a memorable time for us that got even better when the film became a small hit, even garnering an Oscar nomination. I used the money from the film to buy the Cabrillo. To the surprise of many, especially Dana, I also had no interest in ever making another film. I was a contented one-hit wonder.

"Dana, we've been through this a million times. The muse is gone. I like what I do now much more than filmmaking."

"Harry, it's not working."

"It will. Ok, it might. Besides, this neighborhood and the regulars, the staff, they are like family. For both of us. The Cabrillo is my *Cinema Paradiso*. It's my life."

"Yes, your life, not mine."

"It used to be yours."

"Not really."

That was more or less the flow of all our conversations lately. We had mastered the art of patterns, irresolution, and dead ends. I knew I was on borrowed time financially with the Cabrillo and emotionally with Dana.

But I also had my own psychological analysis as well. I thought Dana was using the theatre and her desire to leave the city as a mask for what she really wanted to leave.

Me.

And perhaps I was wearing a similar mask.

We kept soldiering along our plateau for a while as couples do until it all changed one cataclysmic night when the plateau suddenly turned Himalayan upon the arrival of Jackson Halifax.

*　　*　　*

I was setting up for this week's reading. It was just our sixth one since launching the bookstore-gallery-bar plan. We only had room for about 20 seats and had not filled them all yet for any reading, but I expected tonight to be different. Our author was my old friend, Jackson Halifax, who was back in town after disappearing for a decade or so. I predicted our biggest crowd for our first author who wasn't really just local. Jackson had a good national following of loyal readers and had left his mark in San Francisco back in the day. While he had been gone a long time, Jackson was one of those people whose wake never quite dissipates.

He and I had been friends back in those heady emancipated days when I moved to San Francisco right after college. Days of gloriously vague plans and open road futures. I was working odd jobs and flirting with the Kerouac screenplay, but mostly I was studying Kerouac and the Beats while spending time with a coterie of artists of all kinds that hung out at a Judah Street café in the Sunset District, just across Golden Gate Park from the Cabrillo. The hippie owner of the café let us organize readings and informal, any-kind-of-art-goes gatherings that we fashioned after Dada. We romanticized it as our own personal Cabaret Voltaire. Those gatherings and the two issues of our journal, *Confluence*, caught the attention of a local paper, which ran an article that dubbed us the Sunsetters. The few moments of notoriety swelled our egos and deluded us into thinking we could be a new kind of Surrealism, but a movement we weren't. Most of us were just looking for individual success. Artists can be as greedy as Wall Streeters. Not long after the article, the Sunsetters were no more, splintering in different directions and varied pursuits, barely a footnote in the history of San Francisco art scene.

Jackson had been the de facto leader and had the most success of the group. He had written two well-received novels and was reading at the Cabrillo to promote his recently published third book, *195*. However, he had informed me via email that this would be his last novel. In Ken Kesey fashion he had decided to quit writing. His goal now was to "transcend the need to write in order to live a more authentic life." I replied with a lot of questions about this strange decision as well as trying to fill in the gaps of the last ten years. He ignored most of them but did say that he would be sticking around San Francisco for a while and asked if I knew a place he could crash. I offered him one of our two rentals, a small one-bedroom unit above the theatre and adjacent to our apartment that had just become vacant. He immediately pounced on the offer. We didn't talk price. I would take whatever he could spare per month, but I wasn't expecting much, if anything, knowing Jackson. Given our financial situation and Dana's antipathy for Jackson, I knew this wouldn't go over well with her.

*   *   *

Jackson showed up about ten minutes before the reading. All the seats were now taken and there were even a few people standing in the back. It was our best crowd yet. There were also more young women than usual, which was clearly due to Jackson. His novels had a cult following in the hip millennial crowd and he was a good-looking guy who always had women in pursuit. I also noticed a couple of guys settling into the back row that didn't fit our scene. I had seen them at the bar drinking a lot of beers, noisier than most of our patrons. They'd asked for Buds but settled for Anchor Steam after complaining about the price. They were middle-aged, down-and-out, pot-bellied Irish pub types who rarely came to our more highbrow, less divey scene. One had long but thinning red hair with a thick beard. He looked like an aging lumberjack. The other was all bald on top with a baby face contradicted by a gin blossomed nose.

As I was staring at them I heard, "Harry Gnostopolos, my favorite Greek in the whole world." I turned, noticing the tough guys turning that way, too.

"Jackson, my old friend, it's been too long!"

"Life gets in the way sometimes, but not anymore."

We hugged. Jackson had a great hug. Really pulled you in and squeezed. No bro hug mediated by a handshake to avoid the male loins getting too close. He didn't give a shit about a little ball and cock friction.

He still looked good, but I could see the ten-year absence in his face. His skin looked tanned though weathered with crow's feet emerging. While his eyes still had that puckish glimmer, darkness colored below.

When we pulled apart, Jackson locked both his hands on my shoulders, keeping the distance close. "Harry, really happy to be back home. We're gonna reconnect even better than before," Jackson said with a clearly intended devilish gaze.

"Great, I think."

"No need to worry, Harry. We're on a different raft in the thirties."

"What kind of raft is it?"

Jackson laughed. "A raft in progress, my brother. No need to play the whole hand now, but let me be upfront on the literary scene."

"Do tell."

"This is my first and last reading."

"Really? I know you said something about quitting writing, but I figured you'd still be pushing the book."

"Quitting the entire game, not just the words."

"Well, I am honored that we're the only reading, but don't you want the book to sell? Nothing wrong with royalties, right?"

"Not at all. Nothing wrong with money. Anti-money days are long gone. In fact, I am more about money than ever before, but that's the point. Readings won't do shit. Nickle and dime nonsense. There wasn't going to be any huge book tour with my publisher anyway. I'm just a mid-lister. So I told my agent I was doing one reading at the Cabrillo for my friend, Harry Gnostopolos. After that, the book would sell or flat line on its own. My agent will do the social media thing anyway. He'll post this reading so we hit the Fakebookers, Twitter birds, and all the other digital bullshit. One reading covers the globe, right? The millennials don't go to readings, do they? We'll hit 'em face to phone as they like it. Plus, we'll plug the Cabrillo."

"Great. Plug away. We need it."

"Consider it done."

"Hey, by the way, I loved *195*, man. You shouldn't stop writing. You're too good."

"Actually, this is the perfect time to stop. The trilogy is complete. Time to melt this armor."

"What armor? You were always practically naked," I said, laughing.

Jackson grinned. "Yeah, well, I fooled 'em all, even you. It's a sacred time, Harry. No room for lies."

"Yeah, but how does writing ruin it?" I persisted. "Your stuff is about seeking transcendence, not story-telling. You're one of the few that carried the Beat baton."

"I gave it a shot, but it's fraudulent. It's, ahhh, mendacity," he said with a wink that I didn't know how to interpret. "I want authentic and pure experience, not just gathering material for creation. Such a phony life. Wolfe said you can't go home again. It's really only writers that can't go home again. We're such a dishonest lot."

I shook my head. "Man, I don't buy that for a second."

"Harry, it's a ruse. Time to demystify youthful dreams. Anyway, whatever, we can wax and wander philosophical and artistic another day. Let's do this reading and then we'll really get into the important stuff."

"Sure thing. We've got our best crowd yet," I said, scanning the room again. There must have been 40 people crammed into this corner of the lobby area. The two oddballs still stood out. "A couple of strange cats though in the back row. Do you know them?"

Jackson turned, and took a good look as they did to him. The bearded one seemed angry, almost snarling, but it wasn't so clear from this distance.

"Ever seen them before?" Jackson asked, turning to me.

"Nope. First timers for sure."

"They seem familiar to me, but I can't place them.

This could be interesting. Be ready."

I furrowed my brow. "For what?"

"I don't know. How about we find out?" Jackson said with a wry grin, seemingly happy about the unpredictability of what might come next. He hadn't completely changed.

"Okay, we're late anyway. Do you want a beer, or glass of wine while you read?"

"Sure, how about a Malbec? Really into Malbecs these days. Down on Syrahs. Did you know I had a winery?"

I stared incredulously at Jackson, shaking my head. "You're kidding, right?"

"Not at all. Lots to talk about."

"Indeed," I said, pouring Jackson a glass of the only Malbec we had. I tried to focus on the task at hand—making my way to the podium and introducing Jackson.

"Cheers, old friend," I said as I headed to my emcee duties. Jackson raised his glass and nodded a thank you. As I set up my notes, I took another peek at the Irish Pub guys and saw that they were still staring at Jackson, who was now oblivious to them. He was swirling and sipping his wine as if he really was a vintner.

"Welcome everyone. Thank you for attending tonight's reading. We are delighted to have Jackson Halifax join us at the Cabrillo. I've actually just learned that this is a particularly special event since it's the only stop of Jackson's book tour. One and done just for us. So Jackson's first book was a tribute to San Francisco and its bohemian culture. It was a collection of short stories about artists of all kinds—writers, painters, poets, auteurs, journal keepers, dreamers, and searchers of every ilk all set in our city back in the pre-invasion days when artists could still eke out a living here."

I heard a little muffled talk from the back row and looked up at the suspicious guys. They glared at me and suddenly Babyface seemed more familiar, but I still couldn't place him. He shot me an odd, crooked smirk that I ignored in favor of pretending to look at my notes.

"Ahem, so Jackson's second novel moved to Prague and revolved around a coterie of eccentric artists, one of whom was battling insomnia and existential indecision. The new novel that he will read from tonight, *195*, is about a writer traveling the entire world, in fact literally all 195 countries trying to satiate wanderlust in one giant all-encompassing journey while simultaneously transcending the need to write. *195* is quite personal to Jackson because he lived much of novel by traveling to almost all of the world's 195 countries and, not only is this his last reading, but rumor has it that *195* is Jackson's last novel. Transcendence apparently accomplished."

I heard a few murmurs of surprise from the audience. One woman plaintively said, "That's terrible news."

"Ladies and gentlemen, please welcome my friend, the unpredictable Jackson Halifax, to the Cabrillo."

To a round of applause, Jackson calmly walked to the podium clutching his novel in one hand, the Malbec in the other. I decided to avoid eye contact with the back row and as I consciously looked at the front rows, a woman stole my attention. I had never seen her before. She had long black hair that flowed down the front of her shoulders and nearly over her chest, forming an alluring dark frame around her fair, almost ivory skin. She was so striking that I couldn't pull my gaze away, transfixed by her presence and lured further in by large smoky eyes. It had been a long time since I was stopped helplessly in my tracks like this. There are beautiful women everywhere, but something was different about her, something even beyond the immediate surface beauty, that suddenly multiplied my pulse and shortened my breath.

"Harry, you okay?" I heard Jackson say amidst laughter at the spectacle I created, suddenly realizing I'm in a crowd and looking utterly ridiculous, if not creepy. I finally looked away, but just before doing so I noticed the woman smile sheepishly, instinctually putting her hand over her mouth to hide her embarrassment. We made eye contact for a fleeting, but appreciable moment.

I took a deep breath, trying to gather myself. "Sure, sure, ahhh, my apologies. Got a bit distracted, yes, but I'm fine. Sorry. Hmmm, ahem, yes, it's all yours, Jackson." And then I started clapping aggressively in the hopes of redirecting attention away from my schoolboy idiocy. It worked. Lemming instincts kicked in and everyone followed my lead. I took a seat in the front row, stealing one more unrequited glance at her before sitting down.

As Jackson began to speak, I immediately began plotting a way to meet this woman while also wondering how much of this sudden and intense attraction to another woman had to do with the state of Dana and me.

"Well, that was quite the moment," Jackson began, darting glances back and forth between the woman and me. "Something seems to be in the air tonight at the Cabrillo."

I glared at Jackson imploring him to move on and spare me.

"Ok, so that's a tough act to follow, but hello everyone. Thank you for coming tonight. My friend, Harry, is kind of right. I'd like to say I transcended writing, but I missed the mark on such a lofty state. I'll leave the transcendence to gurus and yogis, but I have at least successfully quit writing with no compulsion to do it anymore. I grew weary of a dishonest and ungrounded life lived in order to recreate it, umm, or manipulate it into a readable reality all for the affirmation of others. I now prefer something much more authentic, life for life's sake. Simultaneously I wanted to cure my perpetual and disruptive wanderlust so I could settle down in one place and attempt the greatest challenge of modern times, a normal life. So, well, the protagonist visited all 195 countries and the result was this," Jackson said, holding up the heavy tome of *195*. It wasn't quite *Infinite Jest* length, but its 800 plus pages came damn close.

I could hear more grumbling from the back row. I turned, slowing down to sneak another peek at the magnetic woman, who was now looking at Jackson and not noticing me. The two hooligans were in dialogue with each, distracting those trying to focus on Jackson.

Jackson ignored them and began reading from *195*. He was barely a few sentences in when their chatter got louder. He tried to power through it while some folks in the audience tried to shush them, but it had no effect. Eventually it became impossible for him to continue. I was about to say something, but Jackson beat me to the punch.

"Gentlemen, is there a problem?" he asked. "Do you have a question?"

Redbeard stared at Jackson, clearing his throat, which sounded like old tires grinding against a gravelly road, and then blurted out, "We're more interested in the first book."

"Great. I'm sure there are copies available, right, Harry?"

"Definitely," I said pointing to the table near the podium carrying all three of Jackson's books.

Redbeard continued, "We read it. In fact, just finished. Such interesting characters," he intoned with what seemed sarcasm and glanced at his partner in disruption.

"Glad to hear it. Maybe you'll like this book so let me continue."

"We don't give a shit about this book."

Jackson put down *195* to some muffled sighs from the audience. "Do I know you?"

"Take a close look," Redbeard said, standing up.

Jackson stared and shook his head. "I don't know you from Adam."

"Fuck, Adam. You know me, you son of a bitch," Redbeard barked, pulling Babyface up to stand next to him. "You know us!"

We, the audience, were turning our heads to the front and rear like it was a tennis match, but clearly this had the makings of a much less civilized sport.

"Why don't you quit the games and tell me who you are?" Jackson asked calmly, not a shred of nerves in his voice. "You're making a scene."

"You know us better than you should," Redbeard insisted.

"What the hell does that mean?"

"Yeah, t-t-t-t-take a good look, Jackson, you mother fuck-k-k-k-er," Babyface said, stuttering wildly, his face all painfully contorted while trying to get over the high hurdles of the letters T and K.

Recognition quickly etched on Jackson's nodding face. "Sean and Reilly, my God! I'll be damned. It's been a while. I'm amazed you're still alive. Really am. Had my doubts all these years later. I thought the booze would have taken you down by now. AA?"

"Those aren't our names. They're your names!"

"You'll always be Sean and Reilly to me. Can't even remember your real names. Doesn't really matter."

I stole a glance at the raven-haired beauty who, like the rest of us, was mesmerized by the exchange. I also now remembered Sean (Red Beard) and Reilly (Babyface). They were characters from Jackson's first book, which had a story about a seedy bar and its hardcore regulars. The barflies befriended a young bartender-writer (Jackson) passing through San Francisco during his peripatetic youth. Together they schemed to steal money from the pub and its evil owner because he was planning to sell the historic pub to a TGI Fridays-type corporation.

Sean and Reilly were drawn very close to reality, from beard to stutter. I even remember going to that pub where Jackson bartended, or as he said at the time, "gathered material." His fiction was always virtually romans-à-clef. And now these characters had come to life years later, right off the page in a mutiny against the author, reminding me of Woody Allen's *The Purple Rose of Cairo*.

"You disrespected us and stole our identities."

"That's ridiculous."

"You're such a prick, Jackson. Always were. We told you things in confidence and you used it all practically as we said it. You exposed our secrets, you piece of shit!" Sean said.

"Yeah, we t-t-t-trusted you. We were f-f-f-friends," Reilly added.

"It's fiction, boys. You inspired characters. Take it as flattery. And I didn't expose anything. No such thing as bartender-drunk confidentiality."

"Flattery my fucking ass and what is said at the bar, stays at the bar. Fucking bartending 101."

Jackson shrugged and smiled. "Didn't know the protocols. All apologies, but what's done is done."

"You cost me my girlfriend after she found out about it and read the bullshit."

I stood up. "How about you guys talk about this after—"

"Shut up," Reilly interjected, stutter-free.

"You guys need to leave. Get out of my theatre before I call the cops!" I yelled.

Jackson put his hand up towards me and continued, "Was it the same girlfriend you used to whine and cry into your beer about? She left you 'cause you treated her like shit. Glad she finally woke up. Had nothing to do with me I'm sure."

"That's bullshit. You remember things the way you want to. You never knew me, Jackson, other than what you chose to steal."

I started feeling a little sympathetic for the guy while I could see Jackson's calm demeanor shifting to anything but sympathy.

"Are you guys done? Feel better after venting like fools?" he jabbed.

Jackson drank, but he wasn't a heavy drinker. His father, though, was a hard-core alcoholic. He rarely talked about him, but I learned through his fiction about their complicated and tense relationship. Those hardcore lushes from the bar probably hit too paternally close to home for him.

Sean and Reilly looked at each other, nodded, and then rushed towards the podium. As they went by, I stuck out my leg and tripped Reilly, who went headfirst careening into the wooden table that had all of Jackson's books on it. The table flipped and the books flew in the air while he settled supine and dazed, covered with scattered copies of *195* and the other two books.

Meanwhile, Jackson was readying for Sean, who lunged at him throwing an off-balance and awkward punch. Jackson leaned back, easily avoiding the punch by several feet while Sean stumbled forward, almost falling, but regained his footing as he and Jackson squared off.

"I'm going to kick your ass, fucking thief," Sean yelled.

Jackson just stared him with steely-eyed focus. Sean was a big, thick guy with a well-earned beer belly. He probably outweighed Jackson by 50 pounds, but Jackson was muscular thin.

Sean threw another punch, slow and looping over the top that left him off balance again. Jackson was ready with his right hand calmly cocked near his chin and his weight on his back foot. As Sean regained his balance, Jackson unleashed a whipsaw right hand, his weight shifting synchronously with the punch. I wasn't a big boxing fan, but it seemed like perfect pugilistic form. His fist landed with a cracking thud on Sean's left eye, seemingly lifting him erect for a fraction of a second before he collapsed in a heap and a thud, motionless and out cold.

The audience reacted with gasps and cheers. Moviegoers crowded around to the live show in the lobby. A moment later I noticed Reilly had recovered from his tumble and was taking aim at Jackson from behind. Several people and I yelled, "Jackson!" The warning backfired as he turned towards the voices while Reilly flew at him like a football player going for a tackle. His shoulder struck Jackson squarely in the lower back. They both went down, but Reilly took the worst of it. His head struck the corner of the podium. He was moaning and groaning, holding his head as a rivulet of blood streamed down his baldhead. I noticed several people filming the whole thing on their phones, others talking on them. The woman that mesmerized me was now checking on Jackson. A few regulars attended to the fallen characters. One of them checked Sean's pulse to make sure Jackson's punch wasn't lethal.

"He's alive, but probably very concussed," he said as Sean started coming to.

2 — Nadine of Casablanca

Soon enough the police and EMTs arrived. After the police arrested the feeble pair and put them in the squad car, one cop asked the necessary questions to Jackson, me, and a few other witnesses while the theatre was still abuzz. Once the police left, we went on with the show. I got Jackson set up for the book signing while the growing crowd was still fired up. We sold hundreds of books thanks to "The Arthouse Brawl" as the SF Weekly later headlined the story. The article began with, "Two characters attacked their author at the Cabrillo theatre, but their insurrection failed…"

While I was busy dealing with all the chaos and excitement, I managed to keep an eye on the woman. She had been milling about and then went to the bar, having a glass of wine and chatting with a local poet, who had given a reading here a few weeks ago, but with considerably less drama.

When things started to settle down, and Jackson was finally done signing books, I noticed that she was gone. I was scanning the lobby when Jackson grabbed my arm and led us to the bar.

"I know who you're looking for. Man, what the hell was that?" he asked, now putting his arm around my shoulders in brotherly fashion.

"I know. That was one hell of a reading, huh?" I deflected.

"You know what I mean," Jackson persisted.

"I don't know what you're talking about. I'm just trying to get things under control since your characters clearly have serious issues with their creator."

"Indeed they do. Brought some excitement to the Cabrillo though and drummed up some business, no?"

"No argument there. Great for business."

"Anyway, never mind that stuff. What about that woman who had you under a spell? You're not escaping that part of the drama."

"Well, I'm trying to. It was embarrassing. Kind of lost it there."

Jackson sighed. "To say the least. You practically melted before everyone's eyes."

"I know, I know, but I pulled it together eventually, didn't I?"

"Not really."

"Well, yeah, she got me good. So, who is she? It seemed like you know her."

"Indeed, I do," Jackson confirmed with a sly smile.

"Hmmm, I guess I'm not surprised," I said, trying to hide some disappointment.

"No, no, no. Not that way, brother. She's all yours. I've got my hands full in that area. Trust me."

"Trouble with Celeste? You guys still together, or kind of together, or whatever it was that you guys were?"

"Defining it doesn't matter anymore. We're not together."

"That's too bad, Jacko. I always liked her."

"Yeah, me too," Jackson said, breaking eye contact

with me. After a long ruminating pause, he asked, "So, anyway, how's Dana? I don't remember you as the deviating kind. At least not years ago?"

"I'm not. We're together, but it's been a little off or I don't know. It's complicated," I said, feeling a twitch in my eye and wondering if it were visible to Jackson.

"Always is and then again it really isn't. Sometimes we just want complicated."

I shrugged. "Maybe so."

I got us a bottle of Malbec and Jackson told me about the mystery woman. Her name was Nadine Chakir. He had met her in Morocco when he was passing through Marrakesh after a few days in Tangier. It was there in the North African phase of *195* that his living novel got delayed significantly by a woman named Samira, who was Nadine's best friend. Unlike most of Jackson traveling trysts, this one stuck.

Jackson and Celeste had an open relationship that allowed for affairs when they were out of town. What happened on the road, stayed on the road for both. No questions asked. They viewed their itinerant polyamory as liberation from the doldrums of monogamy, but regulated by keeping it out of town. I even remember Celeste saying back in the Sunsetter days that it not only made their relationship more exciting, but actually strengthened the bond since they always came home to each other.

But their free-spirited phase inevitably fissured. "I fell hard and fast for Samira. Just like you did tonight."

Samira visited Jackson on many of the *195* stops

after the Marrakesh affair. Between visits, she was the muse propelling the novel. His separation anxiety and mad craving for her catalyzed into a fury of passionate creativity.

When the travels ended and the novel was finished, he was back with Celeste hoping home would break Samira's spell, but this one had an iron grip. He couldn't fight it anymore and confessed it all to a shattered Celeste. Their end was brutal, and the guilt broke him down for a while, but his passion for Samira was more powerful than his love and guilt. Jackson and Samira eventually moved in together in Big Bear, outside of LA.

As for Nadine, Jackson had spent a little time with her in Marrakesh when he first met Samira, but got to know her better when she visited Big Bear. During her stay, they all road tripped to San Francisco and Nadine was quickly smitten with the city, which was no surprise. It was preordained since she also happened to be a big fan of the Beats. Her family had a summer home in Tangier and she got hooked on Beat lit at an artsy bookstore that was a kind of City Lights descendent. Kerouac and many other Beats and Beat peripheries like Paul Bowles had spent a lot of time in bohemian Tangier in the 50s and their footprints were easy to find as I knew from shooting *Kerouac* on location there. Nadine studied literature at the oldest university in the world, University of Karaouine in Fes, but was keen to earn a Ph.D. specifically in Beat Literature with a focus on the underappreciated female Beat writers. San Francisco State had one of the few American Lit programs in the States or anywhere for that matter that allowed a focus on Beat Lit.

"Man, are you kidding me?" I sincerely thought Jackson was messing with me. "She's a damn Beatnik? I thought I was the last one standing. What are the chances?"

"Maybe those similar passions are part of the alchemy that hypnotized you," Jackson posed.

"So much serendipity."

"Well, not exactly. She already knew you before tonight."

"What? Jackson, what the hell is going on?"

"Yeah, she knew you because of *Kerouac*. Of course she had seen it and one night it came up. I told her all about you and our friendship. She was very curious. That's why she came to the reading. She wants to meet you. She didn't just stumble in."

I took a big gulp of Malbec. "Are you fucking with me?"

Jackson furrowed his brow and laughed. "Not at all. Take it easy. Look, she's Beat to the core and loved your film. I think she even wrote a paper on it in college. When she found out we were friends, you bet she wanted to meet you."

I rubbed my face as if it would remove all the stress and disbelief welling up inside. "Well, I don't know how to handle this. I need to focus on getting Dana and me back on track. Nadine certainly won't help that process. It was just a momentary lapse."

Jackson rolled his eyes. "A big moment and a huge lapse. I think there's probably more to it than you're willing to admit."

"Everybody's a therapist these days."

"Look, just meet her and say hello. We're not talking about having sex tonight. She just wants to meet you, that's all. You have no choice anyway. She went to get cigarettes and will be back any second."

"Here?"

"Yeah, where else? Like I said, she wants to meet you. Even more now I'm sure."

"Fuck, I'm embarrassed as hell!"

"She was flattered. You made her feel like Helen of Troy for Chrissakes," Jackson said, letting out a hearty laugh. "What woman wouldn't want that?"

I really wanted and really didn't want to meet Nadine. I didn't trust myself and wasn't ready to walk away from Dana even though lately it seemed like we were in quicksand, slowly and painstakingly sinking while just a few seconds in the presence of Nadine was all flight and velocity. Despite fantastical notions disjointing my mind with inflamed ideas, I couldn't undo all the years Dana and I had together so fast.

As Jackson was chatting with a few customers about the book and the fight, I noticed his knuckle was bruised and swollen. When they left, I pointed it out.

"Sean has a goddamn thick skull," he said.

"Hey, so where did you learn to fight like that? You really kicked that guy's ass."

"He's an old fat drunk. I should hope I could handle him."

"But you looked like you knew what you were doing."

"I boxed for a spell," Jackson admitted casually.

"Really? Boxing and bought a winery? A new woman? Damn, times have changed."

Jackson shrugged. "A decade does that."

"Well, not so much for me. Been pretty damn flat lined."

Jackson nodded, massaging his modestly grown, grey-flecked beard as if it helped him think, before saying, "I foresee verticality."

Jackson started unraveling the mysteries of his winemaking and boxing adventures, which were both intertwined with his relationship with Samira. He was talking slowly, his mood turning pensive, almost solemn, but before he could get very far, Nadine arrived.

"Am I interrupting?" she asked.

Jackson's spirit seemed to get a jolt with Nadine's arrival. "No, not at all, perfect timing," he said. "Nadine, let me introduce you to a great American filmmaker, Harry Gnostopolos. So good that all he needed to do was one film and then retire."

"Really nice to meet you," Nadine said, hand extended. We shook hands while my heart raced like it belonged somewhere else. I couldn't understand why this was happening. I meet many beautiful women. The city is full of them, but something was different with her. The visual attraction traveled visceral depths.

"Likewise," I said, hoping I was camouflaging

what was happening within while trying to quell the emotional anarchy.

"I loved your movie. I'm a big Kerouac fan, the Beats in general. It was so good." Nadine's voice pitched towards masculine. Deep, a bit husky, but still feminine and very sexy.

"Thanks. So glad you liked it."

We were silent for a bit and then both of us kind of looked at Jackson for help.

"Are you kidding?" he said to both of us.

"Jackson, don't be a jerk," she said, playfully shoving him.

"So how about a glass of wine or a beer?" I asked.

"Wine would be great," Nadine answered.

I got up, pulled my chair out, and motioned for her to sit, which she did with a smile. I went behind the bar and asked her what she preferred.

"Whatever you two are drinking is fine with me."

I opened another bottle of Malbec, poured her a glass and went to refill Jackson's. He passed his hand over the glass before I could pour. "My friends, I am gonna call it a night. Let you two get to know each other."

Neither of us protested. Jackson finished his glass with one final healthy gulp.

"Jacko, I've got the apartment all set up for you. Let me show it to you and get you settled."

To Nadine I said, "I'll be back soon. Can you stick around a bit?" I couldn't stop myself.

"Sure."

I walked Jackson upstairs and got him settled.

"Stay here as long as you want," I said. "Mi casa es su casa."

"You're a good man, Harry. You know, things have been kind of rough lately, financially. I don't have much for rent right now."

"Never mind the rent."

"Nonsense. I will pay my share. I have a plan, an epic one actually, just need to finalize some details. I think it will interest you, too."

Shaking my head, I responded, "I already have plenty on my plate with the Cabrillo. Business is not so great when we don't have brawls."

"Well then you'll be very interested, but that's a conversation for another time. One step at a time."

I nodded and started walking away, not giving this "epic plan" any thought, when Jackson said, "Hey, Harry, is Dana okay with this? I don't think she's my biggest fan."

"She's fine with it."

"You're a bad liar, Harry."

"Well, she's out of town and doesn't know you're staying yet. So as of right now, ignorance is bliss."

Jackson laughed. "Thanks, man. Enjoy Nadine."

*   *   *

A few staff were still around cleaning up, but the place was quiet. The movies were finished for the night and no customers were around.

"Hungry?" I asked upon returning.

"Very," Nadine said. "Starved in fact. With all this drama I never ate dinner."

"Well let's do something more about that." I went behind the concession stand and put two hot dogs in the warmer, grabbed some assorted candies and chocolates along with a bucket of popcorn, two bottles of water, condiments, and laid them all out on the bar in front of us.

"Bon appétit," I said. "A movie theatre picnic."

"This is great. I love it."

I couldn't believe I was alone with her. I was so curious to know more about her past, the attraction to the Beats, life in Morocco, future plans and anything and everything else. I hadn't met someone new in a long time. Rather, I hadn't really gotten to know someone new in a longtime. I spent most of my time with the Cabrillo staff or the regulars that frequented the theatre. What little extra time I had beyond that was with Dana. My life had become very provincial. Nadine was a sudden and refreshing exotic exit.

We indulged in the junk food, not saying much at first, mostly just smiling and laughing foolishly, but not so awkwardly. Then we started talking about the fight and how she met Jackson. We chatted about San Francisco, the Beats, and *Kerouac*; I asked about bohemian life in Tangier today and told her about my experiences there. We talked on and on and shared our lives and stories. At this point she told me that she was involved with an American woman, Christine, whom she met in Tangier while Christine was doing a semester abroad. It was her first relationship with a woman, which I was so relieved to hear. They were long distance for now until Christine finished grad school back east. "We're bi-coastal, among other bi's." Christine planned to move west after graduation.

"Are you guys solid, if you don't mind me asking?"

"Ask me anything. Yeah, we're solid I guess. More like stable, but maybe too stable."

"I get that. Dana and I are in a similar plight of stability."

"Plight or plateau?"

I ruminated on this for a moment and then said, "The plateau is the plight."

"Indeed, it is," Nadine agreed.

Before we knew it, a hint of sunlight snuck up on us.

"Wow, it's almost six. We sure can talk," she said. "I need to go, Harry. My god, I have class in a few hours and I still have some reading to do on no sleep."

"Don't go. You can stay here."

Nadine laughed. "Are you crazy?"

"No, no, I don't mean with me. I have an extra bedroom. Dana is out of town so you can just crash."

Nadine paused, "Ummm, not a good idea. To be honest, it's too tempting."

I nodded in agreement.

"Have we really been chatting for five hours?" she asked.

"Yeah, it raced by."

"Will you walk me home? I'm just down the street towards Ocean Beach."

"Of course. I don't care if it's to San Diego."

"You're cute. And dangerous."

We stopped at the door to her building. You could see the legendary Cliff House perched above Ocean Beach from her place. "Thanks for a gourmet dinner," she joked. "It was an aptly ridiculous meal befitting a perfectly strange evening."

"Strange indeed. You know, I'm sorry about before."

"About what?" she asked, probably knowing exactly what I meant.

"At the reading. For staring and embarrassing you. It was probably creepy."

"No, not creepy at all. To the truth, I was flattered. Embarrassed, but very flattered. That's never happened to me before."

"I'm surprised."

"Well, maybe because most people are more discreet than you!" she said, gently slapping my shoulder.

"Of course. I don't know what the hell happened, something just, umm, kind of, clicked in me, intensely and immediately."

"Now I am embarrassed again," she said, looking down and then glancing up and making eye contact, before looking away again. Every gesture attracted me more.

"I don't know what to do with all of this," I confessed.

We looked into each other's eyes. "I don't either. Let's just say goodnight."

"Doesn't seem like the appropriate way to part after all that happened."

"No, it doesn't. I hope we see each other again soon," Nadine said and then headed up the stoop towards the door.

"Me, too," I said, starting to walk away.

Just a few steps later, I could hear footsteps approaching from behind and then a hand pulling on my shoulder. When I turned, Nadine whispered, "Let's make it more appropriate."

It was a long, dizzying kiss, so much so that when we stopped, I felt unstable on my feet, stricken with actual vertigo. It was the most intense and powerful kiss I'd ever experienced. Nothing had ever come close.

"Wow," I said taking a deep breath. She looked a little disoriented and I sensed she was feeling exactly what I felt.

We kissed again for a long time. It was like an opiate that let you trespass utopia. When we stopped, I pulled her in so that her head was against my chest and neck. We hugged tightly, as if letting go would have tragic consequences. She smelled so good and the curves of her body pressed perfectly into mine.

When we finally pulled apart, she said, "Good night, Harry. Really, good night." She was shaking her head as she opened the door and entered without looking back. I sat on the stoop in front of her building, watching the morning sky brighten, trying futilely to compose myself.

When I got home, I poured myself a scotch and climbed into bed with it, relieved that Dana was gone so I could just lay there alone and undisturbed, letting the events of the wild evening unfold like a movie in my mind.

3 — Big Bear

Jackson decided during his journey around the world that he would replace writing with wine making, convinced that quitting fiction to work the land and produce something real was his new destiny. He joked that it was like the old Berlin song, *No More Words*.

But his commitment was no joke. It was infused with passion and preparation. Jackson was always an autodidact and had been studying wine making for years, but he took it further by enrolling in courses at UC Davis' Department of Viticulture and Enology while making the final revisions on *195*. After the novel was complete and in the hands of his publisher, Jackson wandered the California coast in search of wineries to purchase. He was ready to leap into his new life, but never mentioned to me how in the world he got the money for something so expensive. At this point I never asked.

He started as far south as one could possibly grow viable grapes before the climate simply got too hot. Once you were further south than the Central Coast, specifically Santa Ynez and Santa Barbara counties, any available land for a winery got cheaper and cheaper. Most of the wines made at this latitude were fruity ones from plums or pears. LA and vicinity were certainly not on most vintner's maps, but according to some renegade UC Davis research and blogs from a few offbeat amateur enophiles, there were radical theories that Big Bear, east of LA and ensconced in the San Bernardino Mountains, had the potential to be the next big wine thing. Some speculated that the soil would be perfect for Syrahs. The Central Coast was tapped after the *Sideways* phenomenon while Napa and Sonoma were old news and over the top in cost. So Jackson and Samira moved to Big Bear to research the land in search of the hidden gem of terroir that would produce a new masterpiece. The mountains, the not too distant ocean breeze, the moist air from Big Bear Lake, cool evenings and warm days all might conspire to create a great American Syrah.

It was a gamble, but Jackson rolled the dice.

He found the spot, in the far northwest edge of Big Bear. He loved the peaceful area and even fell for the name Big Bear, which would be the namesake for the new winery. Jackson thought he had found his own personal nirvana, a simple kind of transcendence. Writing was finished, demons exorcised, wanderlust tamed, a new and real purpose, and the right woman to spend the rest of his life with monogamously. Simplicity had coalesced.

"Samira was now my words and wanderlust. The land my new day-to-day life."

Meanwhile, Samira had given up her life in Morocco for this adventure. She had been working menial jobs but dreamed of being a painter. She had studied art in school but had never focused on it. She thought this would be her opportunity. She loved Jackson and the whole idea of creating this winery from scratch. She would work the land with him during the day and paint landscapes of the process by night. If nothing else, she envisioned her work someday adorning the Big Bear Winery tasting room.

They had invested a lot of money, time, and sweat preparing the land and planting those first grapes. It was an exciting time with so much promise, but those early dreamy days soon faded into a disaster of drying vines. The days were too hot, and the rainfall too little to cool the terroir. The first harvest produced an undrinkable wine. Jackson tried some experimental techniques to rescue the great winery adventure, but he knew he needed a miracle of cooler weather amidst a global warming world and more rainfall in the drought-stricken land of Southern California.

Jackson had known all along that it was a long shot, but he really believed (or wanted to believe) in Big Bear. He also wasn't forthcoming about the risks to Samira. He convinced her that this was a can't-miss opportunity, but he lied about how the climatic odds were against them. He wanted her more than truth.

Big Bear took its toll financially and emotionally on the couple. Samira fell in love with a writer, but now she was partnered with a seemingly reckless winemaker who had quit writing. She was second-guessing everything about the relationship and impulsively uprooting her life. She grew angry with him and angrier at allowing herself to be seduced into this fantasy. Her painting turned from serene landscapes to frustrated abstracts. For Samira, Jackson's once shiny romantic spontaneity had tarnished into unattractive instability.

The bloom was off the bohemian rose.

*   *   *

Jackson was having beers and bemoaning his plight with locals one evening in the tiny Big Bear downtown (a general store, pub, pizza joint and laundromat) when he heard about Homer Gaines' gym. Gaines was a famous boxing trainer whose prize pupil was gold medalist and light heavyweight champion, Anders McKenna. The professionals trained on one side, but there was also an amateur section for novices to work out and spar that helped fund the gym. He told Samira about it and she suggested he join to help him deal with all the anxiety over failing Big Bear. It could be therapeutic for both of them. She also craved space from Jackson, spending more and more time secluded in her studio that they had built next to their house.

Jackson had always been a boxing fan and particularly of McKenna. He wasn't sure if he was more excited to release his stress on the speed and heavy bags or just at having the chance to meet McKenna.

He joined, got a personal trainer, and learned boxing techniques while taking out his winery frustrations with ten-ounce gloves on. The trainer taught him the academics of boxing – angles, positioning, feinting vs. attacking, and situational punch selection. He shadowboxed for many hours to improve his footwork and hit the mitts for proper timing and hand speed.

"Man, I was a quick study. I processed it fast and was quickly converting it all into muscle memory as if I'd had a boxing lineage. In hours, I could hit the speedbag like a pro. You know, the rat-tat-tat-tat thing they do. Felt great. You get into this very Zen rhythm. Kind of a kinetic TM state."

Jackson was hooked. He started working out daily, every morning at the crack of dawn, and then laboring at the fledgling winery all day and evening, trying to transform the terroir into the soil of a noble grape. In the process, he got into amazing physical condition. Impressed with Jackson's progress, his trainer recommended that he take some real fights in the local amateur league. Jackson obliged and even knocked a few people down, one guy out, and was put on his ass a few times as well but discovered that he had a good chin—something innate that can never be taught. He could absorb a punch and not see stars or get spaghetti legs.

"You never know what kind of man you are until you get punched in the mouth. We all have a fight or flight instinct. Mine was fight."

Then the highlight came. Jackson was training one day when Homer Gaines came over to the amateur side looking around for sparring partners. It was early in the morning and there weren't many options. Anders McKenna's regular sparring partner had gotten hurt, and Anders was moving up in weight to fight for the light heavyweight championship. Jackson was the perfect size among the few guys training at sunrise. Gaines tapped him on the shoulder and asked, "Hey, man, you want to spar with the champ?" The next thing he knew he was in the ring with one of the best boxers in the world, one who had never lost a professional fight.

"No wonder you kicked those old drunks' asses.

You're used to fighting champions."

Jackson laughed. "Definitely a giant step down in class with Reilly and Sean. On multiple levels."

"How'd you do?"

Jackson rolled his eyes. "He toyed with me, of course. He's a genius in the ring. Constantly and quickly shifting his stance to get the precise punching angle while simultaneously maintaining an impenetrable defense. It was like a junior high basketball player suddenly in the NBA. He was just getting in a workout and taking it easy on me, but then in the last 40 seconds or so, he decided to work on his offense for real. Every time I tried to block a face shot, I'd get caught in the ribs and vice versa. He did the head-body attack until I was on the canvas, finished."

"I remember the head-body thing from *The Fighter*."

"Yeah, except Mickey Ward was all gritty warrior, you know, take two or three punches to get one in. Anders is like Garry Kasporov with gloves on. He doesn't get hit. He's always two or three moves ahead of his opponent."

*　　*　　*

Boxing therapy helped keep Jackson's fragile psyche from total breakdown, but the vineyard continued its downward spiral.

"Syrah is not like Cabernets that grow anywhere like weeds. Syrah is a complicated and beguiling red. She beat me worse than Anders McKenna did and so much was at stake. I lost everything, Harry. That's why

I am here. I had a great woman, a giant bank account, conquered obsessions, and was ready to work my own piece of Eden to create something so real, not some fictional perversion. I made it back to the land and blew it. Fucking blew it, big time!" Jackson said, shaking his head and gritting his teeth in disgust.

"Sorry, Jacko, that's a big loss. So sorry."

"I should have blended it. I jumped in too quickly. Thought I did the research, but there are so many variables with wine, and none went our way. Goddamn climate change! Global burning was scorching the soil and the droughts were worse than ever. The skies just wouldn't open up. I even learned a true Native American rain dance from the Lakotas and tried it night after night like a madman. Can you fucking believe that?" Jackson asked, looking up at me and laughing uneasily at himself. Before I could respond, he looked away again, and went back to venting. "The vines were so thirsty, and I couldn't quench them with sprinklers. We were running them round the clock some days, paying fines, county folks were up my ass. The first harvest took a beating, money got tight, and then Samira and I collapsed. Dominoes, Harry, dominoes. Who could blame her? Gave up everything to be with a rain dancing fool," Jackson said, laughing hard and almost maniacally.

"You were desperate."

"No, I was a ridiculous jackass. When she left me, I fell into a deep depression. Couldn't work the land, couldn't box, couldn't and wouldn't write, couldn't do anything. Couldn't get out of bed. Darkness was too visible. I had no outlet. I'd sit and stare all day at the dying vines and spend evenings in Samira's studio hoping she'd change her mind. And now Eden is 150 acres of brown wasteland in Big Fucking Bear."

"Is it really over? Where is Samira now?"

Jackson didn't answer.

*   *   *

A few days had passed since the kiss. I hadn't heard from Nadine. She could have asked Jackson for my number or just come up to the theatre to see me, but there was nothing. I did walk by her apartment building a few times, thought about ringing her, but resisted. Dana would be home soon and I opted not to complicate things. I wanted to talk to Dana, heart to heart about us, and then be intimate. We hadn't had sex in so long that I couldn't remember the last time, but I knew we needed that and a lot more. It was time to shake up the relationship in one direction or another. Maybe Nadine was the spark we needed to get on track.

Or off.

I also didn't see Jackson much. There was a separate entrance to his apartment in the rear of the theatre via the fire escape. I texted him a few times, but he never responded. I knocked on his door a couple of times, but nothing.

Finally, one morning I saw him. I had heard him walking up the fire escape around sunrise, so I roused myself up to go see him before he left again. The door was slightly ajar, so I nudged it open. He was sitting on the floor, cross-legged yoga style with his back to me.

"Hey Jacko?"

He slowly raised his hand, putting an index finger up. Clearly, he was in some meditative state and wanted to be left alone though I wondered why the door wasn't closed.

I went back to my room, texted him again asking to meet later, and then went back to bed. Late in the morning, I went to work with still no reply from Jackson. The first movie was playing at 1:15. The concession folks, ticket person, and manager were all doing their jobs. I watched the operation run and still got a thrill when I saw things in motion in a theatre that I owned. I had planned to meet with my accountant today to go over the books and see how deeply in the red we were, but my mind was elsewhere in a conflated realm of Nadine and Dana. The meeting was in an hour and I wanted to cancel on Mariana Jimenez, CPA, but opted not to. She hated cancellations, unplanned changes, or any kind of deviation. She was an accountant to her core.

"Harry, did you see the news?" Joel, our manager, asked.

One of the things that Mariana wanted to talk about today was Joel's job. She wanted me to cut expenses and suggested I take over managing to eliminate Joel's salary. She was trying to save the Cabrillo and, "if enough revenue wasn't coming in, then expenses had to be trimmed. It's that simple, Harry. What goes out must be less than what comes in or we end up chapter 13, dead."

I liked Joel and didn't want him to lose his job. He had all sorts of neurotic issues and, ironically, he had an unrequited crush on Mariana that distracted him from doing his job well, but the last thing he needed was to be let go. The Cabrillo was his family after all, as it was for a lot of us, including and especially me. Besides, I didn't want to be the manager. I wanted to be the owner. I had spent many of the early years as the manager and every other role there was to cut costs. I'd done everything from sell popcorn to rip tickets to clean the theatre when I couldn't afford a cleaning crew. I still did these jobs when necessary to fill in for folks, but I didn't want it as a permanent job. I wanted progress, not regress.

"No, I haven't, Joel. Let me guess, we're on the news."

"You bet we are. You are and your crazy friend, Jackson. The whole thing is all over the net. Video is going viral. Even saw it on the local TV news. Our online sales are crazy. Sold out all shows today already."

"Really? Every showing?"

"Every single one, both theatres!" Joel shouted and fist bumped me, wide-eyed and giddy.

"That's great. We need it. We never sell out downstairs. We can do all the planning we want, set up all the gimmicks and pitches, but it's the unplanned that saves the day."

"Life is what happens when you're busy making other plans," Joel said.

"Indeed, John Lennon."

"And the Chronicle called. They want to do an interview with you and Jackson. We have to ride this thing for all the publicity we can."

Joel gave me the Chronicle reporter's name and number.

"Ok, I'll give her a call."

"Hey, guess what else, Harry?"

I knew what was coming. Joel really cared about the Cabrillo, but whenever he was truly happy, it had to do with one thing. "You went out with what's her name last night and had a good time?"

"Yes, Karissa, but not last night, this morning. Went on a long bike ride in Golden Gate Park, across the bridge and then had coffee in Sausalito near the houseboats."

"Sounds great. Progress?"

"I think so. I think things are heading in the right direction."

"Excellent. Keep me posted."

I gave Joel thumbs up, went outside to look at the marquee and see our ticket person in the old style outdoor kiosk. Woody Allen's *Irrational Man* was playing in the main theatre. We were showing Brando's *The Wild One* downstairs as part of biker week. *Easy Rider* tomorrow. The downstairs theatre was always weekly themed old movies.

"Harry, not one ticket left for either show tonight. Can you believe it? It's a Tuesday!" Sandy, the ticket queen, said. "Your friend put us on the map."

"I know, I heard from Joel. Crazy. That's what happens when you have a good ole brawl at a movie theater book reading."

"Hey, you were pretty good. I saw the video. That was a nice trip that sent the guy flying."

I laughed. "Sandy, that was no big deal."

"Don't be humble."

"My friend, Jackson, was the star of the show. He's why we're sold out."

"Won't argue that," Sandy agreed.

As I took in the theatre from the outside, something I did almost every day before any crowds came, I saw Jackson coming out of the main doors.

"Hey," he said quietly, sounding and looking dispirited. Apparently, the meditation or whatever it was didn't do its job. "Lunch?"

"Sure, you okay?" I asked.

"Yeah, yeah, fine. Moods have to flow. Won't do any good to dam them."

"Let's go to McLellan's. Great little Irish pub a few blocks up. A whiskey pick-me up will do the trick."

"Maybe."

As Jackson walked by the ticket kiosk, Sandy opened the door and raised her sexagenarian hand for a high five. Jackson obliged on the fly with a measured smile. Sandy said, "That's some punch you have."

"Thanks. Just a lucky shot."

"No sir, you know how to punch. You're like Russell Crowe in *Cinderella Man*. Who's the real guy?"

"Jim Braddock," Jackson answered.

*   *   *

McClellan's was a dark Irish bar with one small TV, two beers on tap (Guinness and Harp), a great selection of Irish whiskeys, and a decent batch of scotches. They served just a few appetizers and sandwiches, keeping the food very simple. It was just there for padding to have another drink. Dana and I both loved it and hung out here often during better days.

The bartenders were usually all straight out of Dublin and their brogue certified the authenticity of the place. Photos of Joyce, Wilde, Bowen, and their ilk adorned the walls. It unpretentiously managed to pull off literary.

We each ordered a Guinness. Shawn, the bartender, poured them with craftsman-like precision holding the glass at a 45-degree angle, pulling the tap forward until it was 75% filled, patiently letting it settle, before pushing the tap forward and topping it off so that the frothy and creamy head was perfectly delineated from the dark body of the stout. He once told me "pouring Guinness quickly and incorrectly is criminally prosecuted in Dublin."

While I was watching the bubbles cascade down the side of the glass and then surge upward, I noticed Jackson watching CNN on the inconspicuous corner TV. There was something about John F. Kennedy being reported.

"What's up?" I asked him.

He shushed me with his index finger while staying glued to the story so I turned to the TV to find what was so important. The story was about Trump pushing the FBI and State Department to release the remaining confidential documents on the Kennedy assassination.

A portion had been released after pressure from Oliver Stone's film, *JFK*, but many more were under lock and key due to "national security." The documents were set to be released in 48 hours.

When the story shifted to Trump and the ridiculous border wall, Jackson's focus dissipated. "What do you think?" he asked.

"About what?"

"Trump finally doing something right and getting these docs released. Maybe finding out who really killed JFK."

I shook my head. "Not a chance there's anything revelatory in there. Why would the culprits incriminate themselves?"

"Good point."

"Didn't know you were so into the JFK conspiracy?" I asked.

"Lately I've taken an interest. You were always into it as I remember."

"Yeah, because of my dad. He was a big conspiracy buff and Kennedy fan."

Shawn finally delivered the perfect Guinnesses. "Here's to reunited old friends," Jackson toasted.

"And to you single-handedly boosting sales at the Cabrillo," I added as we tapped pints.

"Really? The reading drama did that?"

"Indeed, it's gone viral. Doesn't take long these days. Sometimes it spreads even before it happens," I quipped.

"Crazy world. I miss the pre-viral days." Jackson

said.

"Yeah, well, we're getting old school coverage, too. The local press is eating up. It's going to make the Chronicle tomorrow, local weeklies, you name it. Hey, wait a minute, if the movie theatre is getting a bounce, I bet your book is flying off the shelves, or rather getting downloaded like crazy. Have you checked Amazon?"

"No."

"Jacko, come on, you're not opposed to sales, are you? Just 'cause you quit writing doesn't mean —"

"Look, sales are fine," he interrupted. "It's just not enough. Doesn't cut it. Samira did it for me. I want her back and *195* as a bestseller won't do it. I tried to tell her that this morning, but it didn't go well. But maybe getting the winery up and running will."

I took out my phone and searched for Jackson's book on Amazon. "Do you know what your rank was recently?"

"No," he said dispassionately.

"Come on! You gotta have an idea. You must check it once in a while out of curiosity, right? You have no ego?"

"I don't because I don't give a shit."

I found it on Amazon. "Ok, take a guess."

Jackson sighed at my persistence. "You tell me."

"Come on, just guess, man."

"500,000."

"Not even close. 758."

"Highest ever probably," Jackson conceded with a hint of enthusiasm breaking through his guard.

"See, we're both going to make some money on last night's drama."

"It's peanuts, Harry. It will translate into hundreds, maybe a few grand in royalties for me. Hell, I still haven't made enough to cover the advance. Bohemian days are over."

"Well, it's —"

"No, it's not better than nothing. It's still nothing." Jackson nearly yelled, downing the rest of the pint. He ordered another and then looked at my still nearly full pint. "Yeah, just one," he told Shawn. He was cranky, but I could tell he wanted to talk, just not about sales and royalties.

He filled in more gaps of the last decade. He started with alcohol. The first drink he'd had in over three months was the Malbec at the reading. He had been on a very serious holistic detox routine for 100 days, a complete holy trinity of the mind, body, and soul. Prior to that, the failed harvest and post-Samira depression had taken over. He had quit boxing and its requisite discipline, and started drinking heavily and using whatever drugs he could get his hands on, especially coke and pharmaceuticals. Everything had fallen apart, and he temporarily staved off a breakdown by narcotizing himself. He knew he was nearing the change-or-die precipice, but he couldn't stop the train racing for the cliff.

Homer Gaines did that for him. Gaines was looking for him to do some sparring and heard that Jackson now spent his time at The Lakeside, Big Bear's local dive bar. Gaines walked into the bar one afternoon and saw the wreck Jackson had become. He stood there shaking his head and not saying a word for a long time.

"It freaked me out. I mean not a word. Just staring at me, no through me, like an oversized black Yoda."

Finally, Gaines handed him a business card with a website on it and said, "If you want to live, go here and follow it. Don't half-ass it." He put his hand on Jackson's shoulder, squeezed it a few times and then said, "Godspeed," before departing.

The next day when Jackson woke up feeling the usual hangover horrible, instead of immediately grabbing a beer to ease the pain and start the day's journey into the void, he went on the webpage. It was a healer's site that fused Eastern and Western panaceas. He read every word on the website, and followed the plan immediately, going cold turkey. If anyone besides Homer Gaines had suggested this, he would have blown it off, but Gaines had that presence and Jackson was deeply touched that he took the time to do that.

"His showing up at the bar was the most paternal experience I'd had since probably grade school. Maybe ever."

Jackson went through the brutal 72-hour detox and then stayed pious to the plan, which went well beyond abstinence from just alcohol and drugs. It also preached celibacy and a proper diet (no processed foods, red meat, soda, sugar, heavy on fish and raw fresh organic foods), but the most unique part was monthly colonic cleansings, where they stick a hose up your rectum and blast the colon with antioxidant and mineral infused water.

"It's like a river flowing north up your ass, through the intestines, and then south from whence it came. Nothing weirder that that, but there is no better cleanse. You feel light and pure inside, like someone scrubbed your guts clean." 24 hours before and after each cleanse, he only drank a special volcanic water.

"The hunger was torment, but it was great disciplinary torment and you feel so purified."

The spiritual element was intensive Transcendental Meditation. He studied with a devout TM group in Big Sur and meditated dutifully at dawn and dusk every day.

He stuck to this regimen and got himself whole and clear-headed for the first time in a long time. "I felt great, Harry. I didn't solve the riddle of existence or make sense of why it all is, was, and will be. There were no epiphanic lies, but perception became clear. It was beautiful catharsis. I now knew what I wanted."

"What was that?" I asked.

"Well, right now it's some good whiskey. My colon needs a different kind of elixir. The 100 days are done. Wisdom through abstinence has shifted to wisdom through excess, at least occasionally. Can't ignore Blake forever."

"Shawn, two shots of Bushmills, single malt, please," I said.

"21 or 16 years?" Shawn asked.

"Let's go old."

Shawn smiled. "Celebration?"

"Yeah, a celebration," Jackson said, perking up. "I'm back home."

Shawn refilled our Guinness' without asking and then poured two shots of Bushmills, one ice cube in each, and one neat Jameson. "I'll drink the blue collar stuff while you enjoy royalty."

"To friends, Irish Whiskey, and a San Francisco reunion," I toasted as we all raised our glasses.

Homer Gaines had started Jackson on the right path, but Nadine closed the circle. She stayed with Jackson for a couple of weeks at Big Bear upon her arrival in the States until she settled in San Francisco. They talked a lot about Celeste, Samira, writing, family, everything. She was a great listener. Together they realized that he was still madly in love with Samira and she was his truth. The best way to get her back was to get his life back on track first. That's when he knew rebuilding the winery would be his mission. He wrote Samira and told her his plan. For the first time after many unanswered attempts, she responded wishing him the best, but asked him to give her time. That little response was all he needed to believe there was a light at the end of their tunnel.

"She didn't shoot it down. That's all I needed. Now it's all about the winery, plain and simple. I will fix the past to save our future."

I nodded but wasn't convinced his plan made sense. I wanted to ask how he was going to fix the winery this time and what guarantee he had it would bring Samira back, but I had another curiosity on my mind.

"I hope it works out, Jacko. But tell me something, how close did you and Nadine get?"

He laughed. "Not that close. I mean, don't get me

wrong, she is very sexy, smart, funny. I see all the attraction you have, but I didn't want to ruin our friendship. I needed that more and all I could think about was Samira anyway. To be honest, some nights, sleeping in the same house, lonely as hell and sober as a judge, I did think about it, but I knew better than to mess it up. I'd fucked up enough things over the years by disrespecting boundaries."

"Well done."

"Besides there was another roadblock to any romance with Nadine."

"What's that?"

"She's into women now."

"I thought she was fluid, as they say these days." I said, flashing back to the kiss, which wasn't a great mental leap since it had been on my mind on some level every moment since it had happened.

Jackson elaborated. "I don't think so. I think she changed teams permanently. Last I heard she was very serious with an American ex-pat she met in Tangier. But, you know, if she were ever gonna go back, I think it'd be you," he said, getting up and pulling out his wallet.

"I got this, man."

"Ok, but next round is on me. We have other matters to discuss. Fiscal matters."

"Like what?"

Jackson just tapped my shoulder reassuringly a few times. "All in good time, old friend."

"Ok, but one question now. How did you get the money for Big Bear in the first place? You said yourself your books couldn't have paid for that, right?"

"Not in a million years. Let's just say I kind of hit the lottery."

Before I could probe that mystery, Jackson said, "Here, take this," as he clicked away at his phone. Seconds later my phone dinged with Nadine's contact information.

I stared at it wondering if I should delete it.

Jackson gave me a couple of back slaps and headed out the door. Before he left, he turned and asked, "By the way, when does Dana get back?"

4 — Who's Afraid of Virginia Woolf

Dana tried to be quiet as she returned from the shower, but our creaking bedroom door woke me up. Usually I just rolled over and buried myself in a pillow, but I caught a glimpse of her out of the corner of my eye. She was wearing one of the sexiest things a woman could wear—a white towel. Wrapped breast to thigh, Dana wore it well. The top of the towel connected tightly at her cleavage, her breasts elevated and accentuated. The bottom tantalized at the peak of her thighs, hinting at so much while revealing her firm feminine legs,

I hadn't taken the time to really look at my partner of nearly a decade. The routine had dulled the powers of observation, but this morning I had the urge to focus on her. I thought this could be the moment to resurrect our sex life.

Now wide-awake, I continued staring. Her normally light brown hair, dampened to dark auburn, edged along her shoulders, drops of water sliding down her breasts and into the towel-pressed cleavage.

Besides our asexual detour, I hadn't even seen her this close to naked in a long time. I was usually asleep when she was getting ready for work since she had a normal 9-5 schedule and I had the vampire theatre life. Despite all the distance and sub-textual tension in our relationship, all I saw at this moment was a beautiful, sensual woman in front of me. A woman I'd been with for so long, but hadn't truly *been with* in ages. Maybe sex would be the first step on our road back to togetherness. Maybe it would exhume us.

I imagined getting up, gently kissing and touching her, slowly sliding my fingertips down her arms, pulling the towel slowly off and then tenderly kissing her all over before lingering at her breasts, circling the edges of her nipples in the way that used to turn her impassioned and heavy of breath. She loved to lie supine across my desk, a perfect height so I could get on my knees, kissing her thighs and gripping her wrists firmly, before my tongue glided just barely inside, slowly up and down until she'd pull my head in to go deeper at exactly the right time and spot, just the way we learned during our early days when we were figuring out our bodies, exploring and understanding our mysteries in the ecstatic, yet tragic pursuit of demystification...

But that was all just an old movie in my mind, hyperbolized by the deceptive perfection of nostalgia. The mysteries were gone and all that remained were memories that got us through the day-to-day grind. Sexual adventures now only occurred alone after Dana had left for work.

But today Dana was here, and she looked magnificent. Today had to be different, a return to those novel yesterdays.

"Hey, are you awake?" she suddenly asked.

"Very," I said.

"That's unusual. Couldn't sleep last night?" Dana asked as she bent her head down and vigorously towel dried her hair. She was in her panties and bra now.

"Slept fine last night."

"You were staring," Dana said casually while putting on some lipstick. "Caught you."

"Well you look fantastic."

Dana shrugged, half-smiled, and muttered something indecipherable, my flattery barely registering a reaction.

I sat up in bed and looked at my cell phone charging on our makeshift nightstand. It was 6:22.

"Seriously, you're so sexy. My god, I am a lucky guy."

"Morning horniness?"

"No, it's more than that. It's you. I miss you. I miss us."

"Come on, Harry. I've heard you taking care of business when you thought I was gone."

"Whatever, I'm telling you, it's you. I don't want to masturbate. I am tired of it. I want you." I sat up and pulled the covers down, exposing my boxers rising high.

Dana laughed. "Well, I'm flattered, but your timing is terrible."

"I think you said that the last time."

"Because it probably was."

I shook my head and sighed. "Well, apparently it's hard to fit into your schedule. What time is your flight again? 10?"

"9:35."

"We still have time. Come here. Come to me."

"Harry, I need to get dressed and in an Uber in 20

minutes."

"Give me 10."

"Great. I get all messed up so you get off and all I get is to be behind schedule and risk a missed flight. Sounds dreamy, sweetheart," Dana said, focusing on putting lotion all over her body, massaging it in deeply. At one point we caught eyes in the mirror, but she looked away quickly.

"It'll be all about you," I promised. "I'll take care of you, then myself after you leave. All about you, honey."

As she rubbed moisturizer on her face, Dana said, "That's sweet, Harry, really, ahh, kind of sweet, and I believe you intend for that, but once we start, I know how that little fella works. He'll take over."

"Little fella?" I said. "Jeez, not exactly the description guys like to hear."

"Harry, come on, I don't have time for this. Besides, you know I won't come when I am rushed and not in the mood. How can it be about me right now? It's about you. It's about your dick. Is that better? Let's be a little real for a change."

"That's what I'm trying to do."

"Yeah, on your schedule."

"I promise it won't be that way. I won't even use the *little fella*," I said as I got out of bed. Dana had put on a tight skirt and was buttoning a silk blouse as I approached from behind. I put my hands over hers and pulled them from their buttoning efforts to behind her back, as if she were about to be cuffed. I held both wrists in my left hand, slightly tightly as she used to like it. Dana always liked it a little rough, sometimes more than a little, and never used to oppose us wandering down that path. She used to say, "I like when you ravage me in bed, but are gentle out of bed."

Holding her wrists, I gently kissed the nape of her neck and slowly unbuttoned her shirt.

"Harry, please, when I get back—"

"Shhhh." I slid my hand across her cleavage and then slowly down her stomach until I reached under her skirt. She took a deep breath. I could feel pleasure chipping away at her resistance.

"Harry," she sighed sensually.

"Dana, sweetheart, we need this right now. It's been too long. We really need this," I whispered.

"Harry," she said more softly. I released her hands and she turned facing me. We kissed, and I started to nudge her towards the bed.

"I miss you so much, Dana," I said, kissing her down the front of her neck as she tilted her head back in a sexy surrendering way. I slowly slid her blouse over her shoulders.

"Harry," she cooed.

I continued kissing her as the blouse fell to the floor.

"Stop, Harry," she whispered.

I ignored her, thinking she was being playful, while I ran my fingers through her hair. Then I started to unzip her skirt and felt her hand grab mine with a tight grip.

"Harry," she said a little louder and sterner.

"Dana, I thought—"

"Just stop!" she yelled as I stepped back, startled.

"Honey, I thought —"

"What are you trying to rape me?"

My eyes widened incredulously in shock. "What?"

"You heard me."

"Come on, Dana. Rape?"

"That's what I said."

"Are you crazy? I was trying to seduce you, but failed miserably. You seemed to be getting into it, but clearly I misread the signals."

"What signals? I kept saying no!"

"I heard and felt otherwise."

"Because you heard and felt what you wanted."

"I'm sorry. I really didn't mean it."

Dana twisted her skirt back to its proper form, and buttoned her shirt.

"It felt like rape," she repeated.

I shook my head and sighed with exasperation. "Come on, are you kidding me? Christ!"

"How do you know what it felt like to me?"

"I should have a pretty good idea after all these years."

"Apparently not anymore. And I think I know my feelings better than you know them. I hate how you presume you know me better than I do."

"I didn't presume anything. You used to like it a little aggressive. Hell, you used to like sex, period."

"I used to like a lot of things. Why don't you try living in the present? When was the last time we were rough?"

"I don't know. I don't even remember the last time we were not rough."

"Well, maybe that's a sign."

"Of course it is. I was trying to change things."

Dana took a deep breath. "Why don't you just listen to me, my feelings, instead of what you think my feelings are? Do you hear yourself?"

"Jesus, you just did a serious 180. I swear you were getting into it. I know that. I could feel it and hear it in your breath and voice. It wasn't my imagination. And then something clicked in you telling yourself not to enjoy it or something weird like that."

"No, I told you I had a plane to catch in 20 minutes. How is that a 180? You ignored me and did what you wanted to do," Dana said, her gaze returning to the mirror and fixing herself up.

"Fine, I'm sorry." I leapt into bed, spinning and landing on my back. My hands were behind my head, fingers interlocked. "Shit, Dana, what the hell is up with us?"

Dana took another deep breath, exhaling loudly. "Look, I'm sorry, too, Harry. It's just not right."

I ruminated on that one for a bit. "This moment or in general?"

Dana didn't answer. She looked in the mirror and fixed her hair. I'd lost her. I just wasn't sure if it was this morning or forever.

"You know I can drive you. Forget the Uber. We can talk on the way."

"It's not necessary, Harry, but thanks."

"Why not?"

"Don't worry. It's covered under my expenses."

"Screw the expenses," I said angrily, ticked off that she wasn't getting my point or that she was just purposely avoiding my point. "Dana, it's about saving us, not a few dollars for Christ's sake! What the hell is going on? You feel a million miles away from me."

"I have a trip to take, Harry. Calm down, stop thinking about yourself and let me get ready. You're such a goddamn selfish pain in the ass."

"Fuck, Dana, throw me a bone here. I'm trying."

I knew we were doomed once we crossed the profanity precipice. Dana shot me a look in the mirror to confirm things. "Your timing sucks. Why now? Why when I am rushing out the door. Because you have a hard on. Fucking unbelievable!"

She began applying makeup and eyeliner. I probably had about 10 minutes before she was gone. I wanted some resolution, something clear before she left, one way or another. I couldn't get out of my own way.

"So where's the conference?" I asked

"Vancouver."

"Aren't you worried about us? Don't you think we're in a rut?"

"Yes, and yes," she said, corroborating it with a steely glare into my reflected eyes. She then sat on the far edge of the bed as far away from me as possible.

"Harry, we've had this conversation before."

"I know we have. That's why I wanted to be intimate. That's why I didn't want words. They've been getting us nowhere."

"Sex won't solve anything either."

"Who knows? Maybe it will reconnect us. I always feel closer after we have it."

"Look, I am sorry about the rape comment. That was over the top and dramatic."

I nodded appreciation.

"But your timing did suck. If you wanted to save us, you could say, let's move out of this stupid apartment, instead of let's fuck."

"Dana, moving is not that simple. It's what you want, not what I want. It's a logistical nightmare for me as we've discussed ad nauseam."

"So we want different things. That's a sign."

"Maybe."

"Harry, to tell the truth, I find your gephrophobia—"

"Gephyrophobia," I stupidly corrected her.

"Whatever the hell it is, I find it oddly convenient. Who the hell has a fear of bridges?"

"14,000 of us."

"How do you know that?"

"Research. There's a website for us freaks."

"Ugh. So confront it. Get over it if you want to save us. If you really and truly wanted to save us, you would make that a priority, but I don't feel you really want to save us, Harry. I mean this last-minute attempt at sex, maybe you timed it so it wouldn't work out."

"It was unplanned and therefore I didn't time anything. I was going with the moment."

"Think less superficially," she instructed, picking up her phone and typing something quickly.

"Ahh, I see, Dr. Dana, it was the unconscious setting sex up to fail because even though I think I want it, deep within the dark recesses, I really don't want it."

Dana rolled her eyes, stared at the ceiling, and then closed her eyes while take several long and slow breaths. When this mini-Yoga session was done, she said, "And now Jackson is going to stay with us. That's really going to help things," sarcasm ruling her tone.

"Just a few days."

"I know what that means. Remember last time. A few days was a month."

"That was ages ago. And you used to like him when we first met."

"You always direct everything back to the beginning. It's exhausting. People change, Harry. And that's not really true. Your memory is not 20-20. I tolerated him at best. He's draining and self-serving, but that was back when you were a filmmaker and there was the excitement of *Kerouac* coming out. I could put up with him and a lot then."

"Those were good days."

Dana nodded. "They were. I used to like the whole Kerouac Beat thing. I thought it was cool and hip when we met. I mean, you made this film and you knew all about this odd group of artists that I was clueless about. It was intriguing and quirky and I loved our collaboration on the movie. It made you different, but to be honest, now I'm so tired of them. You still read all the bios that come out saying the same damn things about all of those guys and tirelessly talk about the Beats with your Cabrillo regulars. The truth is now, years later, I think they were just a bunch of juvenile misogynists who never grew up."

"It's not just guys. I read the female authors and the feminine critiques. I get the flaws."

"Not sure you really do."

"Wow, from intrigued to judgy."

"Change, Harry, change happens. Life isn't static, but you are. You're exactly the guy I met, but I'm not that woman anymore. A decade has passed. We should change."

"I've changed. I went from filmmaker to theatre owner. That's a huge change."

"Yeah, I know. Don't remind me. When is the obsession with Kerouac gonna end? I mean enough already. It's a little weird."

"I'm not obsessed."

"Harry, please," Dana sighed.

"Ok, maybe I am. So what? PhDs have an area of expertise and it becomes their lives. The Beats are my area."

"So get a PhD then."

"You're being ridiculous. I feel like I am under indictment for being who I am."

"Anyway, that's just the periphery of all of this. It's not the point. We're missing the point."

"What is it then, Dana? What is the elusive point?"

She looked at her watch and then at me. "Harry, I

think on a subconscious level you are very upset about how your life turned out."

I laughed. "Maybe it's more on a conscious level you are very upset about how my life turned out. You want me to be someone other than who I am."

Dana didn't respond at first. She got up and stuffed a few more things in the outside pocket of her carry-on. She rolled the bag to the threshold of the door, took her shoulder bag and flipped through some folders for the meeting. Then she stopped and looked at me. "Maybe so. Maybe you're right. Uber will be here in minutes," she said, before heading to the bathroom.

This certainly didn't go as planned, at least consciously. Maybe Dana's subconscious analysis was right. Who knew, but I did get the feeling that our relationship was closer to ending than it had ever been before.

When she returned from the bathroom, I opted for the innocuous. Maybe I was ready to surrender, too. "So you looking forward to the conference?"

"More like looking forward to Vancouver."

"Great city."

"Yeah, but it's no San Francisco, right?" she pushed.

"Well, nothing is," I said, playing the subtext game.

"Yeah, it's really become so cool with all the techies invading and the prices skyrocketing. It's a city of the 1%ers now, not the city you moved to years ago. It's actually parody of the Beats. I'm surprised it doesn't bother you."

"Well it does, but our little enclave here still has some integrity and soul. It still has a taste of old San Francisco. The Cabrillo is helping maintain that. It's one of the reasons I don't want to sell or move."

"It's cute, Harry, even a little noble that you are trying to fight the present and future by creating the past on one block of San Francisco."

"Thanks," I said sarcastically to the insult wrapped in compliment. "Actually more like a few blocks."

"Bravo."

We were silent for spell. Perhaps resting for the next joust. Dana was peering out our bay window overlooking Cabrillo Street looking for her Uber, not trusting the app.

"So do you have any other ideas to save the theatre?" she asked.

"Not right now."

"Well, you've tried everything."

"Maybe not. I don't know what I haven't thought of yet."

Dana laughed. "Good luck thinking of what you haven't thought of yet."

"So who's going to be at the meeting?" I redirected, probing the one area left that was a bone of contention between us. Might as well expose the whole skeleton.

"A lot of people."

"I mean from your office."

"You specifically mean Stephan, right?"

"Yeah, Stephan. Is he joining you in Vancouver?"

I had caught Dana flirting several times with Stephan

at a few of her office parties. We had a few fights about it, but nothing major. She always countered with one of the poets in the neighborhood, whom I was friends with and really enjoyed her company. I didn't push hard on the Stephan thing because I liked my freedom and the fact that Dana wasn't the jealous type. However, whenever I saw her texting extensively, big smile in the process, I suspected it was Stephan.

"Yes, he is."

"That's nice. You know his plans."

"He's a colleague. We work in the same office. Of course, I know his plan. The whole staff knows who's going. We're not going down that road now, are we?"

I was about to respond, but Dana beat me to it. "Look, Harry, we're killing each other here. Every word has venom, subtext, frustration. All the hallmarks of a dysfunctional couple."

"Agreed. We're heading towards *Who's Afraid of Virginia Woolf*."

Dana rolled her eyes. I suspected it was at my movie reference. I remembered when those references inspired intrigue rather than annoyance. "That's the wrong direction," she said.

"Good, we agree on something," I said with a smile hoping we could at least laugh at ourselves, but it elicited no such levity from Dana.

Her phone chimed, signaling Uber was close. She aggressively yanked up the handle of her carry-on, dropped the shoulder bag on top of it, and dragged the two bags in tow as she headed towards the bedroom door. Just before the threshold, she paused. "You know, Harry, if we can only agree on the fact that we're fucked up, that's a pretty bad sign."

I nodded. "Well, let's try and do better when you get back. Maybe the time apart will do us some good. A little break always used to help. I'll have better timing next time. That was really my bad. All apologies."

Dana was looking down at the floor, not moving or saying anything.

"Hey, you ok?" I asked.

"I don't think so, Harry. This isn't about timing. Forget all that."

"When you get back, how about this? We go up to Bodega Bay for a couple of nights. No cell phones, no Ipad, just you, me, the ocean and time. We'll talk, make love, reconnect and see if we can get back on track. We used love Bodega Bay."

Dana half nodded with an inscrutable expression forming on her face.

"Sound good?" I pushed, approaching her for a make-up hug, but foolishly misreading the signals. She stopped me with a hand in my chest, literally keeping me at arm's length while shaking her head slowly, and staring at her feet.

"Then what? What do you want to do? I'm out of answers," I said with my hands out and palms up in supplication.

Dana headed out the door, but suddenly stopped just beyond threshold, turned and looked at me. After a long pause, she said quietly, "I slept with Stephan."

"What?"

"I slept with Stephan," she said a little louder.

I looked at her, speechless. Then I closed my eyes as if not seeing her would help me process this. Unexpected and odd images flashed across my interval vision: Nadine and I kissing and then to Steve Carrell jumping out of the car in *Crazy, Stupid, Love* when Julianne Moore won't stop talking about her affair.

This wasn't a movie though. It was the delicate seams of my life finally fraying.

"Once?" I asked.

She shook her head.

"And Vancouver? Again?"

"Harry, I'm sorry."

I nodded, holding back tears welling up inside. I don't know why, but my entire focus at that moment was not to cry in front of Dana.

"Harry, I need to get this out. I'm not coming back after the weekend. We're going to stay in Vancouver for a couple of weeks. Then I'll come back and get my stuff. I'm sorry, but it's not too late to have another life for both of us. We tried, but we're so stuck. I don't want to lose any more time."

I felt short of breath, similar to the panic attack on the Bay Bridge, and those damn tears demanded their flow.

"Are you okay, Harry? I'm sorry. I'm really sorry. I wasn't planning on telling you this way, but there is no good way to do it."

I took several deep breaths and rubbed my eyes trying to dam the tears.

"Are you okay?" she asked again. "I'm really sorry."

"You don't need to say sorry anymore. Please don't say it again. And don't ask if I'm okay. What a stupid question."

"Fine." Dana's phone rang jarringly. "Look, I've really got to go."

"Go."

"We've been over for a while. It was inevitable that one of us would meet someone else."

"Right" I said, wanting her to leave immediately before the tears broke free.

"I know, I know. I am handling this the wrong way," she said amidst a relentless slew of text rings. She dialed the driver, "I'm coming in one minute. Please wait."

"One last thing, Harry. Let's make it clean and drama free out of respect for the good days we once had."

I wanted to say *go fuck yourself*, but resisted.

She continued, "You can buy me out of the theatre and property. I'll give you a good price." Dana now seemed emboldened by her confession. "I just want to keep it simple and move on. No offense, Harry."

"Not a fucking chance, Dana."

"Goodbye Harry."

And she was gone.

I lay back in bed, arms at my side, corpse-in-coffin like. I thought of going after her dramatically like it was a movie, but there was no physical reaction to the thought. I heard her descend our steps, the suitcase hitting the floor of our entry hall, the wheels rolling, the heavy door to the street opening and closing with a thud, and then a car trunk slamming shut, followed shortly by two car doors closing. The sound of her Uber got lost in the blur of other cars heading up and down Cabrillo Street in the morning San Francisco rush.

Tears suddenly emerged, slowly at first, but gaining momentum to an uncontrollable sob as if they had breached an ancient levee. Once it was over, there was the therapeutic effect of calming the panic I'd had, but the anxiety shifted into hollowing sadness accompanied by deep nostalgic dread. Memories of better times with Dana taunted me. It felt like the death of a close family member or best friend, especially one you were once so close to and then had lost touch.

Or maybe I was mourning the part of me that had died with our end.

Then over time I just got swallowed up in the disconnection of all relationships. Regret that my mother and I had drifted to the superficial, that I wasn't closer to my father, lost opportunities to be a better brother, friends that had been lost to time, even some random memories of minor relationships that could have been more.

5 — Anti-Social Media

I stayed in the apartment for a few days, drinking, smoking, binge watching film noir (*Night of the Hunter* and *Rebecca* multiple times) or doing my version of *Rear Window* through our bay window. I didn't see any murders in front of the theatre or along Cabrillo Street, but there was the lure of a neon sign advertising for a psychic, Madam Francois, across the street. I'd always been mildly curious to check her out for the hell of it. During these few days, it was the only temptation for me to leave the apartment, but I resisted to avoid running into people I knew. I just couldn't stomach human contact. My misery and I were getting cozy and we needed our cocoon more than Tarot Cards.

I did text Joel that I was down and out with the flu and available only for emergencies.

Finally, four days after being dumped, a morning email from Dana snapped me out of the funk.

> *Harry, there is no easy way to end things. At least, it won't drag on longer than it already has. Reminds me of the Seinfeld metaphor we love that breaking up is like trying to push over a coke machine ☺. I don't mean to make light of things, but I feel like we broke up a long time ago and have been rocking the Coke machine for far too long. Someone had to knock it over and guess it ended up be-*

ing me. For too long we refused to end it for the sake of what we had, rather than keeping it for what we have. It took me a while to realize how disconnected we'd become. Surely you must see this, feel this, right? Unfortunately, I had to meet Stephan to fully realize just how wrong we had become as a couple. We deserve so much more than we gave each other. I wish you only good things, I really do. I hope you find a relationship that is right for you. You are a good man, just not the right man for me anymore and I am not the right woman for you. Sometimes it is quite simple.

As for the theatre and all the assets and money stuff, let's worry about that after I get back. Gives you time to process all of this and then we'll figure that out. I just want my half after we sell. This can be simple too. 50-50 as it should be.

Drama free, agreed?

Fondly,

Dana

I immediately wanted to delete it. I had my finger on the button and then pulled back. I read it again. And again, getting angrier each time. Sure, Dana nailed it that we had emotionally broken up a long time ago and were held together for years through denial, laziness, fear of aloneness and whatever else lurks and loiters in the subterranean. Such is the human relationship tragicomedy.

What really got me was the happy-face emoji and the "fondly" farewell. Wasn't this a moment that should be free of idiotic emojis and weren't all of our years together worth more than a goddamn "fondly"?

But, of course, those were just pitter-patter jabs that softened me up for the knockout punch: She wanted half of the Cabrillo, sneaking it in at the end after saying we don't need to worry about it. Sure, let's not worry about it as long as you know I am dictating the terms at 50-50!

I knew she was entitled to a share of the theatre, some sort of payout or percentage, but 50-50? No way! *Kerouac* had paid for the Cabrillo. Hell, she had protested like crazy when I used the windfall to buy it. We had almost broken up over that. And then in those early days of the theatre, Dana had grudgingly helped out on occasion, but she hadn't actually done any work of significance in years, which was also clearly tied to her pulling away from me (and toward Stephan).

I took a deep breath and tried to ponder this 50% request more seriously, less reactively. The more I thought about it, the more I realized she was probably going to get it regardless of my protestations. She could point to her salary picking up some slack lately and, regardless, I'm sure there was some common-law California marriage rules that entitled her to half of everything no matter who or how we paid for it. The seismic consequences were sinking in. I would have to sell the theatre in order to pay Dana off. I was already overextended on loans and had burned through much of the property equity. There was no way the bank would give me anything else. I had to parry Dana's demands and find a way out of this financial mess. I couldn't lose the Cabrillo, but right now it was all too much to think about it.

Instead, I just wanted to see Nadine.

I wondered if Dana hadn't been with Stephan, would I have pursued Nadine? Would I have been the one to break us up? Dana was right. One of us was eventually going to knock over the coke machine. She just pushed first. Maybe even my last-ditch effort to save us was just guilt over kissing Nadine, guilt over wanting Nadine so much.

What had she been thinking about since our kiss? Did she still see it as potent and dizzying as it had been in the moment? Or had hindsight twisted it into a fleeting, wine-inspired late-night tryst not meant to go anywhere?

She may have even regretted it for cheating on her partner, repressing it like I had in order to focus on Dana. But now there was no need for repression on my end. I had nothing stopping me from pursing Nadine, except her.

*   *   *

It was time to exit the self-imposed exile. I looked in the mirror and the reflection was pathetic. I hadn't shaved or showered during hibernation. My eyes were bloodshot and puffy dark bags bigger than carry-ons hung below. My head straddled the blurry boundary between hungover and drunk.

It was high time to clean up and face reality, or at least clean up and see a movie.

I shaved, leaving a goatee behind for no particular reason other than wanting a different face. I took a long, hot shower and inspired by Jackson's 100-day plan, drank glass after glass of water to give the innards a shower. I was so dehydrated that the water was like fuel.

After a proper breakfast of eggs, ham, and toast, I went downstairs to the theatre to do some work. On the way I detoured by Jackson's apartment, but he wasn't there. I texted him, but it strangely bounced back as if the number no longer existed. So I called and disconnection was confirmed. I left a note under his door to contact me. All I wanted was Nadine's contact information (I had deleted it shortly after he had given it to me), but now I was also wondering what the hell was happening with him? Was he gone for good? If so, it wouldn't be shocking in the context of younger Jackson, but this time I had really gotten the feeling that he was sticking around, determined to share some plan with me.

*   *   *

It was too early for any staff to be in yet so I had some time to ease back into societal discourse.

I made a pot of coffee at concessions and spent the rest of the morning working with some actual focus. First, I did my customary walkthrough of the two theatres, lobby, ticket kiosk, every inch of the Cabrillo to make sure things were clean while looking for any defects or areas that needed renovations or innovations. We had a great cleaning crew that came early every morning so I rarely found any issues on that end. In fact, looking for issues was really just an excuse for me to check out the theatre, slowly and methodically, alone and quiet. It was therapy, my version of TM.

Then I went to my office, which was behind the lobby concession stand. I purposely put it there to be close to the action, hear the corn popping, fountain soda flowing, customers chatting, the melody of the movie theatre experience. But right now things were far from melodious for the Cabrillo. My accountant, Mariana, had been pressuring me to meet and discuss in detail our financial distress. I had been avoiding it for a while, but she was persistent and I knew I had to face the music.

Mariana would say something like, "Harry, we are so in the red that we are bleeding," rolling the R in red, true to her Colombian Spanish roots.

In preparation, I started reviewing our recent sales and the news was actually better than I thought. Sales continued to be stronger post-brawl and all through my four-day exile. Consequently, concessions and bar sales were 30-40 percent higher than normal each day. However, I noticed a slight drop over the last couple of days. The sell-outs had stopped. Crowds were still higher than normal, but it appeared that the Jackson effect was starting to wane, and my bet was that we would gradually return to our old normal. Jackson was a temporary jolt, an espresso on a groggy gray morning.

Perhaps it was delusion or denial or some sort of foolhardy cockeyed optimism, but I still had hope that we could build on the jolt, not let it fade, and keep the new audience. Maybe more advertising. I could do those damn Google Ads that everybody does, but had been resisting out of silly contempt for all things social media. I checked Amazon and *195* was still higher from the last time I looked a few days ago. That was a good sign. But deep down in the recesses where truth patiently lurks until willfully and forcefully summoned, I sensed I was just buying time in order to stave off dealing with the reality of losing the Cabrillo. Jackson's dramatic appearance wouldn't save the day. Its effect ultimately just a mere drop in the financial bucket. I had no idea where I would come up with the money to buy Dana out. I needed a winning lottery ticket and I never played the lottery.

Just then my phone buzzed. I checked hoping it was Nadine even though she didn't have my number.

It was Jackson texting from a new a number.

Jackson: *Hey, man, it's Jackson. Had to get a new phone. Long story. Meet me at Ocean Beach in a half hour. By the surfers. I'm bringing lunch and big news.:)*

Me: *Where you been?*

Jackson: *Big Bear. Winery stuff. See you soon. I hate texting.*

*   *   *

On the way to meet Jackson by bike, I glided by Nadine's apartment, staring at her building and replaying our scene there. A block after I had gone by, I almost hit a parked car, skidding to a stop and nearly going headfirst over my rickety handlebars. I turned around and biked back up Cabrillo Street, enjoying the painful burning tightness in my thighs. When I got to her building again, I stopped and walked to the steps exactly where the kiss happened, hoping to feel the memory more. I sat on the stoop, eyes closed, feeling her and the kiss until the moment got derailed by the intrusion of Dana and Stephan together.

Fuck both of you. You guys did me the favor of freedom. Thank you.

Back on my bike, I headed downhill to Ocean Beach, straight into a tear-inducing headwind.

There was no sign of Jackson yet, so I sat on the beach wall, close to where the shore met the legendary Cliff House restaurant. Surfers were paddling out and riding in. The waves were modest, and no dorsal fins were in sight. A few folks lay on the beach much closer to the ocean than the wall.

While watching the surfers, thoughts of Nadine were interrupted by Dana again, but this time it was her money demands. How the hell would I pay her became my mantric question.

Suddenly, I felt two hands clasp down hard on my shoulders and neck from behind.

"Hey," I yelled, my hands pushing down hard on the cement beach wall to brace myself from falling forward.

"Just ole Jackson, here," he said in a calm voice. "Relax, Harry, I'm gonna crack your neck and ease your entire body into an instant peace. Just trust me."

"Do you know what you're doing? Actually, I'm fine. Loose as a goose. Thanks anyway," I said trying to turn around, but Jackson's grip was tight.

"Bullshit. You're as tight as nun's puckered ass," Jackson said as he massaged my neck and shoulders. He had strong hands, always did, and probably more powerful now thanks to boxing and working the winery land. "Don't worry. I learned this from an old Norwegian fisherman friend in the North Sea while travelling for *195*."

"I remember that scene." I tried to relax, slacken and let Jackson do his thing, hoping I wouldn't be a paraplegic as a result.

"So you really read the book?"

"Of course."

"I didn't know people actually did that anymore," Jackson said wryly. "Okay, muscles are loose enough now." He slid his hands to the side of my neck, rubbing his palms quickly back and forth, the friction warming my skin. Then with his palms pressed hard below my jawline forming a makeshift neck brace, he pressed his thumbs at the base of my skull and jerked my head left, then right — "Pop-pop-pop-pop," crackled the vertebrae as I yelled, "Fuuuuuck!"

Jackson then jumped up on the wall with ease into standing position, awaiting my response.

"Wow," I said, rubbing the back of my neck.

Jackson put his hands together, Namaste style, and bowed.

"I thought this was a Norwegian thing."

"Norwegian who learned it in Osaka. Come on, Harry. Globalization."

"Damn, that was good. Scary as shit, but good.

Thankfully I can still move my limbs."

"Wish I could do it to myself. Instead, I found this chiropractor down in Big Bear who works with the boxers. He's decent. Had him align me yesterday. I'm feeling pretty good."

I rotated my shoulders and felt a newfound ease in my neck muscles. My shoulders seemed lower than before.

"Now you're really loose as a goose," Jackson said.

We walked down the steps to the beach, sitting with the high cement beach wall as our backrest at Jackson's insistence. "Good to have our backs protected." He pulled out two hoagies and a six-pack of Sierra Nevada wrapped in a t-shirt from his backpack. We ate and drank while Jackson filled me in on the winery trip. Coincidentally he also had a meeting with his accountant to make a new financial plan for the winery. The results weren't good. He could sell the land, but it would be at a loss because the failed vineyard decreased the value. The land now had bad grape juju and investors were gun shy. He'd be in the hole by about a million. He could foreclose knowing he'd probably never be able to buy anything with a loan ever again, or he could raise some money and try for another harvest. Maybe hire some experts this time and not go it alone.

"What are you gonna do?" I asked.

"If I lose Big Bear, I lose Samira. So it's simple. I get Big Bear up and running right this time. I just need money."

"What about Kickstarter?"

"Spare me the digital panhandling social media bullshit."

"Yeah, it's annoying, but it's not begging. It's an investment for the millennials. Everybody's into wine or pretends to be. You can offer, say, free tastings for life at Big Bear if they give, I don't know, $100. Maybe a few bottles from the first harvest if they offer $500. Something like that. You can milk the wine fad."

"No."

"Then start writing again," I suggested, hearing myself give the same kind of advice I hated hearing from Dana.

"No, no, that's not the answer. Writing is not the solution, it's the problem. I'm done. Don't people get that. It's not a damn lark. It's real. You of all people should get that," Jackson said, perturbed.

"Yeah, I get it. My bad. Funny thing is that I am meeting with my accountant today, too. I need money to save the Cabrillo. Might be as much as you need or more."

"You're kidding?"

"Wish I were."

"I didn't think you were in that deep. You guys seem busy."

"Well, thanks to you kicking your own characters' asses, lately we are. But it's a temporary boost. We need a long-term surge. If not, then I need an infusion of capital."

"How about your own advice?"

"Which is?"

"Kickoff."

"Kickstarter. Shit, maybe I should. Never thought of it for the Cabrillo."

Jackson looked me in the eyes, a bit wide and wild-eyed. "It's bullshit."

"No, really, I heard some success stories. This LA writer, Nick Miller, got his book off the—"

"Harry, we're not talking about plugging novels. We're talking major debt here. The Social Media billionaires are already killing the San Francisco we knew and loved and mythologized. They're wrecking our myth. Let's not play their game. I got an old school plan that will get us the money."

"Ok, what's ya got?"

He didn't say anything, but stared at me again with an intense, giant-eyed gaze.

"You going all manic on me?"

"Why not? Manics get shit done. Manics change the world. Normal is a flat, straight road to nothing."

Jackson paused, took a slow, deep breath while staring out at the Pacific. He suddenly seemed lost in thought, as if I weren't here anymore. Then he took a long swig of his beer, downing half the bottle, before turning back to me. "This is perfect. Confluence at Ocean Beach. Oh, I've got a tale for you, Harry." Jackson then crossed himself and said, "Bless me father, for I have sinned. My last confession was, ahhh, never."

"What are you talking about?"

"I accuse myself of numerous, no countless sins, but there's one big one I need absolved, so I can do it again," Jackson said, diabolically grinning.

*   *   *

It all started in Barcelona, in another kind of confluence. Jackson had coincidentally run into our old friend and fellow Sunsetter, Arsen Satorian. I remembered Arsen very well. A damn good painter and Jackson's best friend back in the day. Arsen and I weren't that close, but we had the Greek-Armenian kinship, sharing similar cultures and ancestors both slaughtered by the Turks, though his folk got the worst of it.

Jackson's globetrotting *195* journey stalled in Spain after only 25 or so countries. Stuck in Barcelona, wandering and wondering along Las Ramblas, he ran into Arsen sitting in a café.

"Café Zurich, actually. So I snuck up behind the melancholy Armenian and gave him the neck treatment."

Arsen had left San Francisco to follow a beautiful bipolar Spaniard whom he'd fallen tragically in love with. When things fell apart, he stayed in Barcelona trying to figure out his next move, with suicide on the table of options.

That meeting with Arsen set up a series of events that Jackson said were already in motion. He and Celeste were living in this kind of secretive, neo-Beat Hotel in Harvard Square called The Brattle Arms, the name befittingly conjuring up film noir.

It was run by a mysterious and hermetic woman whom no one had seen in decades. Jackson called her Madam X. You had to apply to stay at The Brattle Arms.

It was like getting an artist's grant and no small one at that: room, board, and a decent stipend. Sort of an underground NEA grant, except much more valuable, albeit with a few strange and dangerous strings attached.

Jackson's string was crime. In covert fashion, Jackson had some money to support his work, but a larger sum, much larger, was also offered if he would steal a Picasso from Harvard's Fogg Museum. He couldn't confirm Madam X was behind the plan because he had never met or spoken to her. She worked through proxies, but he was pretty sure it was her gig.

"Shit!" I silently yelled, realizing what he had done. "You fucking stole *Rest*? Holy shit!" I had read all about it in the news and followed the case closely. It was a huge deal, the biggest art theft since *The Scream* heist in Oslo and the biggest one in the States since the Isabella Steward Gardner job in Boston, just across the Charles River from The Fogg.

"Shhh," he said, nodding.

"Arsen, too?" I whispered.

"Among others, yes."

"Wow, fucking incredible. And you got away with it."

"Touch and go for a while, but we did our homework."

When the smoke cleared and no one was charged, the artists-turned-art thieves got their loot, 2.5 million dollars each.

I was still trying to process that old friends were mastermind criminals. Jackson ate his sandwich quietly, perhaps sensing I needed silence to absorb this. Maybe a few minutes passed when I opened up two more beers, raised my bottle and whispered, "To stealing Picasso."

Jackson smiled, met my bottle solidly, and we drank.

"I have a thousand questions, but I guess you don't want to tell me everything."

"No need to," Jackson said. "You know all you need to know.

"But why tell me anything?"

"Good question, Harry. Past is prelude."

We finished our sandwiches and the second beer. Jackson looked around, first behind him, peering above the wall, then directly in front at the surfer area before looking down the long stretch of beach to the south. There were a few folks near us, but far away enough so they couldn't hear us.

Jackson looked lost in rumination again, fixated blankly ahead at the ocean. Finally, he said, "Let's take a walk to the other side of the Cliff House. I don't like the vibe here."

*   *   *

We walked past the restaurant and then headed down the steep rocks along the cliff to a tiny patch of beach, no bigger than the size of an average living room. I'd never been down here before. We sat on the sand with our backs resting crookedly against jagged rocks. The ocean was like a placid lake on this side, but the tide was slowly, almost imperceptibly creeping in, wetting the beach to within about five feet of us.

Whenever the tide was coming in, my mind always darted to the film, *Blackbeard, the Pirate*, or more specifically to the end of the movie when Blackbeard is finally captured and sentence to slow, torturous death by rising tide. His captors dug a deep hole along the shore at low tide and buried Blackbeard in it up to his neck. He helplessly watched the tide gradually come in as he slowly drowned.

"I think we may be washed out of here soon," I warned.

"No, we're fine. The tide should be peaking now. Have you been to the new and improved Cliff House?"

"Yeah, the views are better with all the glass, but the food still sucks. Dana and I went once for anniversary or something. Good place for drinks though."

"You guys ventured really far for a special occasion," Jackson jabbed.

I shrugged and didn't take the bait. "I like this spot right here though. Nice and secluded."

"Precisely," Jackson said and then shifted his position so that he was sitting cross-legged and facing me, zeroing in his eye contact. "So here's the deal. Madam X got in touch with me or at least I'm guessing it was her. Whoever it is, we'll just call her Madam X."

"Fitting."

"She's got another job for me."

I rolled my eyes. "Come on, Jackson."

"What?" he asked, looking sincerely confused by my reaction.

"Are you kidding? You got away with a huge

crime and you were a damn amateur. And now you're gonna go to the well again and push your luck? You got thieving fever or what?"

Jackson laughed. "Maybe a little bit, but I think it's less about fever and more about opportunity."

"You're crazy."

"Harry, come on. You're not the snap judgment kind of guy. That's not very San Francisco of you."

"Well, San Francisco ain't very San Francisco anymore."

"Touché. Anyway, just hear me out."

"No need to but do as you please."

"Look, I'm not an amateur anymore. I've got one under my belt."

"Yeah, a real veteran now."

"Actually, it's two jobs this time so I'm double dipping in the well. How's that?"

"Fucking crazy."

Undeterred, Jackson explained the first gig. He and his crew were going to dismantle all the speed cameras in San Francisco. They would open up the metal boxes, cut the wires, do some damage, and leave a small sticker of Mark Zuckerberg's face."

"X has some high-powered lefty friends," Jackson said.

"Sounds more like tea party quacks."

"Kinship of the extremes."

"Well, I can't stand Facebook and all that, but boy he's been taking some heat lately."

"Well deserved."

"Gotta say the whole thing sounds kind of goofy."

"Kind of fun, actually, and I loathe those damn cameras. Neal Cassady must be turning over in his grave." Jackson knew what strings to pull with me.

Jackson explained that there were 45 speed cameras throughout the city. "We" didn't have to get them all. X told him to just get enough spread throughout the city to make headlines and give it the appearance of a planned job with multiple groups; a conspiracy by definition.

Jackson had already done the research. He had taken photos of all the different types of speed cameras, had secured the tools to quickly break into the boxes, cut the wires, crack the lenses, and then spray an instant freeze chemical all over the machinery. The masterminds wanted enough damage to keep them out of commission for a spell. He had uniforms that exactly matched the city electrical workers' jump suits. It would look like routine maintenance or repairs especially since it would be a daytime, plain sight job. No one would think twice of it. He had five people, including himself, already in and needed one more to have three crews of two.

"So?" he said with a smile.

"So what?"

"You in?"

I scoffed. "I want nothing to do with this."

"Well, of course, because you don't know the reward. We wouldn't do it just for the adrenaline rush or a political statement. This isn't the 60s."

"No, I'm not doing it because it's crazy."

"Not at all. This is pure sanity. You need money, right?"

"Not this kind of money."

"What, you're looking for pure, clean money? No such thing, Harry."

"Right, I'll tell the judge that philosophically speaking all money is tainted and corrupt, so my crime is just the crime of everyday existence."

"You're not curious at all?"

I paused and then said, "Fine, tell me how much for kicks."

"Ahh, a chink in the armor, huh Harry? Show me the money, right? We bohemians are such frauds after our twenties," Jackson said, with a hearty laugh that he quickly muffled with his hand. "The combine slowly pulls us in."

"I'm not doing this, Jacko."

"300 grand. Each."

I didn't say anything, just stared straight out at the Pacific.

"It's a two-part gig. The speed cameras are just a low-risk warm up for the big one. The first one tests our mettle and creates chemistry for the group. Call it a tune up fight before the championship."

I could feel Jackson looking at me while I followed one surfer standing up and riding a small wave to shore. He never fell, just beaching the board and walking off it.

"Do you have a record?" he asked.

I shook my head. "Of course not."

"Good. If we get caught, the absolute most we do is pay a fine and a community service slap on the wrist. And we keep the 300K. But we won't get caught. I have been prepping this for months. There is no sure thing, but this is as close as it gets."

I turned to Jackson staring directly into his eyes and said, "The money is barely a dent in my dilemma." Then I turned towards the Pacific and followed another surfer, cresting a decent wave before falling somewhat dramatically. I took a big gulp of Sierra Nevada.

"Add a zero for part two."

I almost spit out my beer.

"Got your attention now."

I looked at Jackson, shaking my head.

"This is our ticket, Harry. The Wonka Bar golden ticket out of the quagmire."

"3 fucking million?" I asked.

"Well, 3.3 to be precise."

"Might as well tell me part two now."

Jackson grinned. "Can't do that yet."

"Why not?"

"Can't say what I don't know. X won't reveal that until it's time to do it. If we fail at part one, there is no part two."

"Let's just say I agree to the first one. We do it and then I don't want in for the second one after I find out the plan. Do I still get the money?"

"Of course. Madam X is a straight shooter. You do the work, you get paid."

300 grand wouldn't solve things, but it would buy

me some time, pay for lawyers to deal with Dana's demands, and pay off a few urgent debts. But 3 million solves everything. I downed the rest of my beer.

"Kind of crazy not to do part one, right?" Jackson asked, his voice calmer, less persuasive since he knew he had hooked the fish. "Easy money, a good civil liberty cause, and a slap in the face to new San Francisco from the old guard."

I shrugged.

"Oh, and one last thing. We'll be in three teams of two. Your partner would be Nadine."

"What? You're kidding!"

Jackson shook his head slowly. "No time for kidding."

"Now you're playing dirty."

"Money and love, brother. Art's a seductive lie. That's what it all boils down to anyway, right? Everything else is window dressing."

"Why is she doing this?"

"Needs the money and wants the adventure. Why else? She's Beat. She's one of us."

"Right, come on, Jackson. What's her money problem?"

"Everyone has a money problem besides the one percenters? But if you insist on specifics, I think her dad is in some kind of trouble. You can ask her yourself." Jackson said. "I need to meet with a few other folks, Harry. We're ready to move on this. What do you say?"

"Is that why she came here? Is that why you introduced us? Just to lure me in to do the job."

"Don't be silly."

"I'm not. Was the reading all part of the plan to get me—"

"Harry, stop. Control your paranoia. It's not a conspiracy. You and Nadine's connection is organic, real. I had nothing to do with your chemistry."

"There's just too much happening all at once. It's all too connected."

"Embrace it. Nothing was happening for too long, right? You were tired of the plateau. Now you're off it."

"And riding a rollercoaster."

"Look, take a night or two to process. Madam X sets things up to succeed. She knows people on the inside, cops, politicians, pays them off, and carefully crafts the conditions for this to work. I'm no criminal mastermind. I got away with *Rest* because she took care of all the variables. She makes it work behind the scenes and we just execute."

Jackson got up using my shoulder for balance. He gave me a couple of reassuring taps and said, "Harry, we got this. I got your back and it will give you more time with Nadine. Love and money," he said, before ascending the cliff.

Despite Jackson's assurances, paranoiac rhythms were flowing in my quicksand mind. The kiss? Was the whole Beat thing made up, too? Jackson knew me well. He knew the buttons to push. Who was this woman Nadine? Questions were manically multiplying. I shook my head vigorously side-to-side, cheeks slapping my jaws, trying to physically dispel the maddening trapdoors in my mind.

It was all too film noir, but I couldn't deny the energy from stepping off the plateau and into living a screenplay.

And then there was Madam X. Real or a fictional ruse from Jackson? Just like the Mr. X character in the film, *JFK*, a character invented by Oliver Stone to tie up the loose ends. And the same damn variable, too.

My head was spinning. I needed a neural downshift.

I needed to see Nadine.

6 — Organic Cigarettes

I was in my office waiting for Mariana to arrive. It was two minutes before two and Mariana was never late, but I was not thinking of Mariana. It was now all about Nadine and the 3.3 million dollars that would save the Cabrillo. How was I going to say no to this opportunity?

"Hey, Harry," Mariana said from my office doorway. "Everything okay?" she asked.

"Not really."

"Yeah, you look deep into it. Didn't even notice me standing here."

"Come on in. Have a seat and let's get into it."

Once she settled in, she looked me in the eyes and said, "Harry, not sure you want to hear the news I have."

"I don't have a choice. How bad is it?"

Mariana scrunched her face as if she were in pain.

"I know. Lay it on me."

Mariana pulled her laptop out of her bag and set it up on my desk. She turned the screen towards me with a PowerPoint loaded and ready to give all the gory details in a tragically clinical narrative of graphs, charts, and tables—an irrefutable financial apocalypse.

"Harry, even if the surge from your friend's fight drama carried on and we sold out every show from here to eternity, we'd still be in trouble."

"Nice movie reference, Mariana."

"Wish I could meet my Burt Lancaster, but that's

another story. Anyway, ok, Harry, I have some ideas. Just hear them out."

"I'll hear 'em, but not sure I'll listen."

"Of course you won't, but I'll voice them for my own sake. I would like to suggest carving out more movie theatres. Not a multiplex, but four or five instead of two. You need to appeal to more tastes and increase ticket revenue."

Before I could reject the idea, Mariana beat me to it. "But I'm not going to suggest it because I know you would hate that. And you would start your anti-cookie cutter, multiplex, small-business-hero rant, bringing up all the old San Francisco theatres back in the day like the Coronet, Alhambra, etc. and how you are carrying their baton."

"Well said. You know the script. And I'm glad you didn't suggest it by not suggesting it."

"You're so predictable."

"Mariana, you know damn well two becomes four, and then four slices into eight little shoebox theatres showing Fast and Furious 14 and Jurassic Park 12 and on down the slippery slope we slide into cinematic conformism, drinking the Kool-Aid, betraying the entire—"

Mariana put her hand up. "Stop. Please stop. Look, it has its own financial challenges, too. We'd have to buy out neighbors again and expand and we don't have the capital for it anyway. So I really wasn't suggesting it. Just ruling it out."

"Good. Ruled out. We agree."

"Now just listen to another idea, a real one, Harry,

and don't go all manic on me."

"I already know the answer is no with that lead in."

Mariana sighed. "Ay, Harry, you're not in the driver's seat here. Debt is driving this car and you are a pedestrian about to get run over."

"Nice analogy. Run me over."

"You keep just two theatres, but expand them. Get more seats. Get rid of the old movies downstairs, move the current indie film downstairs and show a blockbuster upstairs. Charge the same price for both. Theatre 2 is killing us. It's rarely even half-filled and we don't charge enough. We charge less and get less customers. That's the opposite of a successful business."

"Not gonna happen. We'll lose our entire identity."

Mariana took a deep breath. "You're so stubborn. Terco como una mula!"

"Look, Mariana, your suggestions only make financial sense on paper, but we'll just be like everyone else. Why would they come here? The locals come because of what we are, or better yet, what we aren't."

"We need more than locals, Harry."

"If we show a blockbuster, we might as well open a Starbucks in the lobby while we're at it."

"Fine. Then the next move is to fire Joel and you take over managing. Save his salary, benefits cost, and we keep your current salary even though you'd be managing. You basically pay him to chat with the customers anyway while you do most of his work. Wouldn't be a big change other than cutting expenses, which we desperately need to do."

"How can you say that?"

"Say what?"

"That Joel doesn't do anything."

"Ahhh, because he doesn't do anything, Harry."

"He's crazy about you. You know that."

Mariana's expression suddenly had the look of eating rotten food. "Si! Dios mio! He's so creepy. He used to be shy about it, which was a little cute. But lately he's been all eyes on me."

"He really likes you."

Mariana sighed. "You know, it's my romantic plight to have someone like Joel like me. He's not my Burt Lancaster."

I laughed. "Well, that's for sure, but your bar is pretty damn high."

"Not really. Anyway, you should fire him to save money and spare me."

"Come on, Mariana. Joel's part of the family. You're being harsh."

"I'm a woman in the business world with a Spanish accent. That's two strikes. I can't afford to be soft."

"Well, the customers like him and so do I."

"Harry, you're too ideological and too nice. Everything is emotional when it needs to be logical. You need to straighten your spine, use your head, and get your heart out of everything. Okay, forget the theatre ideas for now and we'll keep creepy Joel. Let's try the apartments," Mariana said, taking a deep breath of frustration and exhaling loudly. "We need to raise the rent on the couple in apartment 2 and what about apartment 3? Is it rented yet?"

I liked how Mariana used the first person. She was tough, but I knew she really felt part of this. She was a good woman trying to help. I just hated all of her ideas.

"The Feldens have been there for four years and are great tenants and customers. They're at the theatre at least once a month. I don't want to gouge them."

"Fine, apartment 3?"

"It's rented," I said, a bit sheepishly.

"Okay, finally something good for a change. How much? The way this city is going you can easily get five grand for it."

I hesitated. Sometimes I felt like I was talking to my father instead of Mariana. Or, at least a father.

"What's the deal, Harry?"

"My buddy Jackson is crashing there for a while."

"What are you charging him? Don't say nada. Please, not nada!"

"He has nada."

"Jesucristo, Harry! If you're not going to do anything differently, we will continue to sink like the Titanic. I give it six months before rock bottom."

"Then what?"

"There is nothing after rock bottom, Harry! That's the meaning of rock bottom! You won't be able to pay your bills. You will have nada. The bank will foreclose on you and the Cabrillo will become a health club."

"What happened to *we*?"

"You've made this about you, not us," she said, clearly exasperated.

"I can borrow from the equity. I own the building. Best investment I ever made, right? You always say that. I'll always have the real estate, right? Land is real," I parroted.

"You borrowed on the equity several times already. You only own about 10% of the building. The bank owns the rest. You owe creditors more than the 10% equity. Los Americanos never own anything. It's always borrow, borrow, borrow."

"This is getting serious. We're up shit's creek."

"You passed shit's creek about a year ago. Dana has been trying to tell you this, too. You don't listen. Listen to your woman, Harry."

I grinned. "Yeah, right. I know. I get it."

"If you really got it, you would bite the bullet, sell now and take the money and run. You might have created a little bubble of an opportunity from the notoriety from your friend who pays no rent. It's perfect for some nostalgic movie-lover buyer who just watched *Cinema Paradiso* and wants to throw away a few million to fulfill a childhood dream. Those types will overpay."

"I am that type minus the money."

"No, you're much more genuine, to a fault. We need some fraud from Silicon Valley or a Social Media millennial who has millions to burn on an impulse buy and wants to show off the theatre to friends. Harry, seriously, you need to get out before it all collapses. We're on the brink. The rest of your life is at stake here."

I was shaking my head slowly during Mariana's futile attempt at rational persuasion. Then I looked her in the eyes, deeply, poker-faced and quiet.

"Harry, stop it. One Joel is enough! And you need to be serious."

"Por qué I have nada if I sell. Nada y nada y nada pues nada."

"Harry, spare me the existential nada. This is about money nada."

"It's true. I would have nothing. No purpose. No meaning. This is not about business, or even about money. It is truly existential. It's about raison d'être. Mariana, I feel a panic attack looming."

"Ok, ok, then, keep the wine and beer bar and bookshop. Do the readings and run the place. Maybe turn it into a bistro. But sell the theatre to survive."

I laughed. "You're not getting it."

"You're not getting it!"

"Each idea is worse than the other. The bar and books are peripheral. Open up a bistro? Che loca! It's all about the movies."

"Fine, then write the goddamn second screenplay for Christ's sake! That's instant money. Your wife is right."

"We're not married."

"Dana's right!"

I told Mariana to leave me the PowerPoint. I'd review it carefully, reconsider her ideas and try to come up with some new ones. And then I asked her how much cash would get me out of the hole and back in the black.

"A Million is a big help. 1.5 saves the day for several years. You got a benefactor hiding somewhere? A rich, lonely aunt about to die?"

"Maybe," I said with a shrug.

"Well, tell her to hurry up."

"She's stubbornly hanging on."

"Those damn old people," Mariana said, giving me a hug. "Sorry to be so pushy, but it's time, Harry."

I nodded.

"Let's meet next week."

"Sure."

"Harry, this is not a movie. It's real life. You need to make a decision."

"Mariana, you're absolutely right."

*   *   *

As soon as Mariana left, I found Jackson's text with Nadine's contact information. I powered through hesitation and texted her, asking if she were free to meet for a drink anytime soon. Surprisingly, she responded immediately and said she was free. "At this risk of appearing too anxious, how about it in an hour?" We decided to meet at McClellan's.

To kill time and anxiety, I took a walk around the neighborhood, ending up at a little neighborhood market on Cabrillo and 42nd that sold individual cigarettes for 50 cents each. There had to be at least a 100 in the plastic box at the counter marked, "50 cent fags." The shop owner was gay and British. He liked to get a reaction from non-locals. I dug out four American Spirits. Might as well go organic while inhaling the carcinogens.

Dana and I both used to smoke them back in the early days until she quit. She'd read an article that debunked American Spirit. They were owned by the behemoth RJ Reynolds, had no affiliation with Native Americans despite the name and logo, and there was no proof that the organic and chemical free aspect of the cigarette had any less negative effect than Marlboros or whatever.

"They're frauds," Dana said.

But they were still my cigarette of choice. I put three of them in my shirt pocket and smoked one on my way to McClellan's.

As I inhaled, I noticed my right hand holding the cigarette was shaking.

Fortunately, Nadine wasn't at the bar when I got there. It allowed me to settle in, get a drink into the system to try to quell the quivers inside and out. I ordered a Harp from Shawn and took a few quick, but big gulps. I didn't know whether to bring up the kiss or just pretend it didn't happen. *Just let it happen, Harry, organically, like the cigarette.* I took another gulp of beer and then saw Nadine coming into the bar out of the corner of my eye. I swiveled to greet her, perhaps too fast.

"Hi Harry," she said with a smile.

"Hi Nadine." I half-started to stand up, paused awkwardly mid-stand, and sat down.

"You can give me a hug if you want," she said, looking a bit bemused.

"Sorry, I wasn't, I, ahhh, don't know exactly. Never mind. Gladly." I finally stood up, abandoning my attempt at language, and gave her a hug. A good hug, holding her in for a few moments. She seemed to settle willingly into my body. Again, the top of her head was right below my nose. I inhaled her scent, the smell of her hair, the smell of Nadine. If pheromones triggered this internal rebellion of runaway attraction, then there was a chemical revolution going on in my heart.

When we pulled apart, we looked at each other.

"Picking up where we left off," she said, giggling cutely.

"This is crazy, isn't it?"

"Completely," she said.

"Nadine, right?" Shawn said, interrupting the magnetic field.

"Yes,"

"Welcome back to McClellan's."

"Thank you."

We both sat down.

"What's your flavor tonight?"

Nadine looked at my beer. "I'm having a Harp, but I was thinking to switch to wine for the next one," I said.

"Wine sounds perfect," she said. "Malbec?"

"Malbec, it is," I said to Shawn. "A bottle."

"How high up the ladder do you want to go?" He asked as he slid the wine list to us. Nadine took the list and chose a higher rung bottle. She told me it was on her since I had covered all the drinks the other night. I argued, but she ignored me. Nadine did the tasting ritual and then Shawn poured the wine and left us alone at the end of the bar. We raised our glasses and she said, "To a new friendship."

"I'm not sure that's the right term for us."

"Probably not."

"Definitely not."

Nadine laughed. "I like how we have just jumped right in and completely disregarded any pretense of small talk."

I looked outside and then said, "Pretty good weather today. A little foggy as usual, but patches of blue sky in the Richmond for a change."

She laughed. "I've been feeling foggy for the last few days."

"Me, too. And simultaneously crystal clear."

"Exactly, foggy clarity," Nadine said, before taking a healthy quaff of the Malbec. "So, Harry, since we're cutting immediately to the chase, you kind of caught me off guard the other night. Actually, really off guard."

"Yeah, me, too. I still have a touch of vertigo."

"I haven't kissed a man in a long time. To be honest, I've been kind of off men for a while."

"I've been kind of off women for a while."

Nadine laughed. "Really, that's too bad. How so? Jackson said you more or less married."

"Sort of, and definitely regarding the lack of sex part."

"Hmmm, okay. And can I ask what that means?"

"You can ask me anything and everything, Nadine."

"I'll remember that. Might cause you some trouble."

"I didn't say I would answer," I parried.

"Touché."

"So put it this way, I can't remember the last time

Dana and I kissed. Really kissed."

"The new has to get old sometime."

"Doesn't have to end though."

"How long have you two been together?" Nadine asked.

"Almost a decade. I don't even really remember the last time we had sex. I know the last time we tried. Or I should say I tried."

"So are you guys in trouble? Sorry, can I ask these questions?"

"Anything and everything." I thought about telling the truth. I really wanted to, but something held me back on this one aspect. Maybe I thought it would overwhelm her and make her retreat because I would be so fresh on the rebound. Or that I wanted us both on the same playing field of cheating. "I don't know. I get the feeling something will happen soon one way or another. We're teetering for sure."

"Well, whatever happens, I wouldn't factor in the other night. Or this little connection we have."

"Why not? And I wouldn't call it little."

"We need to keep our heads on straight. I don't think we should get all carried away and crazy about a late night, wine-soaked kiss, you know."

"Sure," I lied and felt a wave of disappointment darkly pass through me, gravity rudely yanking me from my dreamy perch. It all seemed to matter more to me than her. "What about you? You're in a long termer, too, right?"

Nadine went into detail. She was with the same

woman for nearly three years. They had a good relationship. She called it healthy and loving, maybe a little boring, "but don't they all get that way at some point?" Most of her relationships in the past had been men. She'd only had a few flings with women, usually due to alcohol. All of her serious male relationships were full of drama and craziness. "Completely unhealthy and dysfunctional, but not boring, I guess. I am doomed one way or the other, but I've chosen boredom over drama."

She admitted a lot of it was on her. With men, she became jealous and possessive, insecure, a version of herself she couldn't stand. She found that so odd and puzzling, beguiling enough to consider therapy, but she decided to do the analysis on her own. Ultimately it wasn't hard to connect the mother and father dots. She drew logical conclusions though didn't dismiss the illogical. Nadine took a break from dating and tried to avoid situations like the other night with me, so she didn't slip into something troublesome.

She began focusing on a new career plan and decided to quit the family business and follow her passion by studying literature. She moved to Tangier and enrolled in an MA program in American Lit, focusing on the Beats. She threw herself into her studies and then in her second semester she met Christine, an American expat doing a semester abroad in Morocco. The relationship was immediately peaceful. It just became easy. She didn't turn jealous and trust was not an issue. They had some fights, but it was all very functional and normal, unchartered territory with the men. They could argue without it being the end of the world. She was a much better version of herself with Christine. Obviously, Nadine just concluded she was better a fit with women in romantic relationships. And she was fine sexually without men. "I mean I'm a little weird in bed anyway so conventional male-female sex is not a big loss for me."

"Weird, how so?" I asked, very intrigued.

Shaking her head and grinning, she said. "Out of all that, that's your first question. Such a straight man!"

"Guilty as charged there," I said with an impish shrug.

"Well, that information is only reserved for my lover. So you'll never know," she said, sly grin included.

"Never?"

"Never ever."

"You're cute when you're cheeky," I said.

Nadine swiveled towards me and looked me in the eye for an extended time. "Maybe we should say never to whatever this thing is. If we don't, it will all be so very complicated, and others will get hurt. My dad always said to adhere to the KISS principle in life. Keep it simple, stupid."

"We have a different kiss principle."

"That is definitely true, and we should never do that again."

"Okay, here's to the simplicity of never," I said insincerely as a toast, hoping she wasn't serious, and this was just a game of flirty fun.

"I like that. To the simplicity of never."

"I don't like it at all. Do you smoke?" I asked.

"No, but I would love a cigarette."

We went outside and smoked the American Spirits. I could see a decent crowd around the ticket kiosk of the theatre two blocks south. Nadine seemed to be watching the theatre activity as well. Jackson's offer hung over my head like the pluming smoke and I still couldn't shake the lingering vibe that the theft and Nadine may have been collusively intertwined.

"Your theatre is busy tonight."

"Yeah, the Jackson effect."

We went back inside and ordered a bottle of Pinot this time and some bar snacks. We were sitting closer to each other, our knees were touching; it wasn't consciously done, just our own personal gravity at work. Neither of us said anything about it. I loved talking to her, yet I was also dying to kiss her. I wanted to do both at the same time. Nadine put her hand on my shoulder and then leaned over and kissed me on the cheek.

I smiled. "That won't help the pursuit of never."

"Isn't never a non-pursuit?" she riffed.

"Not in our case."

"Just one kiss for good luck." Then she whispered into my ear, "But don't think you're getting lucky, pal. Remember, men and I don't mix. You bring out the worst in me."

"I would love your trouble in all its forms."

She sighed. "Okay, no more flirting." She straightened her posture, made a serious face. "Tell me something, Harry, to distract me from wanting to kiss you."

"You flirt when you are not flirting."

"It's the wine. After a bottle, all I want to do is play. Wine is terrible for walls." Nadine took a deep breath. "Now, seriously, tell me something."

"Okay, ahh, I've been to Morocco and I love Tangier."

"Me, too. Tangier is my favorite city in Morocco!"

"We shot *Kerouac* on location there," I said.

"I know, I could tell. I knew all the places you shot. Some scenes were right near my campus and apartment."

"Were you there when I was there?"

Nadine laughed.

"What's so funny?"

"No, but you're kind of why I went there."

"You're kidding. Cut it out."

She shrugged. "It's true. I really liked the film. I mean, really liked it. Loved it. I'd been into the Beats before and had read the big ones, *On the Road* and *Howl*, while I studied 20th century lit as an undergrad, but the film hooked me. It inspired me to read a whole bunch of Kerouac novels, even the obscure ones. Don't sleep on *Maggie Cassidy*. Did my time with Burroughs and Corso. I'd already read most of Ginsberg. Then I got into the women — di Prima, Johnson, Waldman, Hettie Jones. The women are so overlooked."

"Agreed! I've read everything by Joyce Johnson and some of all of the others."

"The Beat women need more of voice and that's why I'm here."

"Really?"

"I did my MA thesis on the influence of Beat women on feminist 60s literature. The Beat men are really less sexist than they appear once you dig deeper. I mean, Jack and Neal and those guys were certainly sexist and had some definite misogyny issues, don't get me wrong, but it's more nuanced than that. So, my studies brought me to Tangier and now to San Francisco to get my PhD. And your film is partly responsible."

"That's the biggest compliment *Kerouac* has ever received."

"Now don't let it all go to your head. I am in love with the film, not the filmmaker, silly," she said pushing me on the shoulder.

"Of course."

"I mean, I love Martin Scorsese films, but I am not into Martin Scorsese and I certainly don't want to kiss him."

"So then the other night really had nothing to do with the film?" I asked.

Nadine smiled. "Of course, it did. It's a turn on that you made a film about something I'm so passionate about. But I had no intentions of that. That night you weren't the director of *Kerouac*. You were just this nice guy named Harry who couldn't take his eyes off me."

"Still can't."

"God, you are making this hard."

I filled our glasses with more Pinot. Nadine watched and said, "Uh oh. Walls are crumbling."

"What was it then? The other night?" I asked.

"A moment perhaps?"

"But that doesn't—"

"Explain this right now." Nadine said, finishing my sentence, laughing, in a sexy and unabashed way. Dana was the type to reign in her laugh, instinctively covering her mouth and as much of her face as possible. Nadine's laugh was free and liberated, face fully exposed.

"What's so funny?" I asked.

"I'm finishing your sentences already."

"Incredible. Let's do a test."

"Of what?"

"The other night."

"What kind of test?" She asked, squinting cheekily.

"You know, the kiss, of course."

"Very smooth. That's a good one. Nice try, not gonna happen."

"I'm serious. I mean I would make any excuse to kiss you, but I am honestly curious. I just never had that kind of feeling before from a kiss. Seriously, no joke. I've never felt that before kissing anyone."

"I know. I agree. It was fucking crazy! And it's not right."

"Yeah, it's wrong," I agreed, "but that was the best wrong of my life."

"Must be why people cheat. You feel alive. The danger, the risk, the forbidden element causing the excitement. Maybe that's what turned us on so much. Maybe that was the dizzy thrill."

"I don't think so," I said and leaned in slowly to kiss Nadine, allowing her time to stop me if she wanted to. She didn't. We kissed gently, our lips softly touching, and immediately I felt the connection and soon the vertigo, the feeling that nothing else in life mattered except kissing this woman, that suddenly we were the only people in the pub, the only two people alive. We continued, more deeply, and then I kissed her cheek, and neck, and around her ear. I could hear her breathing intensify and then some whispery moaning before she slowly pulled away, both hands on my chest nudging me away. "Stop," she said with her eyes still closed. When she opened her eyes, she sighed.

"Me, too," I said.

"Even more so," she whispered. "It's narcotizing."

"Indeed addictive."

"Silly man. Silly us."

I emptied the rest of the bottle evenly in our glasses. We toasted without words. We didn't need any.

"Screw it, Harry, I want you," Nadine said, putting her hand on my thigh, slowly moving it up my leg until it easily found my rock-hard erection. "He wants me, too," she giggled. Then she moved her hand gently up and down, until I began breathing heavily, too heavily. "We need to stop," I whispered in between panting. "I mean, ahh, I might just make a scene here."

"Teenage Harry," Nadine teased, kissing me while slowly removing her hand.

"It's you. You turn back the clock."

"Let's get out of here."

*   *   *

We didn't want to go to my apartment even though I told her Dana was out of town nor did we have the patience for the five-block walk to her apartment. "I know the spot," I said. We headed into the Cabrillo, saying a few hellos to staff. Joel was at the concession area, just kind of loitering, his main managerial activity. He turned his attention to us and started approaching when I waved him off. "Sorry, Joel, important meeting right now. We'll talk later."

Disregarding my rejection, he asked, "How did the meeting with Mariana go? Did you—"

"Later, Joel, later."

We walked into my office. I closed the door and locked it. There was a window to the lobby area so I let the blinds down, closing the slats as tightly as possible. I turned on the desk light to dim.

"This is perfectly risqué," Nadine said. "Fucking in the boss's office. Classic porn."

"Nice description," I said laughing hard.

"Let's not be boring, Harry."

"No, never."

We started kissing immediately, passionately. "I'm yours, Harry," she whispered to me.

I led her slowly to the wall so that her back was up against it, pressing her hands against the wall above her head.

"A few shades of Harry. You know, I really like that. Kind of my fetish thing."

"Me, too."

"Take control," she whispered.

I had some neckties in my office closet just in case something came up business wise. Little did I know they would come in handy this way. I took two out while Nadine took her shirt off. We kissed and then I moved my tongue down her neck slowly to her breasts, kissing and caressing until finally reaching around her back to take her bra off. I watched her breasts fall free and then used one of the neckties to bind her hands behind her back.

"We are in sync in every way," she whispered amidst deep breaths.

"Perfectly."

I continued kissing her all over while she got more and more turned on.

"What's the other tie for?"

"I don't know. I just grabbed two."

"Blindfold me. No inhibitions tonight, just fearless trust."

I smiled.

"Is that too weird for you?"

"Not at all. It's good weird," I said.

I cleared off my desk and lifted Nadine onto the edge. I pulled her skirt and panties down and then wrapped the tie around her eyes. She looked so sexy, even more so bound and blindfolded, *9½ Weeks* style.

I stripped while we continued kissing and then she laid down supine on the desk, legs dangling off the edge. I got on my knees and went down on her. Moans turned to screams in no time. Nadine thankfully muffled the passion with her hands so moviegoers and staff wouldn't hear a woman howling behind the popping corn.

I picked Nadine up cradle style in my arms, her

body so relaxed, nearly limp with peace, and put her on the floor. I entered her and finished faster than she did.

I undid the tie over her eyes, and we lay on our backs, breathing heavily.

"I'm usually not that fast," I said. "But you and the neckties, oh my god, Nadine."

"Like I said, teenage Harry."

"Yup."

"I don't care if you take one second, especially the way that tongue works."

I rolled over onto my side looking at her. "I have never been more turned on."

"Me, too. So glad you're into that," She said, kissing me. "But can you do me a favor?"

"Anything."

"Untie me? That is quite a knot. You're like a Shibari expert. I bet you know what that is."

"Guilty," I said, untying her. "Oh those Japanese."

"Harry's a bad boy," she said, laughing, and turning to her side. We were gazing and smiling at each other, perhaps embarrassed at not being embarrassed at all.

"Bondage on the first time. Jesus, we cut right to the chase with everything," she said.

"To hell with step-by-step bullshit."

"Have you done this a lot?"

"Not with others around," I confessed.

"Nothing wrong with a robust imagination."

"You?"

"First time on the first time, that's for sure. You know I've always had this submissive tendency in bed with women and men. I just love to be sensually dominated, not hurtfully or hardcore style. Gently, erotically, just like you did. I hope you don't like the hardcore stuff. I find it nasty and not into it at all. I mean some of the shit you see online is insane."

"Nope, softcore for me. Too much is a turn off. There should be no pain. What we just did was perfect."

"But you know, Harry, out of bed, it's a different story. I'm not submissive at all."

"I see that and I like the duality."

"Even our dualities fit. Did we just meet, or have we been together for a while? I think we were together hundreds of years ago," she said, seemingly seriously.

"Yeah, reincarnation."

"I don't disbelieve it right now."

"Now what?" I asked. "We failed miserably at never."

"Couldn't have done worse."

"I know what we need to do. Dinner."

Nadine left before me, trying to temper the staff gossip mill. I snuck out a few minutes later, fortunately avoiding Joel. We grabbed a zip car, and went to Safeway, picking up some cheese, olives, prosciutto, a bottle of burgundy and headed to Baker Beach on the other side of the peninsula, near the Presidio with a view of the Golden Gate. We picnicked on the beach until the sun went down. When it got completely dark except for the dim of distant streetlights, we went to a secluded area of the beach and made love again.

Without neckties.

*   *   *

We went back to Nadine's and immediately crashed together, a short but deep sleep. She woke early to study at the SF State Library. I left with her and while we kissed one last time sitting on the stoop at the scene of the first kiss, Nadine suddenly detoured.

"Hey, I need a favor," she said.

"Sure. Anything."

"Let's not talk for a couple of days."

"What?"

She explained that she needed time to process and step back a bit from all of this, from all the intensity of our feelings and connection. It was too much, too fast. "I'm afraid my heart will get whiplash."

"Let it happen. Don't try to control it."

Nadine shook her head. "No, it's too much, Harry. We're accelerating too fast. I need some slow."

I nodded, clearly saddened by the sudden turn.

"I'm not breaking up with you, silly. Don't be so dejected, though it's sweet. This was the best night of my life. I have never connected with someone on every damn level, but at the same time, it is scaring the shit out of me. I'm afraid to lose control because of the power of our connection."

"Embrace it."

"I want to, but I can't just do that by telling myself to. It's not that fucking simple," she said, her tone turning angry for the first time.

"If you insist," I conceded.

"Just a little time. I don't want to become who I

used to be. You don't understand. You don't know me. I don't want you to see that side of me and I don't want to see it either. I want this version."

"I don't fucking care, Nadine. I want all of you. All of your versions. The more, the better."

Nadine laughed. "That is really foolish. Trust me, you will care. It is easy to love me this way. You are just blinded by the now."

I shrugged. "I will attempt patience."

"Thank you. It's better for us for the long term," she said, kissing me. "And besides there's the matter of your girlfriend and mine."

7 — Gephyrophobia

After parting with Nadine, I walked up Cabrillo Street towards the theater. When I got there, I decided I didn't want to go home. I should've been exhausted from just a few hours of sleep, but I was wide awake and wanted to be out watching the world start its day. It must have been the adrenalin from the lingering satisfaction of our intimacy. Or it was all the drama of suddenly presented life-changing possibilities. Cataclysm loomed in all its glorious disquiet. Despite Nadine's sudden break from us just when *us* had begun, I felt sure we would be together. She couldn't walk away from our connection because there was no way I could do it.

I clung to her line, "it's better for us for the long term," whenever doubt crippled my confidence. But the cracks were tiny and infrequent. I mostly felt great, riding high from us. My perception cleansed and heart swelled with all our great notions. I wanted to be awake in this state of consciousness for as long as possible.

And a whole day stretched out infinitely before me.

But I needed a plan. I thought of heading back to Ocean Beach to watch the sunrise and the surfers begin their morning runs. It was a typically foggy Richmond morning so the sunrise would be masked in gray, but that didn't matter. I'd still enjoy the early morning beach tranquility and the sneaky thrill of beating most of humanity out of the gate.

I stopped at the Café Zeitgeist across the street and

got a coffee and danish, fresh as can be since they had just opened. After a few sips of coffee, I knew what to do: drive over the Golden Gate. Something I hadn't done in over five years by myself since the gephyrophobic demons had seized control of my driving soul. Today I was fearless and ready to confront those evil spirits head on. Today I was superman staring down his kryptonite.

There were two Zip cars, a Prius and a Rav4. Within moments my superman state was turning fragile. I took the Prius since it was a lower ride and would give me less of a view of how insanely high I would be driving (more like flying) over the mighty Pacific. Gephyrophobia was a first cousin, not removed, of Acrophobia.

I drove up Cabrillo and took a left on 19th avenue, which at this particular stretch was actually part of highway 1, the famous Pacific Coast Highway that wends along America's western edge all the way south to Orange County and north to Mendocino County. However, here in San Francisco, PCH 1 was just simple, nondescript 19th Avenue, traversing the Richmond district to connect to highway 101 and the great Golden Gate. As I cut across the north-south grid streets of Geary, Clement, California, and Lake, fearlessness was losing the battle to anxiety.

Superman was dying.

My palms turned clammy and then downright wet. I tried to rub them dry on my thighs as my heart joined the panic brigade by thumping in my chest like a heavy metal bass drum. I could feel shoulder muscles starting to twitch like individual epileptic cases. Desperately, I tried to distract myself with the scenery. The road turned green and tree-lined as 19th Avenue now swerved a swath through the Presidio, the old Army bases from WWII turned into swanky condos for San Francisco's old money fleeing the downtown 140-character-nouveau-riche invasion. It wasn't working. Breathing became shorter as my overloaded nervous system made the basic act of taking in oxygen a heroic challenge. I thought back to the few failed cognitive therapy sessions I'd had with Dr. Stevens at Dana's behest.

"Concentrate on your breathing, pranayama. Long, slow breaths in through your nose and out your mouth. Let your vibrissae filter the incoming air. Clean, fresh air into your lungs. Concentrate on purity, not fear. Then switch to nadi shodhana, alternate nasal breathing. It will harmonize your cerebral hemispheres, creating the balance you'll need for mind over matter, Harry. Repeat your mantra all the way over the bridge, all the way over the fear. Never stop repeating it."

I began chanting *Mind over Matter* and focused on my breathing, alternating between nostrils hoping to balance those damn hemispheres. I had a bottle of Ativan at home as an emergency. Dr. Stevens wanted me to conquer this medicine-free, but it was there in case this Yogic stuff failed.

I wish I had the drugs. The Eastern mysticism was all fraud right now. All nerves and thoughts aligned in protest to the breathing and mantra, demanding that I turn around, but I stubbornly tried to outflank them, not giving up yet, repeating the mantra louder and louder —

Mind over matter. Mind over matter. Mind over matter...

19th Avenue became 101. It was just 2.4 miles until I was on the bridge. My palms were sliding off the wheel and the stupid fucking mantra and breathing were no match for my sledgehammer heart pumping primal fear into my veins. I forged on praying there wouldn't be a traffic jam on the bridge. I was sure a full-blown panic attack would happen in that case. If I could just stay in constant motion with my eyes focused on the land at the end of the bridge, I might make it. I saw the tips of the orange vermillion towers peaking above the foggy sky ahead. I knew all the data. I had to go 8,981 feet to get to the other side. More than a mile and a half, which at 60 miles an hour should only take a minute and a half. Not much, but for a gephyrophobe, it was a marathon. Deep breaths. Each nostril. I could do this. I used to do this all the time. I drove cross-country alone. Over hill, over fucking dale for more than 3,000 miles. Hundreds of bridges, through snowstorms in the Rockies, Sierra Nevada mountainside roads, high in the sky with no guard rails.

Goddamn it, this was nothing!

I changed my mantra — *Over the Golden, Over the Golden, Over the Golden.* That was much better than the cliché that Dr. Stevens suggested. What a terrible mantra, *mind over fucking matter.* I think I thought my breathing got better, palms drier, and muscles less aquiver with the new mantra. I could see the tollbooth. Now I had a third mantra. *Oh Fuck. Oh fuck. Oh fuck.* I slowed down to pass through the empty tollbooth, wishing someone were there so I could talk to someone. No, a woman, a mother, my mother. Mantras conflated: *Fuck. Over the Golden. Over the Golden. Oh Fuck. Over the fucking Golden.*

I couldn't stop now. There were many cars behind me and I couldn't tell what was ahead of me because the bridge, as usual, was swallowed in morning fog. Maybe a good thing because I couldn't see below me. I wouldn't even know I was on the bridge, except for the sound of the tires rolling across the sliver of cement separating me from a Pacific death, a 4,200-foot freefall into deep, dark shark-infested ocean. Suddenly, nothing but grey. I could only faintly see the taillights of the car in front of me. I felt and heard the road leave the earth. I hated that horrible sound. How do fucking people do this so casually? How can they trust the bridge? *Over the Golden. Over the Golden. Over the Golden.*

I had to be halfway by now. The nervous system was rebelling, but it wasn't full bore revolution. I was doing it. I had it. Thirty seconds or so to go. Then suddenly I saw a string of red brake lights light up like dominos until the car in front fell to red. We were at a standstill. Oh my fucking god! The revolution was full-blast, storming the Bastille, guillotine ready. I wanted to get out of the car. I had to get out of the car. I just wanted to be on land. That's all I wanted was to be on land. I opened the door, ready to escape, while billowing fog rolled into the car. *Stop*, I told myself slipping back into the new mantra and closing the door. The bridge was swaying as was the car. The morning Santa Ana winds were gusty, and the Golden Gate was smartly designed to be flexible, not rigid, in order to withstand earthquakes as it had for its entire 79-year life. But for me, for my fucking phobia, the swinging bridge only made it worse. I closed my eyes, putting my clammy palms over them for reinforced blindness. Now the sway kicked in vertigo and nausea. I gagged a few times, covering my mouth reflexively, but keeping my eyes closed while initiating yet another mantra – *Almost on land. Almost on land. Almost on land.*

Then the swaying suddenly subsided as did my nausea. The new mantra and imposed blindness seemed to be working a little. I reached the edge of panic and came back a bit. It was manageable madness, but I had to open my eyes at some point. Then a loud horn jolted my eyes open. There were no red lights ahead, so I accelerated into the fog. It was wide open. I was going around 30 mph and suddenly sped out of the fog and into the magically blue sky of Marin County. Land ho! In seconds, solid earth was beneath my wheels. Hallelujah! The first exit was Vista Point. I pulled over and parked in the Zip spot. Gephyrophobia was like being seasick, a nightmarish experience in hell that evaporated moments after hitting land, aside from the permanent scar of its memory.

Yes, a panic attack kicked my ass, but at least I didn't jump out of the car and over the side of the bridge plummeting to a pathetic death. I faced the demons, took some shots on the chin, but I wasn't knocked out.

I set the bar low.

I drove down to Sausalito, ditched the Prius at a Zip spot, walked along the waterfront for a while, had a western omelet and a lot of coffee at a little local joint, and then continued walking to the stretch of houseboats further up Shoreline Highway. There was one that caught my eye. It had a nice upper deck rising above the others with a great view of the city. I didn't see anybody on board and the lower deck windows had no curtains drawn so I peeked in. Emptiness. It was probably a vacation rental between tenants. I climbed aboard and up to the top deck. I got comfortable in a lounge chair with a great view of my beloved city. I hadn't seen it from the other side in a while. Dana was right. I didn't get out of the Richmond, let alone the city, often.

The fog was still rolling into the city thick like a white river in the sky. It thinned and turned hazy with some visibility to the east of the Golden Gate. Alcatraz was still shrouded except for its flashing white light, but beyond it, I could see the downtown, the mighty Bay Bridge mocking me from the rear of the financial district's skyscrapers, and just barely the Alameda hills of the East Bay framing the background. I remembered Dana and I renting a boat and cruising the bay in our earlier, happier days, but that memory soon melted into the very new and few, but potent memories of Nadine and me. I closed my eyes, letting the images flitter freely and randomly, liberated from the conscious. Scenes of us living on a houseboat here in Sausalito. She a literature professor teaching in Marin and I commuting via ferry to go to work at the Cabrillo. A life both romantic and real, free of financial worries. The reverie faded into a deep and dreamy sleep until a loud, but mousy voice woke me up.

"Hey, what the hell are you doing?"

I opened my eyes and an angry millennial was staring over me.

"Sorry, man."

"Get off my boat, freeloader. What the fuck!"

I got up and descended the ladder onto the dock. He was already on his houseboat.

"Get a job and get your own boat, Fuckhead!"

"Yeah, maybe I'll do that. Maybe, I'll buy yours. How much you want, asshole?"

He laughed derisively. "There's a surf shop up the road that sells blow-up raft for 20 bucks. That's more in your range."

"Dude, you're such a prick. Are you aware of that?"

"Get the fuck off my property."

"Fuck your property and fuck you. You have ruined San Francisco."

"What the fuck does that mean?"

"You wouldn't understand," I said, walking away.

"Fuck you!" he yelled, now on his cell phone, probably calling the police.

Walking away with my back to him, I waved my middle finger, wagging it slowly in rhythm to the bullshit he kept yelling. In the old days, the owner of the houseboat would have offered me a beer and we would have shot the shit.

Not now. Just anger and me-my-mine mentality.

I found a bus stop nearby and waited to head back into the city, relieved that I was in the hands of someone else to cross the Golden Gate. I checked my phone in hopes of a text or missed call from Nadine.

Nothing.

*　　*　　*

When I got back to the theatre, I took a shower and had lunch. I had a free afternoon before meeting Jackson. I dawdled in my office for a while, looking over Mariana's PowerPoint of the Cabrillo's existential demise. Then Joel popped into the office.

"Hey, Harry."

"Hi, Joel, sorry about last night. I was preoccupied."

"I could see that," Joel said, eyes and grin conveying mischief.

I laughed and lied. "Joel, she's a rep from Sisco trying to sell us some new concession stuff."

"You closed your blinds for that? Must have been pretty top-secret candy."

"Good one. Anyway, what can I do for you, Joel?"

"Not my business, Harry. You're right. I don't judge. We're in San Francisco, judge free zone."

I nodded. "That's good. Our fair city still hasn't lost that."

"They can't take that away from us, Harry. So, on another note, you know what my buddy told me about friends with benefits in America versus in France?"

"Do tell."

"In France, they don't say friends with benefits.

They just say friends."

I laughed. "Oh, those dissolute French rascals."

"Yup, gotta love 'em. Can I sit, Harry?"

"Sure, but just a bit. I think I will see the first show-ing of *Irrational Man*. Any good?"

"Not bad. Okay. A decent crime story, but you'll like it because you love anything by Woody."

"Sadly, it's getting harder to be a Woody fan, but I'm staying the course."

"Sure is. We had some protesters out here the other day."

"Really? I didn't see them."

"Yup, not many and not for long, but the way things are going it may grow."

"Another fallen hero."

"I'll tell you where he fell in the film. The ending. It's really abrupt, but—"

"Shut up! Jesus, Joel!"

"Sorry, I was just—"

"So, what's up? What do you need?

"A couple of things."

Joel gave me some updates and shared some ad-vertising ideas. He wanted to team up with some local restaurants for dinner and movie specials. Not a bad idea. Then he shared a few other not-so-good marketing ideas and the upcoming films we would be showing.

"And then on a non-work, but kind of work related thing, what happened with Mariana? Is she interested?"

I had forgotten all about trying to set them up and Mariana rejecting it. I paused, trying to find a way to let him down easy. "Wait, what about your date the other night? How'd it go?"

"It was okay. We kissed a bit at the end of the night. Kind of awkward though."

"How so?"

"I don't know. It didn't feel totally in sync. It felt forced like I wanted to like her more than I actually liked her and she probably didn't like me at all."

"I know what you mean."

"I mean it's gotta start hot, right Harry? The chemistry has to be there without even thinking about it. That doesn't develop. It should ignite instantly, right?"

"Agreed."

"Ever had that? Did you have it with Dana?"

"I'm not sure."

"Then you didn't."

"It was a long time ago. Hard to remember a feeling you don't have anymore. Anyway, not all relationships begin Hollywood style."

"True, but I want the Hollywood one. The rare ones that transcend everything."

"You're ambitious."

"Why aim for the mundane? That's the default."

"Maybe you need another date with her. Sometimes it can take a few dates to shake off the nerves and let the chemistry happen. Maybe it doesn't always ignite right away."

Joel was shaking his head emphatically. "No way. The chemistry should explode past the nerves, otherwise you start lying to yourself. I know I'd have it with

Mariana."

"Maybe."

"What about her? You're holding out on me because it's bad news, right? Just lay it on me, Harry."

"I don't think she's into it, Joel. She's not dating," I lied.

He was instantly crestfallen. "Really?" he said softly, looking down.

I felt sorry for Joel. He was like a wounded fawn. "Hey, you know what, I say ask her anyway. Maybe she'll go for it. I don't think she likes this third-party shit. Too juvenile for her."

"You think that's it? Did she say that?"

"Not in so many words."

"Then in what words."

"Joel, chill. Just text her later and ask her out. You can tell her I gave you the number."

Joel took a deep breath. He was stressed and reminded me of myself a few hours ago on the Golden Gate, except I was thousand times more neurotic. He started rubbing his hands together as if he were cold. I'd noticed this habit more and more lately. When he pulled his hands apart, I could see some redness on his palms.

"Joel, let me see your hands."

They were chafed to the point of peeling and irritated skin.

"Jesus, Joel. What the hell is going on?"

"Nervous habit. Had it since I was a teenager, back in the dark adolescent years. Got it under control, but lately it's back. What the hell do I do if I get lucky with Mariana?"

"What do you mean? You'll be ecstatic."

"With these mitts? If she lets me feel her breasts, how can I caress them? It'd be like sand paper across her soft skin."

"Damn, didn't think of that. You think of everything."

"I know. That's half my problem."

"Get some moisturizer on them and don't worry about it for now. I think your mitts might be a long way from Mariana's tits," I said.

"Yeah, one step at a time. I'll worry about her breasts later," Joel said. I noticed how he used the word breasts instead of tits or boobs. He was showing respect for the woman he lusted for. Joel deserved a good woman. He was a good guy underneath the neurosis.

"I will send you her number."

"Ok, Harry, thanks. I'm gonna go for it. I'm crazy about her."

"I know."

As Joel was leaving, he turned and said, "By the way, Harry, she's really hot."

"I know," I laughed. "You've told me many times."

"No, I mean the Sisco rep," Joel said, air quoting Sisco rep.

"Man, go do some work. What do I pay you for? To obsess about our accountant?"

"Sure, Harry, sure thing. Thanks, man, you're the best."

As soon as Joel was gone, I closed the door and called Mariana, explaining the situation, even telling her about his hands. I convinced her to just give him one date, and then it will be done with. Even just a coffee.

"Fine, I will, out of my respect for you. I'm dating the guy that you should fire. A guy I find very annoying. Do you realize that?"

"I do. Thanks, Mariana. I really appreciate it." A long silence followed until I broke it. "Mariana, are you there?"

"Were his hands really all red from being so nervous?"

"Yeah, he's really into you."

"Ok, well, that's cute in a pathetic way, but I won't lead him on. I don't want him following me around like a three-legged puppy."

"Who knows, maybe you'll fall for him. Anything is possible."

"Not this time. So, what about your future?"

"Here we go. Scenes from *The Graduate*."

"Everything is a movie with you."

"Of course. They're my life."

"Maybe not for long."

"Ouch. Jesus, Mariana. I hope you go easier on Joel."

"Harry, I'm trying to be a real friend, not someone who says what you want to hear. If you want a yes-woman, you got the wrong girl!"

"Don't ever change. Look, I get it. I've been thinking about our financial crisis a lot. I have an idea," I said.

"Great! Do tell."

"I may ask my old man for a loan."

"Does he have that kind of money? Seven figures, Harry? I thought you said—"

"Not liquid, but the house could help. Maybe he could remortgage it."

"It's a high-risk loan. That's a lot to ask. Are you ok with that?"

"No, but I'm desperate."

"It might be your only chance."

8 — Irrational Man

I concocted the father plan out of the blue as a cover in case I went along with Jackson's scheme. I would need some excuse to explain the sudden infusion of cash. I was already thinking like a criminal. The voice in my head telling me I would never do this was getting quieter. I had to keep all options on the table and right now that was really the only damn one. Maybe I was just easing myself into the felony, the way one goes into the cold waters of Ocean Beach. Who better to manipulate you than yourself?

I looked at the time and realized that *Irrational Man* had started ten minutes ago. I confirmed with Sandy at the kiosk that there were seats. Unfortunately, there were quite a few. The surge had already begun its fade. I grabbed some popcorn, a coke, and a sat in my favorite seat—last row, last seat, far corner of the theater.

I've been a Woody Allen fan since I was kid. I always admired him as a true auteur, doing it all—writing, directing and starring. As a one-and-done-filmmaker, I was in awe of his creative prolificacy, birthing practically every nine months. My favorite film was the underrated M*elinda and Melinda*. I always showed it during Woody week, along with staples like *Annie Hall, Broadway Danny Rose, Deconstructing Harry, Bananas* and *Crimes and Misdemeanors*.

My father was the one who got me hooked on Woody back when we used to go to the movies a lot.

It was a good way to pass our two weekends a month together. Seeing the new Woody film together on its opening weekend became a thing for us. The first one was *Broadway Danny Rose* and our streak ended appropriately with *Deconstructing Harry*. We had a good 13-year run with Woody, but it actually still continues from afar since to this day we chat after both of us have seen the latest one. I looked forward to those talks and really missed going to openings with him.

Guess I just missed him.

Irrational Man was not his best, not top five, but it was very good, an intriguing existential story on how one man can philosophize himself into thinking murder could be a noble decision that would turn a meaningless life meaningful. Some critics thought that Woody was celebrating crime and justifying murder. As the credits rolled, I wondered why the critics ignored the title when making their foolish judgments. Of course, Woody's personal life drama had probably preordained a negative review from most of the critics regardless of how good the film was. Few were separating the art from the artist.

*   *   *

After the movie, I bought four more American Spirits, lit one, and took a walk around the neighborhood. I tried not to turn on my phone, but after a few drags on the organic tobacco, I succumbed. There were two text messages. The first was a long one from Dana.

Hope you are ok. Just want to let you
know I hired a lawyer. Didn't want to bring
it up in the moment. Wanted to let you di-

gest. But I have one just to get through the
financial part of the separation. I have con-
firmed that we are common-law married. I
have faith that you will divide 50-50. Real-
ly no other choice anyway, right? ☺ *Com-*
pletely trust you, just lawyering up for the
paperwork and stuff to ease the bureaucratic
bullshit part. Lots of docs to deal with. Let's
meet when I return in a couple of weeks and
sort this out. I do care about you and want
only the best in your future despite the optics
looking otherwise.

　Fondly,

　Dana.

I read it twice, hating the damn emoji even more,
the word *optics* (Christ, what a ridiculous word to use!),
and that icing on the cake—*Fondly*. What the fuck. After the second read, I promptly deleted it. I had to give
Dana props for helping me eliminate any shred of guilt
over quickly moving on to Nadine.

The second message was from Jackson: *Let's meet*
in 20 on the other side of the Cliff House. Good news.

The good news scared me, but I replied simply: *See*
you there.

As I smoked the Spirit and walked down Cabrillo
towards our meeting point, I stewed over not hearing
from Nadine. As close as we felt last night, closer and
more connected in those moments than I'd ever felt to
anyone in my life, the memory started to feel like a mirage, melting Dali style, as if it had happened to some-

one else. I wondered if she would ever contact me again now that she had time to think and process everything. Maybe it was all just a fling for her. She wasn't a cheater by nature so maybe the guilt won. She was in love with Christine, and she thought Dana and I were still together. I should have told her I was free.

Maybe now she satisfied her crush on the *Kerouac* director, getting it out of her system.

It was crazy, but I wasn't prepared to lose this woman I'd spent about 24 hours with, while simultaneously I was okay, even fine now, with losing a woman I'd spent eight years with. Time was irrelevant, earthly revolutions useless! It was about intensity and transcendence, the rebirth of a soulmate notion, exactly what Joel was talking about.

But then I thought about us being literal partners in crime. If I was on board, I had to see her again. We would work together, thick as thieves. Maybe she wouldn't change her mind about us, but at least I would see her and feel the full and true connection again, solidifying the mirage. Even if unrequited, I would still be in the presence of it.

Oh god, I had it bad.

If I agreed to the crime, it could solve everything. I took a deep breath. Was my rationale ridiculous or was the crime really the panacea, risks and all? *Stop thinking*, I told myself and smoked another Spirit on my walk to the Cliff House. To get out of my head, I called my old man to chat about *Irrational Man*.

We caught up on the theater, his work, and family

stuff for a bit. He was having some trouble with one of his brothers. Ironically, he had to give my uncle a loan to cover some gambling debts. He used the word loan out of kindness to his brother when we both clearly knew he would never see a dime back.

He had seen *Irrational Man* and liked it. We dissected it for a little while and ended as we always did: our updated top 10 list of Woody films.

He wanted me to visit soon, but I told him I had a lot going on with the theatre — expansion, a staff reorg, making some changes to keep up with the multiplexes a little bit while not selling out.

"Harry, the key is balance. Don't go too far either way. Extremes are a young man's game."

"Sure, dad, I agree. But I've got to stay true to theatre's mission."

"Of course. Wouldn't want it any other way."

*   *   *

I paused at Ocean Beach to watch the surfers, but mostly I just got lost in a reverie of being with Nadine. When reality intervened, I walked past the Cliff House and saw Jackson sitting on the little secluded beach.

He gave me a fist bump and a big smile. "My man, Gnostopolos, so glad we're back in action together. You know I love you like a brother."

I smiled uncomfortably, feeling a bit awkward at his instant and unabashed intimacy. "Me, too, Jackson. Me, too," I said, trying to hide the truth.

I offered him an American Spirit. He stared at the cigarette between my fingers, trance-like for a few moments, before taking it and holding it as if he were observing something he had never seen before. "It's been a while," he finally said, seemingly more to the cigarette than me.

Then he looked at me, "What the hell," he said putting the cigarette between his lips while I lit it.

"It's organic, so it's all good," I said.

Then with a suddenly serious mien, Jackson took a puff and said in a baritone pitchman's voice, "Organic carcinogens. We do cancer the healthy way."

We both smoked and chatted small talk about this and that for a change. We put the cigarettes out in the sand, but Jackson took the crushed butts and put them in his jeans pocket.

"Save the earth, right, Harry?"

"Or at least save San Francisco."

"Even more important. You okay, buddy? You look a little tense," he said.

I wasn't sure if Jackson knew what happened with Nadine and me. Had she told him? I didn't think so, but couldn't be sure.

"I'm okay. Damn money issues with the Cabrillo."

"Well, we'll fix that in no time," he said with a wink. "You sure that's it? You and Dana, ok? Isn't she supposed to be back by now?"

I paused. "She might stay in Vancouver a while."

"Really?" Jackson said as if he'd deciphered something.

"Yeah, she's got some friends. Absence makes the heart grow fonder. We could use a little break."

Jackson looked me in the eye for an extended, uncomfortable stretch.

"What?" I asked.

Again, a pregnant pause. Before I could fill the silence, he let me off the hook, "Sure, that can help everyone after so many years."

"So, have you seen Nadine?"

"No, actually. You?"

"Not since the other night," I lied.

"So, what do you think?"

"Of what?"

"Of the surfing conditions." Jackson said looking at the ocean.

"What?"

"Of Nadine, man. What else? What do you think of her? Jesus, Harry, no need for walls. Cut the goddamn bullshit."

"She's amazing."

"That she is, my friend, and like I said, she's crazy about you."

"Jacko, I don't know about that. Are you sure?"

"Very."

"How do you know?"

"Trust me."

"Well, we're both involved so it's complicated."

"You don't sound that involved anymore. Anyway, all the better for you when you get together. All the effort will make it worth keeping. It'll be your sustenance through tough times."

"Huh, never looked it at that way, but you're getting way ahead of yourself."

"Go for it. Go for her. She's worth it."

"I don't know."

"Harry, I never saw you and Dana making the long run. Pieces from different puzzles. I always thought you two were just caught in the momentum of *Kerouac* and got duped into believing it was something more than it really was. Hearts have very low IQs," Jackson said, laughing. "Like that Shawn Mullins song, *My Stupid Heart*. Spot on tune."

"Yeah it is."

"I had a buddy while I was in Madrid for a spell. He was an academic who dabbled in poetry, married this woman from Seville. They were so different, mismatched to the core but they shared the same birthday, same year. They discovered the coincidence on their first date. He said from that moment on he knew they were meant for each other and so did she. The birthday confirmed their destiny." Jackson said, shaking his head. "I mean we'll do anything to think we found our soulmates, especially when we know we haven't."

"Our stupid hearts. Are they still together?"

Jackson nodded. "And miserable, both cheating on each other."

I nodded. "The human tragicomedy, chapter infinity."

"Indeed. Well, I'll leave it to you and Nadine to figure out, but, gotta say, there's something about you two and it's more than a silly coincidence like a birthday. Something very real and true. And hot."

I was glad someone else confirmed our chemistry. It was hard to believe anything was real other than when you were in the moment of its being. But, then again, this might just be part of the Jackson trap to hook me into the crime. Paranoia was a master at undermining any truth.

"So what's the good news?" I asked.

"We're all set. Everything is ready to go."

"That's not news."

"Sure it is, at least on my end. And what about your news?"

I took a deep breath.

"So?" Jackson pushed.

My turn to look Jackson in the eye. I kept a poker face until it slowly slipped into a grin of affirmation.

"Son of a bitch, that's great, Harry!"

"I'm fucking in, man," I said, resolute in word and tone.

Jackson smiled wide with a devilish look in his eye, doing his best Nicholson. "Thatta boy, Harry! Fucking fantastic! I knew you'd come through. Greeks are natural miscreants. How can someone named Gnostopolos not ride the rapscallion American fringe. Man, I'm so glad. I need you. I need old school friendship and trust. Nouveaux friendship ain't the same. Got no roots."

"You got it, Jacko, roots and all."

We fist bumped and then Jackson slapped me hard on the shoulder.

"When do we this?" I asked.

"Tonight, Harry, tonight."

"Really? No way. Shit, that's quick," I said.

"No need to lollygag this thing. The sooner we do it, the sooner we get the money, the sooner I can save the winery and get my life back on solid *terroir* with Samira. We've just been waiting for number six, for you! Now it's go time."

"Not the actual job, right? I need some sleep."

"No, no. We meet and go over the plan tonight. Study it. Reconvene tomorrow night to review. A night off to absorb and process and then any follow up questions. And then we strike Sunday night if all things are in line. Slowest night in copland."

"And on the seventh day, god rested."

"But we don't. Can we meet at the theatre? How about the roof?"

"You've been up there?"

"Of course, it's a great spot."

"Ok, that's fine," I consented.

"I'll tell the crew to meet in the back of the theatre at nine. We'll go in teams of two, quietly in the rear loading dock area. Don't want to be seen too much, especially as a group."

"So, Nadine and I will meet separately at first?"

"You got it."

"Should I contact her?"

"I will text all of us right now. We'll stagger the arrivals by 15 minutes. You two arrive first."

I nodded, so relieved to know that I would see her.

Jackson sent the text and then took off alone, not wanting us to be seen together. I checked my phone immediately, but nothing from Nadine. So I wrote her,

Hey, I know you wanted space, but maybe we can meet before the big meeting tonight? Let me know. If not, I understand. We can just meet at the theatre at the allotted time.

Within a minute, my phone dinged.

How about 7 at McClellan's?

Perfect. I will see you there.

I exhaled and felt whole again for the first moment since we parted ways. Humpty dumpty syndrome. Then my phone dinged again. A smiley emoji.

I felt a mile high. Now I loved emojis!

*   *   *

This time Nadine was at the bar when I arrived. The same spot—one seat from the end at the far corner of the bar staring out at the street-view window. She couldn't see me as I approached and tapped her on the shoulder.

She nearly jumped out of the chair as she turned to me.

"Sorry," I said.

"Shit, you scared the hell out of me." She took a deep breath. "No need to be sorry. I'm clearly anxious and on edge."

"And rightfully so."

There was a pause and we just stared for a bit, slipping instantly into our reverie. This time I didn't hesitate and reached out to hold both her hands, pulling her up for a long kiss. When we stopped, I got my balance and could tell from her dizzied, half-closed eyes that we were alchemically right back where we left off.

We continued holding hands and staring silently for what simultaneously seemed seconds and hours.

Nadine finally broke the silence. "Has to be a past life thing, right? What else explains this?"

"Maybe we should stop trying to explain it."

"And just get a grip?"

"No, not that. The opposite. I mean embrace it free of analysis or fear."

Nadine said, "Free is a loaded word." Then her serious expression slid slowly into a wide smile while she stretched her arms out putting a hand on each of my shoulders. "I hope you never get a grip," she whispered while pulling me in, stopping just before our lips connected, millimeters apart. "Don't kiss me," she mouthed. "Wait. Just wait."

And briefly we did until our magnetic field easily won.

"Harry Gnostopolos, I love your lips. Perfect pillows for mine," she said, laughing childishly.

"We're pathetic," I said.

Nadine started going into details about the song, *Fade into You* by Mazzy Star; how the lyrics and atmospheric music made her think of us. She'd also heard it several times on the radio since our "gloriously notorious first night." Since she rarely heard it on the radio, she thought some sort synchronicity was at play.

"The universe affirming us?"

"Silly, huh?"

"No, not at all, Nadine."

We finally sat down. I ordered a Bulleit on the rocks

to accompany her half-finished Knob Creek neat. Nadine then explained how *Fade into You* was so "exhilarating and terrifying," capturing her usual fear of being with men and guilt over Christine.

"I'm such a killjoy."

"Yeah, stop it. Stop killing joy."

"I know. You're absolute right. I need to stop sabotaging us." Then she lifted her drink, stared into my eyes, and said, "I missed you so much. I didn't know you a few days ago and now you're all I fucking think about."

"To feeling exactly the same way," I said as we toasted.

And on it went, romancing our romance with more futile attempts at understanding it with language, repeated failures that always lapsed into kisses. I wondered how long we could last in this interrupted bliss. Could it be a sustained reality? Naïve impossibilities teased their temptations...

"Hey, but you know what? I'm actually pissed off at you," Nadine said, shoving me on my shoulder in the adorable way that she did. I fell for everything she did, every idiosyncrasy and gesture. I had lost all discriminative skills with her. She was angry because she couldn't focus at school and was falling behind in assignments. What caught her most off guard about us was the physical attraction she felt at the reading soon after my embarrassing display. From my photos online after seeing *Kerouac*, she didn't think that would happen.

"Thanks," I said, defeatedly.

Nadine put her hand on my cheek, "Don't worry,

Harry, I think you're wildly handsome now."

"So, nothing before my spectacle of attraction at the reading?"

"Oh boy, the fragile male ego all locked in its superficial state. Silly man, it was just photos before. I mean, I had an intellectual crush before. Now, I have both. And, I was off men until you. That should assuage your wounds."

"Ok, so I was doomed by gender."

Nadine scoffed, "And then the kiss. The tables certainly turned with the kiss that launched this madness."

"Well, it didn't take a kiss for me. I mean I lost it at first sight as you well know, but the kiss definitely took things to another stratosphere."

Nadine took a deep breath. "Oh my god, it's just crazy. Butterflies just talking about it."

We both smiled and stared at each other. Nothing else existed at this moment besides the two of us. She started shaking her head before leaning in to kiss me. I don't know how long we kissed, but it wasn't long enough.

When we stopped, Nadine said, "Maybe we need one of those slaps like Cher did in *Moonstruck*."

"The *snap out of it* slap to Nicholas Cage?"

"Exactly."

"It'll take more than a slap."

"Maybe we should snap out of it. I don't want to kill joy again, but I see this heading towards danger. It's too much. You know what Liz Taylor said about why she and Burton could never make it last. Why they failed twice in marriage?"

"Yeah, she said they were too in love to stay together."

"Harry, I don't think I can give up on Christine yet, plus you have Dana. It's so complicated. We will cause a lot of hurt. We need time. I mean these moments have been so magical, but we've basically had one date."

"So, what are you saying?"

"My brain told me to end things tonight, and focus on this Jackson thing, but now everything tells me we'll be sleeping together any minute now."

"What the hell does the brain know about romance? It's a very anti-romantic organ."

"Harry, I'm flattered, but I have to admit that I'm worried about you and commitment." I was about to interrupt her when she beat me to the punch. "I know this is crazy because I'm cheating, too, and have no credibility here, but I'm a little taken aback at how easily you are cheating on Dana, you guys have been together for what, eight years? I mean, if we ended up together, that kind of concerns me."

"You're wasting energy on this."

"You don't even mention her. I talk about Christine, but you never bring up Dana. Doesn't it bother you?"

"I'm not cheating on Dana. She cheated on me."

"What?"

I explained every detail to Nadine. She was a great listener, interrupting only for questions here and there. I therapeutically poured it all out about the morning Dana left me, other details about how we had plateaued and how maybe we weren't a good fit form the very beginning, and all the issues we'd had, but there were also good things that kept us going. I even got a little weepy, which surprised me. Sometimes I suspected an avalanche of sadness lay in subconscious wait over the end of Dana and me and that Nadine had just interred it temporarily.

"Thanks," I said when I finished.

"For what?"

"Listening. I guess I needed that. I haven't told anyone, and it felt good to say it out loud. To hear myself say it."

"I will listen anytime you need me, but I am angry now!"

"About what," I said, taken aback at her sudden turn, unsure if she was kidding.

"Now I'm the only cheater."

"Guess so," I said, relieved.

"Great. Thanks for taking the high road."

"Well, Dana gave me the high road. I'd be cheating if she hadn't."

"I need more time, Harry. And maybe you do, too. You just broke up. You're not cheating, but you're on the rebound whether you believe it or not."

I shook my head. "No, no, I knew the moment I saw you and every moment after has confirmed what I instantly knew." I wanted to say I love you but thankfully held back. *Get a grip, idiot.*

Nadine took a sip of her bourbon.

"When are you going to see Christine next?" I asked.

"I don't know. Not for a while. Got a few things going on here," she said, serious in tone and gaze.

"That we do. Let's spend the next few weeks together and see how it goes. That should tell you if this is the real thing. If we have legs."

The air had turned heavy, sad, but it didn't last long. We were capable of quickly shifting across multiple moods in just moments.

"Chemistry has never worked out for me before," Nadine said. "It always becomes a rollercoaster."

"This is different."

"I think it might be, but I probably thought that the previous times. And I have another confession. What I did with you our first time usually doesn't happen. Never in fact."

"Well, I bet bondage is not typical on anyone's first time."

"No, not that," she whispered, "Coming so fast. Oh my god, Harry, I'm never relaxed enough for that until after a few times. Sometimes never with some people."

"I love that, makes up for you not being attracted to me."

"Of course, you do. Don't let it go to your head."

"Too late."

"Ugh, you're pathetic."

We talked on and on about us, our favorite topic, as it should be for new lovers. Love has its own ego. We obsessed over the nature of our attraction, its potency, source, chances for longevity. We loved us and discussed it as if it were this separate entity. But soon the pattern continued as it devolved again into Nadine's fears of hurting Christine and, more importantly, her becoming this "horrible monster" as she had in previous male relationships. She thought it could even be worse this time since our chemistry was so strong. "The more powerful the chemistry, the worse I may become."

"You overthink it. Just let things happen."

"Yeah, let the universe decide, right?"

"*Fade into You* is telling you something."

Nadine sighed. "What a terrible idea. Hippie Zen bullshit. You don't get it." She was shaking her head slowly, before stopping to take another sip of bourbon. "What's really driving me crazy is this gravitational pull towards you," she said before we kissed again for a long time. When we finally stopped, Nadine sighed and said, "Let's not talk about it. When I'm around you, there is no way I can decide not to be with you so it's pointless. You may rue this day, Harry Gnostopolos."

"Not a chance."

"When our gravity fades, then you'll just be stuck with me and all my crazy shit. I'll be your *Betty Blue*."

"Great movie."

"To watch, not live."

"Nadine, I don't give a shit about any craziness. I want all your madness and complexities. It's part of exiting the plateau. Bring it all on and get over yourself."

And then with our legs touching, my left hand on her thigh, and our bar stools as close to each other as possible, we began discussing our other madness.

The crime.

9 — Big Brother Zuckerberg

Leaving the family business (leather goods) and coming to the States was a really big deal for Nadine and a move fraught with complexities. Her father, who was British, wanted her to stay in the family business. He relented ("he had no choice") when she refused to study business at the Oxford, demanding to study literature. Her father viewed her studies as a reasonable distraction of youth, but when she graduated, she would turn practical, forget about studying "storybooks," and start her apprentice at the family business before taking it over. She had an older brother, but her father, who was British, couldn't trust him. He had issues with drugs and the law, and his roguish ne'er-do-well ways seemed to be on a permanent path. So Nadine was the one.

Then the father-daughter clash over the future re-emerged after she graduated from Oxford. She had discovered her passion for the Beats as well as other 50s and 60s picaresque American Lit and wanted to continue studying these writers in Tangier, of course. Her mother mediated the father-daughter battle, part two. Nadine really had the intent to finish her MA and help her father out. She knew the business was struggling to gain a foothold in the new cyber marketplace. Her father was slow to adapt like many in his generation and he was counting on his daughter to lead the transition.

But Nadine's determination and mother's aid, won out. She figured she would satisfy her thirst for knowledge with an MA, take over the business, and then write her own fiction. She promised her father she'd join the business after Tangier.

However, the future often tramples present notions. It was in Tangier where her academic passion narrowed to the women of the Beats. She knew her future was not writing fiction, but in research and writing scholarly works on this topic and that era.

Battle number three with her father didn't go well. He was very angry when she told him that she was moving to San Francisco to get a PhD. She felt guilty over betraying her promise to her father, but she could not live the life her father decided for her. He told her that he would not support her at all. It was the final straw for him. "Dad, I'm not asking for any support. I have a scholarship from the States."

Nadine hadn't talked to her father since that argument.

Soon after she arrived in Big Bear to hang out with Jackson before starting at SF State, her mother told her that the family business was in disarray. Her father had confessed that he had been cooking the books for years, turning the ledgers into his own *storybooks* to avoid paying hefty taxes and mask all the financial issues. Out of desperation, he got mixed up with some unsavory underground characters who gave him short-term loans with long-term consequences. He was now deep in an abyss of debt with no way out. If he didn't come up with close to a million dollars, he would either be in jail for fraud or worse.

When she told Jackson about her dilemma, he had the solution. Jackson was a magnet for those seeking a lifeboat. This dynamic was not by chance. Jackson's whole life was about desperate folks seeking new frontiers. They became his characters. His books were all romans à clef that demanded la vie bohéme types living on societal fringes. Like Kerouac, he loved "the mad ones, the ones who are mad to live, mad to talk, mad to be saved, desirous of everything at the same time, the ones who never yawn or say a commonplace thing, but burn, burn, burn like fabulous yellow roman candles exploding like spiders across the stars "

Nadine told her mother that she had a business opportunity in California that could earn her fast cash and rescue her father. Her mother was skeptical about how she could possibly make so much money so quickly after just moving to the States. "And for a student of literature? What is going on honey? Don't do what he did. It will only get worse."

"Mom, America is still the land of opportunity. It's not a myth. Silicon Valley is full of entrepreneurs, venture capital practically grows on the trees. There is more money in this little swatch of land than probably the entire African continent. It's unfair, but it's reality. Mom, you just stumble into million-dollar ideas."

When pressed further by her mother for details, she was ready with a rehearsed lie. She had befriended some techie folks who had a plan for a start-up where consumers could have their own personal drones. As she elaborated, I drifted paranoically…was it possible that

Jackson had stopped writing because he had writer's block, and all of this was just life material for a future book? Was he gathering plot and characters at our expense? Maybe the reading brawl was staged so he could actualize the drama to write about it. Jackson always said he had a limited imagination. He needed real life to write the unreal. Was he the puppeteer and Nadine and I his marionettes? Or was Nadine making all of this up and complicitly pulling strings from above as well?

But the paranoia defied logic. Why would Jackson write about a crime he was going to commit?

"Do you think it's a good story? Do you think my dad will buy it?" Nadine asked nervously.

*   *   *

We left the bar, bought a few more *fags*, a couple bottles of Malbec, and headed to the Cabrillo roof a little early so we could safely talk about the crime. We grabbed some wine glasses on the way up and then propped open the door with a cement block so that the others could enter. There were scattered and tattered chairs, a few small rusted tables, and a fire pit, long ago leftovers from Dana and me together on many cool San Francisco nights warmed by the rooftop fire.

Nadine arranged the chairs around the pit and then opened the wine while I swept the ashes clean and lit some logs.

"We're in this together, right?" Nadine asked, head resting on my shoulder while I ran my fingers slowly through her hair.

"Absolutely together," I reassured.

"I trust you, Harry. I love that I trust you."

"So glad you do. I'll never let you down."

Nadine sat up, drank some Malbec, and then gazed at me as if she were trying to decipher a code in my eyes. She looked even more beautiful with the glow of the fire and the starry night sky behind her. "Are you worried about prison?"

"Of course. But I think losing the Cabrillo would be a worse prison. And now that you're doing it, I am not looking back. The only thing worse than losing the theatre would be losing you."

"Your words and kisses slay me," Nadine said while caressing my cheek.

"Go big or go home, right?"

"Go big or go to jail, you mean."

"But it's just speed cameras at this point. I mean it's more like a Merry Pranksters thing. Probably just a probationary slap on the wrist since we have no records."

Nadine nodded and continued caressing. "But I'm more worried about the unknown."

"Yeah, agreed, the mysterious part two."

"You know, I made Jackson promise me there would be no guns. I don't understand your country's obsession. If Newtown didn't change the cowboys, nothing will. What a crazy country. Quel pays fou!"

"San Francisco isn't that country."

"I don't think I can live anywhere else."

"Good. I never want to leave her."

"Don't leave her or me."

"Never."

We were quiet for a spell, drinking, touching, kissing and then Nadine asked, "Do you trust Jackson?"

"I think so, but sometimes my mind wanders. Mostly paranoid stuff."

"Do you have that with me? With us?"

"Of course. I'm afraid you'll quit us at any time."

"I love your honesty and your fear. We should do the *It* scene in *On the Road*. Right here, naked physically and emotionally, unravel and exonerate our pent-up emotions and then fuck wildly and freely. The pleasure would be amplified. Reich would be proud."

I nodded in agreement, but my smile turned to a chuckle.

"Are you laughing at me?" Nadine asked, shoving me with both hands, almost knocking me off my chair.

"I like when you do that. It's oddly endearing."

"I told you, the in-and-out-of-bed duality."

"Indeed."

"So, what's the deal? Are you making fun of me for being a romantic fool? For the *It* scene? Is that silly in our too hip times?"

"No, not at all. I'd do it in a second."

"You had it in your movie. What a great scene. Probably my favorite."

"Hipsters look down at Jack now, but I think it's part of the pose."

"So, you'll do it? We'll be naked in every way?"

"Of course." I poured us more Malbec and we toasted to *It*.

Then Nadine followed her pattern and zigzagged right when we were at a romantic high. "But you know, Harry, I'm not ready to leave Christine just yet."

"Ugh, so practical and unpoetic. Are you sure you're not an accountant living in Walnut Creek?"

Nadine giggled. "Are you falling in love with me, Harry Gnostopolos?"

"Don't be silly. It's just sexual attraction and I'm on the rebound. This just gets me back in the game."

"So, you're using me?"

"Exactly."

"Jerk!"

"I am. You don't know what you're getting into. I'm very difficult. Full of dualities, no trialities."

"I like it when you mess with me. I think," she said, vision darting at me.

I took Nadine's hand and pulled her towards me, then put my hands on her hips and swiveled her onto my lap. I kissed her and held her wrists behind her back. I could feel her relaxing, submitting, wanting to be led. "I love when you do that," she whispered. "Is there time?"

I looked at my phone. "Maybe ten minutes."

"I won't need half that."

"Me neither." I got up and took the cement block away from the door.

I hurried back. Nadine unzipped me and then pulled her underwear down, leaving her skirt on. She mounted me and within seconds, she came. I was moments behind.

"Fuck!" She yelled angrily.

"What? No good?"

"Too good. It was too fast!"

"You will have many chances to slow it down."

"You probably feel like Zeus."

"Yeah, lightning bolts in my loins."

"Take it easy, Greek god. It's not you, it's the forbidden fruit, the San Francisco air, I don't know, the rooftop fire, criminal activity, lies, this whole adventure is so goddamn pervy and sexy my vagina is like a roman candle exploding..."

"Shit!" we said in unison, upon hearing a knock on the rooftop door.

We hurriedly got dressed, and then kissed one more time before I opened the door.

There he was—the writer, turned art thief, turned vintner, turned boxer, returned criminal. Jackson strolled over towards us, armed with a large cardboard box and accompanied by his partner in crime, Max Steinhardt, who was carrying two other boxes. Jackson had told me a little bit about Maxy. He was poet-novelist from Ketchum, Idaho, growing up less than a mile from where Hemingway had shot himself to death. He said he felt Hemingway's ghost had visited him on several occasions. Steinhardt had an appetite for gambling, especially the ponies. He had recently inherited a lot of family money, took mushrooms to celebrate, and proceeded to lose nearly all of his million-dollar inheritance at the track. He was on such a utopian psilocybin trip that he laughed all the way to the last race, last bet, and last dollar, celebrating the end of money, philosophically and literally. When his utopian journey ended, he almost killed himself over his financial idiocy.

Steinhardt was a tall, wiry guy with a very long neck and a loping, yet somewhat graceful gait. He had buzzed black hair and throwback, 70s style mutton-chop sideburns that extended well into his cheeks, almost to his chin. Add squinty, narrow set eyes and an aquiline nose and he was quite a striking presence.

"Harry and Nadine," Jackson announced, "this is Max Steinhardt."

"Call me, Maxy," he said in soft, barely audible voice. He looked at Nadine first and then nodded to Jackson. "You're right. She is very pretty," he said in an observational rather than flirty way.

He turned to me, we shook hands, and he said matter-of-factly, "I liked your film. You should make another."

"Thanks."

And with that, communication ceased from Maxy. He sat down in the makeshift circle of chairs that surrounded the fire pit. Jackson sat next to him while Nadine slid her chair slightly away from me, giving us a normal amount of space.

"You can't lose the Cabrillo, Harry. This place is priceless on so many levels. Look at this view, would you."

"Agree completely. Can't lose the Cabrillo."

"That's why we're here, right? Save a theatre, a winery, a family business, and reverse a bad day at the track. Right, Maxy?" Harry put his hand on Maxy's shoulder and massaged it, kneading the trapezius.

"You need a crack, Maxy? A crack from Jack. A crackerjack."

"Sure."

Jackson did his thing. Warming his hands, then the rubbing the sides of Maxy's neck to create frictional heat and then bam, Maxy's giraffe like neck cracked loudly and repeatedly as if he had extra vertebrae. Maxy's eyes were closed the entire time and he kept them closed long after, seemingly in a state of meditative peace.

"Good ole Maxy. You see that, Harry? No fears and hang ups. Just trust."

"I'm good. Still enjoying the last one."

"The vertebral peace is fleeting. Come on, how about another?"

I hesitated and looked at Nadine. "You know on second thought, crack me, Jacko. Fuck it!"

"Thatta boy, Harry. Caution to the night winds."

"Are you sure?" Nadine asked, worry in her eyes.

"He'll be fine. He's already got one under his belt. You're next, sweetheart."

"Not in a million years," she screeched.

Jackson got behind me and started massaging while telling me to relax. "Just relax," he kept repeating in a gentle mantra voice. Then as he continued to massage, "We'll do this right before you go over the Golden Gate as a warm up before you tackle the big boy Bay Bridge. We'll crack your gephyrophobia, pun intended." Jackson slid his hands along the sides of my neck, rubbing long and hard, up and down. Then "pop-pop-pop" on the left jerk and "pop-pop" on the right thrust.

"Amazing," I said.

"You're probably an inch taller now free of all that compression tension. Nadine?" Jackson asked, diabolically toned.

"Not a chance, Jackson," she said holding her hand firmly up in a stop sign gesture. You did that to me one night when I had too many drinks in Marrakesh. Hated it. Freaks me out."

"Try it sober," I said.

"Not gonna happen, boys. Maybe in the next lifetime."

Jackson poured two glasses of wine, gave one to Maxy, refilled ours and then sat down.

Nadine looked at me. "What's this about bridges? What was that? Giraffaphobia?"

"Yeah, I have a fear of long necks. Like Maxy's." I deadpanned.

"What? You're kidding, right?"

"I hate bridges. Gephyrophobia. Long story. I'll tell you later."

"I love bridges," she said.

"Great. You can drive on our road trips."

Then the roof door creaked open, thankfully interrupting any further venture into my ridiculous phobia.

"Here comes my favorite back-to-the-land couple," Jackson announced

Jackson met Curtis and Mercy Bogdonavich. in Big Bear where they were hiking and checking out where Henry Miller used to live. They had been in mid-level management in some successful Silicon start-up but cashed in their chips early and bought some land to grow marijuana in Humboldt County. At that time Proposition 215 allowed "compassionate" growers to cultivate up to 99 plants for medicinal use. The Bogdonaviches were raided and were found to have 101 plants. The county prosecutor decided to throw the book at them and shut down the farm. The debts piled up and their dream farm was now under foreclosure. The Bogdonaviches were suing the county, but the backlog was enormous. While smoking some of the final product with Jackson at Big Sur, they had shared their plight.

And jumped at Jackson's offer.

They certainly didn't look the Humboldt County image where hippies still thrived, and nothing was funny about peace, love and understanding. Instead, they still looked more the geeky Silicon Valley type.

After quick introductions, I poured the Bogdonaviches some wine, and then Jackson asked us to stand up around the fire. He raised his glass. "To the gang of six," he toasted. Everyone echoed him as we tapped glasses.

When we sat down, Jackson asked us to do more detailed intros so we had a story with the face, help connect us and build chemistry. When each of us finished our little bios, he distributed the cardboard boxes to each pair.

Nadine opened our box and pulled out a folder, a yellow jumpsuit, wigs and other disguise materials, an envelope, a tool box, and a license plate. Everyone tried on their jump suit, which had a city of San Francisco patch on the right breast and looked official.

"It's exactly what the city workers wear who repair the speed cameras," Jackson said. Then he scanned everyone in uniform. "Looks like good fits all the way around. Great."

We sat down in uniform as if we were getting into character, which in a sense we were, and looked through the materials in the folder. At Jackson's behest, we opened the folder to a city map of San Francisco. There were ten stars each containing a number from one to ten and all within the Fisherman's Wharf, Embarcadero, Lombard Street areas.

"Each star is a speed camera," Jackson said.

The Bogdonaviches were in the Sunset area. Jackson and Maxy in the Financial, SOMA areas, and Nadine and I were given the tourist spots. Jackson figured since I was the only real local of the group, I was better off in the touristy areas where less of the locals would ever be. Less chance for me to be recognized even with a wig and fake beard.

"Part of everyone's homework is to drive your route until you know it as well as you know your lovers' genitals. The numbers are the best order to do the route, taking into account one-ways, lights, etc. Become an expert."

We then looked at a diagram of the speed cameras. There was little door in the back that gave access. A simple Phillips head screw driver was all you needed to enter the apparatus since city officials never anticipated anyone messing with the machines. Perhaps they anticipated protests and complaints at City Hall, but not an attack on the actual machinery.

"Very simple. Open the latch, snip all the wires, spray the freeze, and then our Zuckerberg sticker on the lens. Should take no more than 5 minutes per unit. That's 50 minutes for the machinery, another 50 for total travel time between the machines and 20 minutes for unanticipated delays. It's a two-hour job. Questions?"

"When do we do it?" Curtis asked.

"Has to be on Sunday. Best time for a crime," Jackson said.

"That gives us enough time to prep and study," Mercy said. "And less time to overthink and get nervous."

"The Bogdonaviches are ready," Jackson said and then looked at Maxy, Nadine and me for confirmation.

Maxy nodded. Nadine and I looked at each other.

"We'll be ready," she said.

"Make sure you drive the area several times. Get comfortable. Use a different zip car each time to avoid the attention of repetition. Spend time at one camera and become familiar with the machinery. They're all the same so don't worry about checking others. Decide on a driver and a mechanic and experience your roles during simulation."

"What if all the cameras aren't the same. Shouldn't we check them all?" I asked.

"Minor differences at most, and you'll have the tool box to deal with any variables. Lock cutters, variety of screw drivers, tools, the works. You don't need to be a mechanic, just damage the thing like a 5-year old and make sure not to forget Zuckerberg."

"What are we driving for the job?" Nadine asked.

"Good question. White vans that look just like city worker vans," Jackson said. "You're a city worker. Act like it. Give a wave or a nod to cops if they come by. Be in character. We have some insiders on that end, too. Risk is minimal."

We went through more questions and discussion until everyone seemed settled and clear. We all stood up and Jackson concluded: "Text me from the burner in your boxes. All our numbers are preprogrammed. Our only communication is through those phones. After you process everything, study, and drive the route, confirm via text by just typing green for go or red for no. Do this by Saturday at 6pm. Once I get the green light from everyone, I will send out confirmation that we're officially on. If you have any questions, text to a shared thread on the burner. If anyone texts red at any time before the job, we abort and reboot. Check your phones for updates. After the job, text a brief summary. If all went well, just say so. No need for details unless issues arose. I don't want a novel. Done with those. Once we've all reported and the mission is accomplished, I'll text with our next meeting info for phase two. Once you get that message, destroy the burners."

Jackson scanned the circle, extended eye contact with each of us, perhaps looking for nervousness and doubt.

"More questions?" he finally asked.

Everyone shook their heads.

Jackson raised his glass and said, "To Sunday."

10 — Family Business

I was in my office playing around with hypothetical numbers, plugging in chunks of my felonious windfall into the spreadsheets Mariana had prepared for me. Laundering would be a piece of cake thanks to the Cabrillo. I had creditors, equity loans, renovations, a monster mortgage, various permutations of how to spread and cleanse the money.

But the issue was that all the money wouldn't be mine. I had to settle with Dana, and I had to settle soon, before the big payoff, otherwise my reduced debts would increase her settlement.

I called Mariana and told her my father was likely to come through. I also decided it was time to come clean about Dana and me. Add Mariana to the list of people who thought Dana and I weren't right for each other.

"Harry, I gotta say now that I can, this was long overdue. Thank god."

"Really?"

"Really! Dios mio, the few times I've seen you together recently you two looked miles apart while standing right next to each other."

I took a deep breath. "Yeah, I know, I've been blind."

"Oh, Harry, I have been blind so many times. Every time actually. Our vision is worst when it's up close. Sex is an instant cataract."

"Well said. Mariana, you're smarter than with just numbers."

"Yeah, in hindsight, but next time, it'll be different. I'm gonna stay 20-20," Mariana said confidently. "Speaking of numbers and Dana, you know she's gonna want her share, right?"

"Of course."

"Harry, be prepared. She's entitled to a whole lot of money."

"Yeah, even though she left me and has been screwing somebody else."

"Are you that upset about it?"

"More than I expected. I'm also upset because she doesn't deserve half."

"Well, I see your side, but the law won't."

"You know a good lawyer?"

"Sure, he did me right during my divorce. And it's the least I can do for you after setting me up with Joel."

"You're being sarcastic. Are you going to get me some lawyer.com idiot?"

"No, no way. And I'm not sarcastic at all."

"Really? I forgot to ask what happened on the big date."

It turned out that Joel had shocked her. He was gentlemanly, courteous, a good listener. He had this marvelous plan that started with meeting at a SOMA gallery for an exhibition on Botero, her favorite artist, the Picasso of Colombia. Since she was Colombian, he figured she would at least appreciate the cultural sentiment, but he really nailed it. She hadn't even known about the exhibit and right away she was touched by his thoughtfulness and awareness of her culture. After the exhibit, they went to dinner at a romantic bistro in the Mission. And then it clicked for her.

"Harry, suddenly Joel became someone I could fall for. He has amazing eyes. I never noticed them before, but he makes such great eye contact. Not creepy, well kind of at first, but then it's just powerful, almost hypnotic. I haven't had someone look at me like that in a long time. Maybe ever."

They went for dessert at the Cliff House, sharing chocolate mousse and port wine as the waves crashed below, and then walked back to the theatre and watched *The River's Edge* after hours.

"Best date of my life, Harry. We made out in the back row like teenagers. Maybe even more than made out."

"Damn, did you guys do it in the theatre!"

"No, no. It was wonderfully high schoolish, but I'll tell you, I wanted to do it. He's good."

"I'm so happy for you and so surprised. Stunned actually!"

"Me, too. I figured it would be a coffee or drink and then I'd cut out, favor done, but he blew me away. I like him, really like him, Harry. And it doesn't hurt that he is a great kisser."

"Wow, Joel the lothario."

"Didn't think there were any nice straight guys left in this damn city. Can't wait to see him. Tomorrow is the encore. He's got this whole winery date planned in

Sonoma and then a walk and picnic in Bodega Bay."
Mariana took a deep breath and then said, "Ok, enough
about me. Let's get back to business. How much money
are we talking about from your father?"

I was thinking I should do something like that for
Nadine. I hadn't really planned anything elaborate,
hadn't really planned anything at all. Joel was totally
outdoing me.

"Harry, you there?"

"Sure, yeah, what was the question?"

"Your dad's money. How much are you getting?"

"Well, not sure yet, but he said maybe, ahhh, a couple of million actually."

"Dios mío! You're kidding?"

"No, señora. He came through big time."

"Harry, this could save us. I didn't know your family had that kind of money."

"Me, neither. They've been holding out."

Mariana said she would redo the projections and
see how best to distribute the influx of capital. Mariana
also warned me to settle with Dana fast in order to get
the money post-settlement. "No need to share that with
her."

"I'm already on that."

She gave me her lawyer's number and then thanked
me again.

"For what?"

"Joel."

"Sure thing. So, Mariana, I take it you don't want
me to fire him anymore."

"No, he's keeper, like I've always said," she said, grinning.

"Right. Of course, Joel's the glue."

"Yeah, my glue now," Mariana said, positively beaming though I think I saw a filmy layer of cataracts emerging.

*　　*　　*

With still no contact from Nadine, I decided to initiate, as always. Together it was so good, but then apart it was as if she completely forgot about us. Or, at least, that was my needy and greedy perception. I texted asking how she was feeling about us after last night and where she was with us now, a day later. I was about to hit send but hesitated at the last second. After taking a deep breath, I added, *I miss you.* Before I could conquer my indecisiveness, there was a knock on the open door.

It was Joel.

"Harry, you got a moment?"

"Sure," I said, putting my phone down and happy that I was interrupted from to send or not to send.

"Are you sure this is a good time?" Joel asked.

"As good a time as any, Joel. Come on in."

Joel sat down and had an inscrutable mien.

Furrowing my brow and narrowing my gaze into an analytic glare, I said, "Hmmm, let me guess. You had a great date with Mariana."

"Harry, better than great. Spectacular. Oh my god, Harry, she is amazing. Wait, how did you know?"

"She told me."

"What did she say? Really? What did she say?

Does she like me?" Joel asked, so amped up that he was talking as if he were on fast forward.

"Slow down, Joel."

"Come on, Harry, tell me!"

"She said she had a great time. It sounded like she had the best date of her life. In fact, I think she said just that."

"Really. She said that!"

I nodded.

"Oh man, oh my god, I'm so happy," he said with a giant sigh followed up by a deep breath as if he'd just emerged from several minutes underwater. "Wow, Harry."

"Breathe, Joel, breathe."

He nodded and calmed himself, averting full blown hyperventilation. "Harry, it went so well. Everything just clicked. The plan, the vibe, the conversation. The museum with Botero. Larga vida, Botero!"

"Yeah, she said—"

Without hearing a word of what I said, Joel interrupted, "And oh my god, Harry, the making out in the downstairs theatre. We were like high school kids, or at least, other high school kids besides me, you know the cool ones. I was so turned on, I almost, you know, lost it," he said, sheepishly.

"Really?"

"Well, it wasn't just kissing. I mean I wasn't Jim in *American Pie*, but it was damn close. There was a lot of touching. Her hands were probing, shall we say."

"Well, sounds like there will be even more probing

next time."

"I know," Joel said, suddenly looking despondent. The euphoric balloon had suddenly popped.

"What's the matter?" I asked. "Are you upset it didn't happen this time? I don't think Mariana would do that on the first date."

"No, not at all. I don't care about that, ahhh, in the usual sense. I'm crazy about her. Whenever it happens is fine."

"Then in what sense?"

"Harry, can I confess something to you? I've never told anyone this."

"Sure, Joel. We're friends."

"No, Harry, you're like an older brother to me. Like a mentor."

"Well, I feel sorry for you then."

"I'm serious."

Joel got up and closed my office door. That has been happening a lot lately. Joel then hesitated on how to begin before spilling forth everything. Once the levee broke, it was a logorrheic flood. Joel was terrified of performing poorly. He had a history of letting nervousness get the best of him. He said sometimes the performance anxiety caused him not to get it up, or the opposite: he came prematurely like a teenager, like he almost did in the movie theatre.

Beyond the erection and prematurity issues, he was so nervous that his palms got all sweaty and that was on top of his already chafed hands from rubbing them all the time. He would get so awkward and uncomfortable that women would not enjoy it and it would ruin everything.

He blamed the neurosis on a few sexual mishaps in his youth and losing his virginity too late, but the lion's share went to Saigon. While backpacking through Southeast Asia, he became very attracted to one particular girl at a "lady bar." Over the course of several nights he came in and sat with her, bought her drinks and flirted, touching more and more with clothes on, while she kept encouraging him to go in the back room for more and 1,500,000 Vietnamese Dong ($75). Finally, on his last night in Saigon, Joel worked up the courage to go in the backroom.

Nguyen quickly took Joel's pants and underwear off and began to stroke, lick, suck, and grind to no avail. After half an hour and exhausted, she screamed and then shouted something in Vietnamese. Joel said, "Sorry, I guess I'm nervous."

Nguyen screeched with frustration. "Never happen before. Why you no hard?" she asked while five or so other ladies barged in, worried for her safety. They all gazed at a dejected and defeated Joel, pants and penis both down. Laughter and mockery ensued. He didn't know Vietnamese, but the laughter said it all. From that point onward, his sexual encounters were usually derailed by a chorus of Vietnamese ladies laughing and jeering in his head, or rather in his loins.

"I do wish we had done it the other night. I was so on my game and had the right wine buzz. Just enough to get it up and just enough not to come. I think I would have done great, but now there's so much build up and anticipation. I'm freaking out and I know the Saigon ladies will be singing their song."

"Joel, you'll be fine."

"Great advice, Harry. That really helps."

I shrugged. "You had a great first date. That can change everything."

"You don't get it."

"No, I do get it. All guys get nervous at least a little bit. You're not alone, but she really likes you, Joel. You've got this Joel. You can do it."

"You think so?"

"Definitely. And since she likes you, she'll be patient. She'll probably find the nervousness cute and a sign of how much you like her. She'll help you through it. It's not a business transaction in a seedy Saigon bar."

Joel nodded, almost confident.

My phone vibrated. It was Nadine. "I'm in the lobby. Are you free?"

What a relief.

"Look, Joel, I gotta go. Just relax. You made her feel great the other night."

"I know, but it was too good. I'll never live up to that again."

"Don't go all Costanza on me now. And keep doing the eye thing," I said heading out the door. "She loved it."

"Shit, it worked. Really?"

"You got some sort of Don Juan meets Dracula thing going."

Joel laughed and then rubbed his hands together.

*   *   *

Nadine wanted to do our reconnaissance. We drove to Lombard Street at the intersection of Union, just below the crooked part where all the tourists gawked and snapped photos. This was the first stop on the map. We made some small talk on the way, new terrain in our intense relationship.

We kissed a bit in the beginning, but it was bordering on awkward and had no narcotizing effect. She told me about her class that day and then we focused on the crime. We went to each of the ten spots. She drove and I inspected the speed cameras. Just as Jackson said, it was easy access with a Phillips head on all but number 8, near Pier 39. That one had a bolt on the little rear door. I took a quick photo of it. When we finished, I suggested we go to McLellan's, but Nadine didn't want to drink. She had a paper to write and needed to focus. So, we settled on a coffee at a café near her apartment.

Something was clearly different. She was obviously backing away. More small talk about her father's business troubles and some talk about Christine's life, which I had no interest in hearing about.

"Look, I think I should go," I said, cutting her off.

She seemed surprised. "I thought you'd want to hang out. What's the matter?"

"Not like this."

Nadine sighed. "Like what?"

"Come on. You're kidding, right?"

"Am I distant?"

"Like a fifth cousin."

"I know. I'm sorry."

"What changed?"

Nadine took a deep breath and stared above me for a while, clearly laboring to put thought to word. "I don't know, it's too much, Harry. The damn thing with J, my father's troubles, Christine, moving here, and now you. Now us. I need to compartmentalize things. I'm over-loaded."

"So, you've chosen to compartmentalize us?"

"Well, that's the craziest thing."

"Crazier than J's thing?"

"Kind of, yeah. No, definitely. I mean we just met. This can't be real. The other shoe has to drop."

"Why does it have to. It can float in the atmosphere forever."

"Yeah, hanging over our heads. You're such a dreamy San Franciscan."

"Some people are just meant for each other. Why not us?"

Staring deeply into my eyes now, Nadine said, "God, I know I'm going to cave, and we'll be having sex in your office in about 10 minutes."

"Let's go to your place. It's closer."

Nadine shook her head, looking directly into my eyes, almost piercingly. "What the fuck is this, Harry? Seriously? Let's cut the bullshit."

Before I could answer, she did. "I'll tell you what it is. It's infatuation and if we follow its course to the con-clusion, it will be bad. I'll end up alone, hurting Christine, and you'll end up alone, too. No one wins."

"I'm already alone."

"No, you're wrapped up in a fantasy with someone you met at a reading right after your longtime partner cheated on you. You need to really be alone. You need to get a grip."

I paused and absorbed the last line. Then I nodded and whispered, "Let's go. We're putting on a show here."

We walked back to Nadine's and at the entrance I said, "I'll see you Sunday. We're ready. Let's just focus on the task as you said." I turned to walk up Cabrillo Street when Nadine grabbed my arm and said, "Wait. Come here." She took my hand and we walked back to her place, sitting on the stoop.

"You really believe this? In us?" she asked.

"100%"

"You're so stupid."

"Yup, full blown idiot."

"The thing is when I'm with you, I'm fine. When we're apart, I unravel and pull away out of fear."

"Then it's an easy solution."

"How so?" Nadine asked with an intrigued, but doubtful look.

"We never part."

She playfully shoved me on the shoulder. "Stop saying all the right things."

I leaned over and kissed her lips, then her neck gently, softly, before whispering in her ear, "Just give in to us, Nadine. Stop fighting it. Stop overthinking us."

"I can't even imagine the look on Christine's face if I tell her about us. She's the best person I've ever met. I don't want to fuck that up."

"I know it's harder for you. Dana and I were basically done, but I confess my greed with you. I want you all to myself."

"Until you actually get it. Christine is so patient with me, my moments, my clinging to life. I don't think you will be."

"How do you know?"

"You need balance. I can see your insecurity, the way you just reacted to my distance. Christine would have pulled me out of it. You wanted to escape."

"No, no, only momentarily. That's bullshit. And I thought you wanted space. I am still figuring out our rhythms."

"Harry, it only takes a moment to mess it all up."

"So thin ice all the time?"

"Maybe. That's been my life."

"Whatever it is, I'm in. It won't change no matter how many red flags you throw at me."

Nadine smiled, and gave me a tender look, as if her guard had finally downshifted.

"So now what?" I asked.

"I don't fucking know," Nadine said, her face falling into her open palms. She then ran her hands slowly through her long black hair as if this would clear her mind. "Here's how I feel. I want you to leave and never see you again. And I want to fuck you and never let you out of my arms. How's that for bipolar?"

"Perfect polarity, sweetheart. I know which pole I want."

Nadine grabbed my forearm with a tight grip, pulled me up off the stoop and led us up to her apartment. We were half-undressed by the time we got through the door.

Later, as she slept next to me, I realized one thing: I was no longer just showing movies.

*   *   *

I left the next morning and we made a deal not to see each other or talk until the crime. Or rather she made the deal and I agreed. It was clear that Nadine's geography was all peaks and valleys, no plains, at least for a while until we sorted everything out. Or maybe this would be our life forever. I was getting just what I wanted but mused if I'd miss the plateau down the road...

While walking home, the patience and steadiness I portrayed in front of her cracked under the pressure of repressed frustration. Its expression was paranoia over everything.

I called Jackson.

He answered quickly. "Hey, everything ok? What the hell, man. No calls, remember?"

"Yeah, yeah. What's really going on?" I asked.

"About what?"

"This whole damn crazy venture. Nadine being into me. What gives man? The pieces are starting to fit together."

"What pieces? What the fuck puzzle for that matter?"

"This whole damn story and hooking me up with Nadine."

"I didn't hook you up. Shit, Dana did a number on you, didn't she?"

"It has nothing to do with Dana."

"I think it has everything to do with her. Or your parents, or—"

"Never mind the bullshit psychoanalysis. Sometimes I think this is all just a set up for your next book. Is this all just another living novel you got me embroiled in? A way to break your writer's block?"

"I don't have writer's block. I quit on my own terms. Are you telling me you think this is a plot?"

"You always said live it first and then write it. Maybe you outlived your material and—"

"Harry, you're going over edge on me. Why would I set up a crime, two crimes and then write about it? I'd be indicting myself. What the fuck, man, think about it?" I paused and realized I hadn't thought this through. Jackson continued, "Jesus, you get some action with Nadine and you're all fucked up. Nothing worse than a man in love. We're worse than women. Take it from me."

Jackson affirmed that all of this was about money and getting his winery and Samira back. He also swore he had nothing to do with Nadine falling for me. "A woman can actually like you for real, for who you are, Harry. Easy on the self-loathing."

"Well, no easy task there," I said, thinking everyone has their own chorus of Vietnamese ladies singing songs of mockery.

"Harry, get some rest and be ready for Sunday. Watch a movie and let Nadine and you fall into place. I need you focused, not all neurotic and lovesick."

"You're right," I conceded.

"Eye on the prize, Harry," Jackson said before hanging up.

*   *   *

Heeding his advice, I took a two-hour nap, had a good lunch rather than my usual bowl of cereal, and then watched *Family Business* in my apartment. It was a good, underrated crime movie with Sean Connery, Dustin Hoffman, and Matthew Broderick. Connery's line had always stuck with me, "If you can't do the time, don't do the crime."

I committed to refocusing my attention away from Nadine and obsessively checking my phone for any scrap of communication. I only had to kill a little more than 24 hours before seeing her anyway. Joel made the task easier by asking me to fill in for him as manager that night. The shift supervisor, who was supposed to be the fill-in, reneged and Joel had his "crucial" second date with Mariana tonight. I cleaned up and got ready to run the theatre for the evening.

Before starting, I went into my office and made a phone call. It rang several times and just when I thought it was going to voice mail, Dana picked up. "Hi, Harry. This is unexpected," she said. "Everything okay?"

"Well, I've been thinking about things."

"And? Are you angry?"

"Not really. Not at all, actually."

"That's mature of you."

"I don't know about that. I think it speaks more about our relationship than my maturity."

"Yeah, probably. You checked out a while ago."

"I guess I did."

"We both did, but I want you to know it was still hard to leave you. And I didn't want to end it the way I did. A lot of years, Harry."

I felt myself holding tears back. "I understand, Dana. I'm sorry, too, that we didn't make it."

I confessed that I had cheated, too, a few nights before our break-up. She was actually relieved to hear that. We started reminiscing about our early days and some good times, but I eventually cut short the nostalgia. "So not to get all practical, but I have a lawyer now. I think we should get this done right away. No need to drag it out, right?"

"Couldn't agree more. I'll be back in town next Friday morning. How about we try and set it up for that day, in the afternoon if the lawyers are on board?"

"Deal."

"Well, that was easy. I didn't expect that."

"A little time helps."

"And are you okay with 50-50? I mean, if not, Harry, then—"

"I'm fine with it. No need to quibble over percentages. You've been a part of *Kerouac* and the Cabrillo from day one."

"I'm kind of stunned. I expected—"

"Yeah, I just want to expedite the process and avoid an ugly and dramatic scene over money."

"That's great. And I will compromise, too. I will give you time, so you can try and make the payments without selling the theatre."

"Won't be necessary, but thanks."

I explained to Dana how my old man was helping me out and that I could get her the money as soon as we settled on the theatre's current value. Dana assured me she would be reasonable and go on the low end of the estimates. We even lapsed into reminiscing about the *Kerouac* days, when we were young grad students in love and committed to the film's success. Back when she believed in it, before all the fatigue and frustration undermined her passion for him and then me, and us. But today was about the sweetness that nostalgia allows.

"Harry, we had so many good days. It was so exciting back then. It just wasn't meant for the long run."

When Dana said that, my mind darted to a line stuck in my head from Hop Along's song *How Simple*:

Don't worry, we'll both get there, just not together.

*   *   *

Those were indeed good days years ago. When I had finished at State, I leapt into turning the short into a full-length feature with Zen focus and manic stamina. It was my version of Jack's 21-day heroic sprint to write *On the Road*. I was so young and artistically romantic that I had wanted to employ *method writing*. I even bought an old typewriter, not unlike the one Kerouac used, and had considered using a scroll to feed it through the typewriter. After a few foolish hours on that clunky, finger-aching contraption, Dana had nudged me back to modernity and I abandoned the purity of my method approach. However, not completely. I had written the expanded script in just 10 nearly sleepless days, albeit with just pots of coffee rather than Kerouac's amphetamine, Benzedrine. Once the script had gone from my own personal vision to the collective of filmmaking, I had to slow down.

Azure Studios agreed to give me enough budget to film on location in many of Jack's cities—Lowell, NYC, Denver, San Francisco, Rocky Mount (North Carolina), Mexico City, Tangier, Paris, and concluding appropriately with death in St. Petersburg, Florida. I wanted the actors and crew to feel the places that Kerouac had been. In Lowell, for some extra cash to the tenants, we even shot in his childhood bedroom. Columbia kindly let us into his freshman dorm for a scene. For the all-important road shots, we shot along the long, lonely western backroads and highways sheltered under those big state skies. Parts of route 66 still grooved their way to the end of the dream of America.

I insisted that we shoot chronologically following the actual order of Jack's life as much as possible. I wanted us to experience the rhythm of Jack's true ebb and flow. I also wanted the film to be simple and linear without a director getting in the way with unnecessary and indulgent creativity. Too many directors nowadays flex their aesthetic muscles to satisfy their ego, not the story's ego. Jack's story was larger than life and didn't need my help. It needed me to stay out of its way. I called this the Buddhist school of filmmaking.

When I had finished the final edits, and handed the film over to the studio, I was satisfied. The film on screen was close enough to the vision in my head. Sure, I wanted to reshoot a few scenes, tweak some dialogue, micro-edit here and there, but I knew it was time to let go and let the audience decide. I was artistically happy, but I had no idea what to expect from the public or critics. On that end, I was full of self-doubt.

Regarding any monetary success, I had a sneaking suspicion that it was not impossible. There had been some recent Kerouac energy and buzz near the film's release. Lost novels like *The Sea is My Brother* and *The Hippos Were Boiled in Their Tanks* had recently been published. The original *On the Road* scroll was released to celebrate the novel's 50th anniversary and the scroll, itself, had sold in auction for an insane two million dollars. Even Cassady's *Joan Anderson Letter*, which inspired *On the Road's* revolutionary spontaneous prose, was recently found and sold for over half a million dollars. There was a passionate cult following that seemed to be poking at the collective American unconscious.

Attempts at filming Jack's novels had all been artistically mediocre at best while completely failing commercially, but I didn't blame the auteurs' abilities, just their decision on what to film. His novels were innately unfriendly to the screen. It was like trying to film *Ulysses* or *Howl* for that matter. The plotless writing had an untranslatable naiveté while the prose crackled with lyrical energy and groovy rhythm, jazzy lyrics blowing off the page like sax notes in a smoky late-night bebop club. Film was a medium bound to fail.

But Jack's life was all plot that howled to be filmed as a biopic. I was optimistic that we would at least do better than the novels turned anemic films.

Beyond my wildest dreams, the damn thing caught fire. We opened nationwide in indie theaters and eventually overseas in over 60 countries. We received an Oscar nomination for best first film, an experimental category that only existed for the year *Kerouac* was eligible. Celestial bodies aligned for us. Dana and I walked the red carpet and sat at a table in the far back corner of the balcony, like the last ones on the list for a wedding, but who cared? It was the Oscars. It was a beautifully crazy time and Dana was ecstatic. We did a few other award shows, winning a SAG for cinematography! The film did well in the States and even better in Europe. Then there were the DVD and on-demand revenues, money flowing from all directions.

Because I had rolled the dice and asked for a bigger percentage of royalties and less upfront money, I struck gold. At the end of the rainbow, the pot filled with more than two million dollars.

That windfall bought the Cabrillo while also sowing the seeds that eventually unraveled Dana and me. She had wanted to buy a house in Larkspur, just north of San Francisco. Her plan was to buy something modest, free of a mortgage, and invest most of the rest in our retirement, and then keep some play money for travel and fun. She would support us with her graphic design job while I wrote the next screenplay. It was all very logical and smart.

But I hated it.

Dana couldn't grasp why there would be no follow up screenplay. The Hollywood life she so wanted for me (and her) would be nothing more than a fling. I had nothing left for another film. I refused to just come up with bullshit for the sake of a contract and cash in with a horrible second movie. I had some offers but wouldn't bite.

"Look, Dana, I'm a one-hit wonder. I'm okay with that. I really am. I knew all along that I only had one film in me. Maybe the muse will hit again. Anything's possible, but I wouldn't bet on it. I'm going out on a high note with integrity."

Dana sighed. "Jesus, Harry, you just got in the game and you're quitting immediately without even trying. I see no integrity in this. One-hit wonders don't stop trying. The success is what stops, but you won't even try."

Shaking my head, I said, "You don't get it, Dana. I don't feel it anymore. You can't force it. *Kerouac* came naturally and that's why it worked. It's not factory work."

"You're a screenwriter, not a poet. You have to grind it out sometimes, nudge the muse into action. You're so dramatic about it."

"No, it actually was poetry for me. It wrote itself and, in some ways, filmed itself. I can't explain it. You either get it or you don't," I said overemphasizing the word it. "You used to get it."

"Harry, what's the truth? Come on, stop with all the poetry, it-wrote-itself bullshit and join us mere mortals. Are you afraid to fail? Is that why you want to quit, or are you just lazy?"

I laughed. "It's not bullshit, but whatever. And nothing wrong with an honest failure. It's noble. Dishonest failure is different. We might as well move to LA if I'm going down that road."

"I don't see any nobility in failure, but that's a foolish philosophical discussion I have no interest in. Another one of our differences. I guess I am LA and you are San Francisco."

"Well said."

"Maybe we need to secede."

"Maybe," I said, not taking the reference seriously.

"You're so annoying," Dana said, her mouth contorted into an odd, inscrutable blend of smile and snarl.

"Yeah, I know. You knew that going in."

"Not to this extent. You really only have passion for Jack Kerouac? Nothing else stimulates you to make a film, but him?"

"I guess not. Not as far as writing a script."

"Isn't that weird?"

"Maybe. I don't know. So let me guess your allusion. I'm gay. Queer for Kerouac."

"Possibly," Dana poked.

"Very superficial analysis. You can do better."

"I just don't get the big deal. Some of his books are god awful, Harry. You even said so. *Visions of Cody*? I mean he transcribes it from some idiotic pot smoking conversations. Worst thing I ever read, or rather tried to read."

"You have to put it into the context of the time. It hadn't been done. It was breaking —"

"That's rubbish. It was embarrassing. And *Tristessa.* Terrible writing and so sexist and unromantic," she said, raising her voice, clearly frustrated with me, with everything.

"Dana, we've been down this road. You used to praise his writing. Now you're—"

"Yeah, I know, I'm projecting. Maybe so. Let me. Just let me sometimes. Damn, Harry, I just need to let it out once in a while without you stealing my anger. You always steal my fucking anger!"

*   *   *

Back-and-forth went the eternal ping-pong match; dead-end conversations chipping away at us. Until one day when I saw an ad for the sale of a movie theatre. A bunch of great old school, single-screen theatres in San Francisco had been bought and converted by Lowe's and other monoliths in order to cookie cut them into tiny shoebox theatres. But one remained unwanted way out in the Richmond. That's when I hired Mariana, who worked for my agent and lived in San Francisco, to see if the numbers would add up. It would take nearly all of the *Kerouac* money to buy and fix up the Cabrillo, but it was possible especially because it came with the apartment in which we eventually occupied and the two other rental units on the top floor as extra income. We would still need a mortgage of at least a couple of million to make it fly, but Mariana said it had a chance. "A risky one, but the real estate value would be the savior if the theatre eventually failed. The Richmond neighborhood isn't hot, but it's still San Francisco, fog and all. And property is the new gold rush."

Dana was disappointed, but I had to act fast. The fights intensified until she finally surrendered, more from the exhaustion of my determination and less from warming to the idea.

"It's your money after all. We'll make it work, I guess."

11 — Clairvoyant

Jackson's text came early the next morning: *Green*. Nadine followed seconds after: *See you at 5 at the theatre.*

I was about to text back but stopped myself. I didn't want to be the last texter for once. I want to show respect for her space, but probably more than that, my ego wanted to assert itself, or at least the appearance of assertion for a change. I powered down and put the phone in my desk drawer, reviewed all the materials for tonight (notes, map, diagrams, and photos), and then took a foggy morning walk to the beach to watch the surfers. I needed to distract myself from cold feet and a clingy heart. On the way I passed by Madam Francoise's shop, Spirit, on the second floor of a nearby apartment building. Though having seen the sign a million times from my bay window, I never once considered going, but today was a day for new considerations.

It seemed they were open, so I rang the buzzer and a gentle-voiced woman quickly responded, "Yes."

"I'm here for, ahhh, the future, I guess. I don't have an appointment. Do you take walk-ins?"

The buzzer sounded, and I went upstairs expecting to see an old, chain-smoking French woman greet me. Instead, a fortyish Asian woman stood beneath a curved archway that led into a dining-cum-living room of an apartment.

"Hello, welcome," she said kindly. She bowed Namaste style and I returned it in kind.

"Are you Madam Francoise?" I asked, trying not to sound too incredulous.

She nodded, bowing again, and then added, "My mother was French."

"Ahh, I see."

"Everyone always looks surprised. Not sure why preconceived notions continue in this day and age. Is this your first time doing something like this?"

"Yes. Is it obvious?"

Madam Francois nodded. "Are you here seriously or for a lark?" Before I could answer, she continued, "Because sir, I take the cards, palms, and stars very seriously. They offer truth in all its universal forms, more so than any other truth these days." She said this with nary a hint of phoniness or levity in her tone or expression. I assumed it was part of the act, but it was convincing.

"Good, I'm here for truth, all truths," I said, equally straight-faced, willing to play the game.

Francoise nodded. "For better or worse. My family is from Cambodia for whatever that is worth to you. I studied in Phnom Penh and right here in San Francisco." She pointed to some diplomas on the wall. "I fuse various seer methods as you will experience."

While I thought palm reading, tarot cards, the Turkish coffee thing, whatever else in this fortune teller ilk were all as absurd as religion, I didn't dismiss whatever gets one through the night nor did I completely disbelieve astrology. When I first moved here there were more of these kinds of kooky cosmic joints, residuals of the hippie, starry-eyed Aquarian daze of the city. I remembered a few other kinds like the I Ching and Gaian Spiritualists, but I hadn't seen them around in a while. Perhaps these have been exported north to more affordable Portland, sadly evicted by San Francisco's money madness.

Madam Francois seemed sincere, seductively so, or at least, she was a very good actor. Besides a small part of me wanted to believe her. *Why not*? What else is there for an atheist to do atmospherically?

Madam Francoise was also attractive, which didn't hurt the attempt to be earnest.

"What is your name?" she asked.

"Harry."

"And?"

"Harry Gnostopolos."

She tilted her head slightly, staring at me through an inquisitive, bemused squint.

"What?" I asked.

"Quite a name."

"It's Greek."

"I gathered that. Does it begin with G-N?"

"Yes! Very few people guess that. I'm impressed."

"Have you studied your name? The etymology and geneaology?"

"No."

Madam Francoise's expression stayed steely in its seriousness. "Do you not believe in Gnosticism? I'm a modern day gnostic."

I shrugged. "I don't know."

Madam Francoise took my right hand and led me into the dining room. Her hand was soft and her grip gentle. She guided me to a certain chair, my back to the only window in the room and facing shelves full of books that were mostly of the mystical kind. I recognized just two authors: Evelyn Underhill and Edgar Cayce.

The room was otherwise non-descript, but it had a warm, lived-in vibe. She sat across from me. A deck of tarot cards to her right, a notepad and pen in front of her, and a large astrological chart on the left. She told me to put both hands, palms up, on the table. She began with the left hand, running her index finger along my palm lines slowly and softly, sending a tingling feeling up my arms and into my head. Then she pulled each hand closer to her bespectacled eyes, studying them up close. When she finished, she wrote some notes on the pad.

"Harry, I also include the eyes in my facilitation of your life situation. May I?"

"Sure."

She got up and pulled a chair close to me, asking me to turn directly towards her so we were facing each other. With her thumb and index finger, she gently closed my eyelids instructing me to keep them closed. Francoise had a grace and tenderness to her movements and touch. She ran a fingertip along the side of my left eye, slowly back and forth as if she were tracing my burgeoning crow's feet. Then underneath my eye, pressing lightly, before repeating it all on the right eye.

She told me to open my eyes. When I did, we were

inches apart, our noses practically touching. I smiled shyly from the intense intimacy, but she kept a poker face and when I looked away, she led me back hypnotically with her index finger. She slowly pulled away from me and then returned to her chair. She wrote more notes and then asked, "When is your birthday?"

"March 14, 1974."

She nodded and looked at her astrological chart before adding notes. Then she took the Tarot deck and started turning cards over slowly, methodically looking at each card, then at me. Out of all of these mystical trickeries, I thought Tarot was the most ridiculous. What the hell do random cards have to do with anyone? Everything else at least had a semblance of cosmic rhyme and reason. My palm lines and eyes were unique to me. Theoretically, they could reveal something. The same with my birthday. The universe was in a particular state of being at our birth, the gravity and energy of that moment could again be revelatory in theory. But Tarot? That took a serious leap of poetic faith.

Francoise laid out three cards and then looked up at me as if I had something.

"What?" I asked.

"Don't doubt the cards."

The three undoubtable cards were: The Magician, The Lovers, and Death. Francoise carefully observed each one, looked at her notes, and then back to the cards. She laid out two more: The Fool and Judgment. Again, from cards to notes several times. She seemed almost academic in her style, as if she were a professor doing valid research on my exposed soul. She made it all so believable like a good evangelist, and now I was getting a bit nervous about what she would tell me.

"Harry, there have been dramatic changes in your life recently—"

"Yes, there have," I confirmed.

"It wasn't a question," Francoise corrected.

"Sorry."

"These dramatic changes are in both your romantic and practical day-to-day life. I believe you are making some big decisions. Think carefully through the decisions but trust your heart and let your instincts lead you. You are ending a period of stagnation. It is a time to shake up your life, both at work and in love. The old roads were heading in the wrong direction."

I was shaking my head.

"You disagree?"

"No, pretty damn accurate," I said, though thinking it was malleable enough to be one size fits all.

She nodded, expressionless.

"And the future? What do you see?" I asked.

"I don't have a crystal ball. I'm not a circus act, Harry. I analyze the moment, your moment. Nobody knows the future."

"Of course. Is there anything else?"

"Isn't that enough?"

"I guess so. I just wish there were some answers."

"There were answers."

Francoise opened a drawer from under the table that I hadn't noticed before. She pulled out a small pad and wrote some numbers down, handing me the bill — $75.

I gave her cash and then we walked to the door.

"Thank you, Madam Francoise."

As I left, she said, "Harry Gnostopolos, trust your name."

*   *   *

After a long walk to and along the beach, I returned home, feeling more at ease after the mystical analysis. Francoise's soothing presence had a lot to do with that, but there was also the momentary appeal of some kind of cosmic possibility universally at work. I could feel how it would make believers a little less lonely, but ultimately I knew this would last no longer than the warmth of a couple glasses of wine.

When I walked into the Cabrillo lobby, Nadine was sitting at the bar, talking to Joel.

"Hey," I interrupted.

"Hi, Harry," they both said, swiveling in my direction.

"So what are you guys up to tonight?" Joel asked, as if we were a couple. It caught me off guard and I froze.

Nadine said, "No plans for me other than writing a paper tonight." Then she turned to me. "You?"

"Ahhh, I have the night off. I might just see a movie or stay in."

Joel smiled as if he were in on the lie. "Harry, you always have the night off."

"Right, of course. Well, actually, I covered for you the other night. So not always."

"Well?" Joel asked as if I should be able read his mind. He was grinning ear to ear and it finally dawned on me.

"Oh yeah, how was the big second date?" Joel always made me ask the question rather than just sharing the news. I already knew the answer from Joel's ebullience. I didn't have to be Madam Francoise to pick that up.

"Well, let's put it this way, all quiet on the Saigon front."

"That's great, Joel."

"What's the Saigon front?" Nadine asked with a furrowed brow.

"Oh, ahhh, never mind that," Joel said glaring confidentiality at me. "Just a silly inside thing with my boss."

"I'm happy for you. Remember, Mariana is one of the best. Treat her well, Joel."

"Of course, Harry. Now back to work," Joel said as he floated away.

I sat next to Nadine who was drinking a glass of red. I ordered one as well from our bartender, Jasmine, who then went to check on some tables.

"What an amateur I am. Sorry. He caught me off guard. Did I look frazzled?"

"Very much so. You need to be cool. We should have met clandestinely, but your staff has seen us together, so I don't think it's that big a deal."

"Let's leave separately and meet at the van."

"Sounds good," Nadine agreed.

We made some small talk about her classes and her dissertation progress, keeping things formal in front of Jasmine and whoever else overheard us. Then Nadine left, making sure that others heard she was heading home to study. I lingered another half-hour before going up to my apartment and then out the back door of the theatre, unseen. It was a half-hour until go time. I took Uber to a small pub on Van Ness about three blocks from the van on Hyde and Filbert. I ordered a club soda and killed some time. The wine was enough to take the edge off, but I wanted to stay clear-headed.

When I got to the van, I dialed in the pass code that was in our materials. I opened the back door and Nadine was already inside, putting on her uniform. She was zipping up the front of the jumpsuit.

"Ready?" she said.

I nodded. "Ready as I'll ever be."

"We're all business tonight, right?"

"Silly question."

After I put on my disguise, Nadine and I sat on the floor of the van and went through the details again several times while waiting for the second text of green or red that would come at six o'clock. She had the route down pat, having done a few more practice runs on her own. I felt like I should have walked it again, taken extra steps like her, but I was still surprisingly confident, even serene about all of this. Maybe it was the Francoise effect.

Don't doubt the cards.

At precisely six the burner beeped. Nadine opened the message and showed it to me.

Nadine went to the driver's seat and I sat on the passenger's side. She drove up Hyde, took a right on Lombard, zigzagged down the crookedest street in the world, and one block later there it was: the first speed camera on Leavenworth and our gateway to criminal activity.

Nadine double-parked in front of the camera to provide some cover. "Wish me luck," I said, all the serenity quickly trampled by a dry mouth and racing heart.

"You got this, Harry. Don't look back."

I walked behind the camera, took out my Phillips head from the tool belt, and unscrewed the back latch. The inside looked just like the blueprints we were given. I cut the wires, sprayed the freezing agent all over before the coup de grâce: Sticking the Zuckerberg on the camera lens.

One down, nine to go.

We hit Jones, Chestnut, Union, and were rolling. Nothing unusual happened until Bay Street. A few passers-by made some anti-camera comments while they saw me doing my *maintenance* work. One said, "I hate those things, man" and another said, "Fucking Big Brother bullshit has no business in San Francisco."

I was ignoring them until one of them kicked me in the ass and knocked me over. He and his buddy were laughing hysterically as I tumbled foolishly. I got up squeezing a screw driver in case they came at me again.

"Hey, you shouldn't fix those machines, you should destroy them"

The irony was too much. "Yeah, well just doing my job."

"You're part of the problem, man."

"Whatever. Go bother someone else, dude."

"We want to bother you," he said as they both approached me.

Nadine jumped out of the passenger side of the van and stood beside me. "Assholes, I have already called the cops. If you leave now, we'll tell them we didn't get a good look at you. If you stay, you're in prison."

The two provocateurs looked at each other and then ran full-speed down Bay Street. I looked at Nadine, nodding approval, finished the job and then we were on our way. All the other stops went without a hitch until the final one on Beach Street. As I was opening the latch, I spotted Sandy walking right towards me with a friend and we briefly caught eyes before I looked down. *Shit*, I muttered. I had faith in the fake beard, cap, and glasses, but just in case I lowered my cap and buried my face as close to the box as possible, pretending to be inspecting something very closely. I could see the four legs approaching, slowing down as they got closer, and then coming to a stop in front of me.

Fuck!

I heard Sandy whispering something to her friend, before she said, "Excuse me, sir." I didn't respond, but my nervous system did by going haywire.

"Harry? Harry Gnostopolos, is that *you* repairing a speed camera? Why would? What's going on?"

I froze for a moment, then pulled my wrench out of the belt without looking and started feigning its use.

"Harry?"

I stopped the faux wrench work and without taking my face out of the camera box, I fished in my tool belt for the first thing I could grip, pliers, and began their pretend use.

"Sir, may I ask you a question?" Sandy was relentless.

Her friend said, "Maybe he has earbuds."

"Harry, it's Sandy," she nearly yelled. "What are you doing here?"

Finally, without looking at them, I said, "Lady, my name is Roger and I'm very busy dealing with electrical issues that are dangerous." I used as deep and different of a voice as I could without sounding ridiculously fake. "I don't know any Harry."

"Sorry. I ahhh, for a moment, thought you were someone I know. It's just —"

"Come on, Sandy. Let's go. Let the guy do his job."

I heard footsteps and chatter fading in the distance. I waited a few minutes, got my breathing somewhat under control, then sprayed the wires, and put Zuckerberg where it belonged. I turned slowly and carefully to see if Sandy was lingering. Fortunately, the coast was clear, and I leapt into the van.

Nadine drove off and said, "Who was that? What the fuck was that?"

"Sandy, who works the kiosk at the Cabrillo. Shit, that was close."

"Did she recognize you?"

"Yeah, I don't know how with the damn disguise. 70-something years old and she's got x-ray fucking vision." I took a deep breath. "But I think we're okay. I buried my head in the damn machine and told her my name was Roger. She seemed to buy it."

"Ok, but what is she going to say when she hears the news about the cameras being vandalized."

"If she does. Not sure this will be on the front page. She'll probably think it's a coincidence. That I look like a guy named Roger with a beard."

"I hope so."

We drove in silence, relieved that we were done. I think we were fully and truly absorbing the potential consequences of our actions for the first time. I could hear Nadine breathing rapidly.

This wasn't a movie.

*   *   *

We got back to the theatre and texted Jackson that all went well, briefly explaining the minor Sandy issue. He responded: *Not worried.*

We went up to the roof with a bottle of champagne. I lit a fire, and we both downed the first glass quickly trying to dial down the adrenaline, which was a twisted mix of euphoria at pulling off the criminal mission, a sort of deviant high, and the anxiety of the Sandy encounter. A few glasses in and we finally diluted the Sandy effect as a minor hiccup in the big picture, convinced (or deluded) that she would never know it was me. One more bottle later and it even got giddy about my ass kicking.

We then mused about part two, throwing half-serious ideas in the air like ticker tape confetti. *A real lion in the home of that Minnesota dentist. Robbing gun shops of all their merchandise and setting it ablaze on Alcatraz. Kidnapping nonbelievers of Climate Change and leaving them stranded on a lonely patch of ice floating in the Arctic Ocean.* We both assumed it would involve some sort of socially conscious protest tinged with humor, but it had to be much riskier and grander since the money was so much more.

The burner buzzed. Jackson: *Job complete. Wednesday at midnight, Theatre 2 of the Cabrillo. Phase 2 meeting.*

"Are you okay with that?" Nadine asked.

"Sure, it's fine," I said, tossing the burner into the fire. "Fuck it."

"What are you going to do with the money if we get the whole treasure?" Nadine asked.

"Save the Cabrillo, once I settle with Dana. I have a meeting with her and the lawyers this week."

"Are you fighting her about money?"

"Not really. I think we'll figure it out. What about you?"

"A lot to my father and stash a bunch for the future. It's more money than I imagined earning in my entire life."

We chatted on, reverting to small talk this and that. She told me more about a paper she was writing on Diane DiPrima's poetry. Then she drifted into her cousin, who lived in Fez, and was getting divorced from his French wife.

But things were different. The chemistry wasn't

there, the magnetism barely active. Maybe it was the champagne buzz, but that should have made connecting easier. I felt a million miles away from her like I was talking to someone I'd just met. Profound, soulmate-like connections were in their essence bipolar: the highs intoxicating and incredible, the lows tragically sad.

"Are you ok?" she asked.

"Sure."

Nadine was shaking her head. "Liar. You're somewhere elsewhere."

I gulped the champagne and emptied the last of the bottle into our glasses. "No, Nadine, I'm right here. Just tired from the intensity and champagne."

"Me, too, Harry. Tonight was a big deal and bigger is yet to come. A lot on our minds," she said, putting her glass down and standing up. "So, I'm gonna head home. We need some downtime to decompress from all of this and I have a meeting with classmates early in the morning."

"Right, good idea to just take things down a few notches."

"Yeah, just for now."

I walked Nadine to the roof door and was about to head down with her, when she stopped me with a hand to my chest. "We better not be seen together."

"Right, of course," I agreed, pretending to be unphased.

Nadine leaned into to kiss me and immediately I could feel the pendulum swing towards the other pole, but it didn't go far as Nadine pulled away first, saying,

"Have faith in us and patience with me," before descending the stairs.

I stayed on the roof sitting by the fire until it went out on its own hours later.

12 — A San Francisco Odyssey

I was in a swanky, but sterile corporate board-room in the Financial District. Dana and her lawyer sat across from my lawyer and me. Two on two. Dana's lawyer, Peter Sweeney, explained the purpose of the meeting and emphasized that his client wanted to avoid court. Her goal was to settle things today, right now, so that "both she and Harold Gnostopolos could get on with their lives."

My lawyer, Ximena Santiago, volleyed back, "We completely agree."

Sweeney was tall and skinny. His fingers were particularly long and bony, well suited for a pianist. He had an affectedly loud voice as if he were trying to overcompensate for his slender frame. Ximena, conversely, was short and stout with a deep voice flowing naturally from her chest.

They were perfectly antithetical just like Dana and I had grown to be.

"Ok, great," Sweeney said. "This should be a slam dunk. We agree on 50-50, right?"

Ximena looked at me for confirmation. She had advised me to go for 60-40, and a higher property assessment, but I refused. We had settled on a value of $250,000 in property equity and I was prepared to give Dana $125,000 of that. We had virtually no other assets besides the equity.

I nodded approval to Ximena, who turned to Sweeney and said, "Yes, we agree on 50-50."

"All right then. We just need a figure. We had two estimates, took the lower one and then cut 10% off that all in the interest of concluding this matter swiftly and cleanly. The lower estimate was $550,000 so we are asking for $247,500, which is half of $495,000."

"Mr. Sweeney," Ximena immediately responded, "are you using the projected estimate of the Cabrillo's property value in 2024?"

Sweeney laughed. "That's cute, Mrs. Santiago."

"Ms."

"Sorry, Ms. Santiago."

"You should also be apologizing for your ridiculous math. I submitted the debt my client has incurred and there is no way your estimate makes sense given the debt-to-appraisal ratio."

I liked Ximena. She was tough as nails and didn't take any shit. She already had Sweeney on the ropes while he pawed back with his estimate based on both the property and the value of selling the theatre. I noticed his voice had gone down many decibels.

"The theatre has no value," Ximena said. "Where do you get that nonsense from?"

"No nonsense at all. Just facts, and as your client knows, Dana was instrumental in the creation and development of the Cabrillo theatre. She devoted much of her time and energy as well as financial and emotional support over many years. This is indisputable. She is entitled to her share."

"Come on, Dana. This is bullshit," I said.

"How so?" she asked. "Please do tell, Harry."

And the fuse was lit. We argued back and forth, shamelessly in front of the lawyers, until each of them calmed their client down.

Ximena tried another angle. "We hadn't planned on going down this road, but if you are trying to squeeze every penny out of my client's theatre, then so be it. Let's remember the Cabrillo is Harry's baby, his heart and soul, purchased from the earnings of his film while Ms. Atkins considers the theatre an abominable albatross. If we want to tally all assets, then we are entitled to half of her 401K. His theatre, her 401K."

"Absurd rationale," Dana said, shooting me a look of disgust.

Ximena countered, "Not at all. If we use your inflated estimate, then 50-50 is for everything, all assets, of which your 401K is one."

Ximena had the 401K in her back pocket and pulled it out with exquisite legal timing. I could see Dana was taken aback by that. I knew her retirement account was getting up there and she obsessively tracked it every night. Meanwhile, the lawyers squabbled back and forth while Dana and I pitched in petty comments here and there. It was like two Seventh graders in trouble with their hopelessly biased parents trying to solve the problem.

Until Dana altered course, "Let's meet in the middle."

"The middle of what?" Ximena asked.

"The original estimates."

Ximena did the math on her phone and told me

that would increase my payment to Dana by $61,250 to $186,250."

I immediately agreed.

"Are you sure, Harry?" Ximena said. "We can go to arbitration. We'll win," her eyes darting an icy gaze to Sweeney.

"I'm sure."

We then began signing a mountain of documents. We agreed on 90 days to pay the money. Dana said she was glad that I didn't have to sell the theatre and that we'd resolved this without court and high drama. Our relationship had fallen off a cliff and shattered at impact. We both had other lovers now and all that remained of our years together was a tug-of-war using a rope worth several hundred thousand dollars.

Now that the money was settled, there was nothing left of us. I watched her leave the room, which might be the last I would ever see of her after being with her almost every day for nearly a decade. There was something profoundly sad about that no matter how far apart we had drifted.

Ximena and I departed together and chatted briefly at the corner of Market and First Street.

"Are you sure you're okay with this deal?" she asked.

"Yeah, I'm okay with it. Glad it's over."

"Ok, Harry, I hope you don't cave so easily during all your confrontations."

*   *   *

I decided to walk down the Embarcadero towards

AT&T Park. I remembered when this area was desolate back in the early days of my San Francisco experience. The Giants still played in the swirling cold winds of Candlestick Park down by the airport. There were a couple of blue-collar burger and beer joints by the water and not much else. It had an *On the Waterfront*, rough-and-tumble, down-at-the-docks kind of vibe. Those were the halcyon days when I was writing *Kerouac*, San Francisco still had a feint heartbeat of bohemia and the Beats, and the Sunsetters had our fling with significance. We were young and dreamy enough to believe that creativity would be our currency while we left the mundane and all the pain adrift in a glorious wake. Is there any youth of today innocent enough to even flirt with these wildly fantastic notions?

Those days now seemed like a lifetime ago. Sometimes someone else's lifetime.

Until recently.

Fancy restaurants now lined the Embarcadero, feeding the crowds of AT&T Park under the looming Bay Bridge. The docks were filled with high-rise condos, hip foodie joints, microbreweries, and all the other dominoes of gentrification. Money had overtaken San Francisco and money was now dictating my life. The only difference was Nadine. Her spirit, our connection, had resurrected my youth. Made me feel alive, desirous to be, an innocence   rekindled. With her, Jackson, and our suddenly thick-as-thieves adventure, my treadmill life transformed into an open road sprint. I didn't want to look back. I wanted to save the Cabrillo and convince

Nadine to be with me all the way to eternity. Grandiose thoughts and poetic rhythms trampled gravity.

I knew today's dreaminess could just be tomorrow's delusion. If so, so be it. Delusion was much preferred to reality.

I passed by a few chain bars and restaurants, kept walking past the stadium, past gentrification, searching for one particular joint from back in the day. It was a cool ramshackle spot on the old docks, all weathered wood and rusty nailed, fishermen nearby, the oddly intoxicating stink of brine, the sizzle of greasy burgers frying beneath seagulls squawking overhead, and distant howls of the Embarcadero sea lions. It was where I met Valerie, the first woman I'd had a serious relationship with in San Francisco (or anywhere).

We were feasting on those greasy burgers and weak beers one Saturday evening, each with our own group of friends. The next thing I knew we had ditched our friends for each other and were at a gay SOMA bar not far from here, somewhere on Harrison. Several shots of tequila later, we were on the dance floor, beneath queer go-go dancers suspended in cages overhead while she was going down on me, her head bobbing in beat with the thumping bass rhythm of house music. I remember looking up at a Freddie Mercury-look-a-like go-go dancer watching the fellatio festivities from above.

Do those places still exist? Had the city of hills plateaued in spirit and perversity. Perhaps it was still happening, but just virtually on the phone, not in flesh and blood. But maybe I was wrong. Maybe I was too ensconced in my little Richmond neighborhood and even tinier Cabrillo world, too detached from the pulse of the city. So much could be going on beneath the façade of the Tweeting Instagrammers. A new underground might be brewing unbeknownst...Hard to believe that though since everything is out there, photographed, selfied, videoed, and announced in the moment. The real experience lost beneath the instant expression of it.

I walked and walked as the road curled south towards the fringe of SOMA. The vibe got less manicured, grittier, more real. Gay clubs and bars were still around. Then I found an Irish pub, O'Donnell's, which looked like somewhere I wanted to be right now.

I walked into an L-shaped bar and saw one man at the corner facing me, but his head was down, buried in a notebook, passionately, almost furiously writing in it. Within a couple of seconds, I knew who the writer was.

Jackson.

I quietly approached while he remained in the absolute vacuum of his words.

"Excuse me, is this seat taken?" I asked.

He didn't flinch.

"Hey buddy, is this seat taken?" I asked with a tap on his back. He looked up and stared at me for a few seconds, confusion etched on his face as if I were a stranger. Then he unscrewed his gaze from its hypnotic-state.

"Harry!" he yelled.

"What the hell, Jacko?"

He got up and gave me a big hug, pulled away, still holding my shoulders tightly, and said, "You okay?

Musculature seems tight. Need a crack?"

"No, no. Spine is fine."

Jackson turned towards the bartender, "Neil, pint of Harp and a shot of Jameson for each of us."

Neil did his job and we raised our shots. Jackson said, "To the next big thing."

"I'll drink to that," I said as our shot glasses met.

"Any word from your employee?" Jackson quietly asked, referring to Sandy.

"Not so far. Haven't seen her."

"I'm not worried. I think she'll forget about it."

"So back at it, huh?" I said, looking down at the open notebook. "So much for quitting words for wine."

Jackson quickly closed the notebook. "No, no, not what you think. This is no novel. This is the next big thing."

"Really? Let me check it out."

"No, sir. Not yet."

"Why not?"

"Not the right time or place, brother. Tonight, at the Cabrillo, you'll find out with the rest of the crew. This is a gem, though, I can tell you that," Jackson said, his voice fading into a whisper as he moved close to my ear. "Harry, we're going to be rich and we're going to redo history. We're going to change the world."

"Shit, kind of ambitious."

"Well, the 60s were."

"Huh?"

"Never mind. A little patience, please. Now what brings you down to SOMA and O'Donnell's. You're usually tucked away in your little Richmond universe."

"I was just thinking that," I said. "Dana. Just met her and the lawyers at the Embarcadero to try and settle the finances. Decided to take a long walk after."

"Didn't go well?"

"It actually went fine. I'll be fine as long we make it back from the rabbit hole."

Jackson smiled and raised his pint, "You'll be free of that weight."

"You're in a good mood. Samira related?"

"Of course. It's always about a woman, right? She finally unblocked me."

"Great."

Jackson had been fruitlessly sending her texts every day that bounced back, but Samira's ghosting finally cracked, and the floodgates opened. He forwarded her all the daily blocked texts he had sent to show his commitment and determination. It worked. She was impressed rather than freaked out and agreed to talk on the phone. He explained how he was coming into money soon, was going to get the winery up and running, the right way this time, and that he desperately wanted her back. She said no for a while, but eventually agreed to consider seeing him once Big Bear was back.

"Jesus, Jackson, it's not very romantic. Basically, demanding money to get back into the relationship. A little too Jay Gatsby."

Jackson looked away, seemingly ruminating on that description. Then he looked back at me, nodding. "Yeah, I like that. I am going all Gatsby on Samira. Most romantic novel ever written, right? Gatsby didn't make the money for greed or the house in West Egg. It was all for Daisy, all for true love. The money meant nothing."

"Very romantic, in the torturous sense."

"What other sense is there?"

"Jacko, I see the desire in all of it. The great mission and all, but Gatsby did this on his own, not from Daisy dictating conditions. That kind of corrupts the romantic purity, no?"

Jackson smiled, closed his eyes, cogitating again. This was something the youthful Jackson didn't do back in the Sunsetter days. He was impulsive, quick with repartee, all spontaneity and Beat-like first thought, best thought. "This isn't literature and love isn't the cosmic elixir that Gatsby wanted it to be." Jackson paused, eyes skyward, then continued, "There's no tuning fork vibrating on a star and my mind is not romping like the mind of god. I am not delusional here, Harry. It's all grounded. If she wants me to prove myself by saving the winery, so be it. What you don't get is that it's not about money, it's about commitment. Big Bear is my commitment to her. It's not materialism for her, it's trust and stability."

I nodded. "Fair enough. Does she know how you're doing it?"

"Of course not. She doesn't need to know everything. Nobody knows outside of the gang of six. That's a rule."

"Good."

"And so, your turn. How's it going with Nadine?"

"I don't know, man. After what you just said, maybe I'm too in love with her. Maybe I'm Gatsbyed, too."

"No, no, you need that. You're in the beginning. Samira and I are passed that. Chronology matters. You need the early days stardust escape so the memory gets you through the later hard-boiled earthly roads."

I nodded. "Damn, you gotta good grip on the whole thing, seemingly everything. Getting all sagacious on me."

"No, no, no, don't say that. Pride cometh before the fall. Strike that from the record," Jackson said with a chuckle.

"Now get a load of this. I've got some other news you're gonna love," Jackson ebulliently redirected. He explained how he had met this young kid, early 20s, right here at O'Donnell's yesterday. The kid had just finished undergrad back east at American University in DC. He was a Lit major and was big on the Beats. He'd taken a course on the influences of the Beat Generation. He saw *Kerouac* and read *195* in the class. Can you believe that shit?"

"Crazy. Our lives aren't totally worthless."

"No, sir. We are canon fodder."

Before I left, Jackson wrote something on a cocktail napkin and gave it to me: *see you tonight at midnight.*

*   *   *

I left Jackson and SOMA, deciding to walk back to the Cabrillo. It was a long trek by foot, but I wanted to see my city again. There was plenty of time before the big meeting at midnight. My perception needed expansion from its *Cabrillocentrism*, and the walk might keep me from contacting Nadine. My mantra was, give her space. I repeated it for the first mile or so and it worked, much better than the gephyrophobia mantra on the Golden Gate. Sometimes we're just not that complicated, no more complicated than Pavlovian dogs.

I walked south along Market Street, past the onset of the cable cars at Powell Street where congregated tourists waited for their historic ride, smiles on many faces, tension on others. I took a right and headed north on Hyde, walking through the Tenderloin, a once notoriously rough and tough area, now shrunken and nearly tamed, but at least free of the Disney characters now running around the once edgy Times Square. I turned quickly on Grove, past the Civic Center and then turned right heading north on Van Ness, City Hall on my right. I thought of Mayor Moscone and Harvey Milk being shot by Dan White, and then White being found not guilty in the absurd Twinkie Trial. Only in San Francisco. I walked to A Clean Well-Lighted Place, the other great independent bookstore in the city. I stopped in front, staring into the store watching people browsing the shelves, sitting in chairs and reading, milling about in three-dimensional life.

Suddenly realizing that I hadn't eaten anything all day, I walked up a few blocks to the corner of Geary and Van Ness to eat at the legendary Tommy's Joynt. I'd had Thanksgiving dinner here alone my first year in the city. One of the best holidays of my life; an eclectic gathering of the weird, lost, and lonely, suddenly kindred spirits on a family holiday, all connected by their move to San Francisco for a fabric of related reasons, joined together at a truck-stop like restaurant that rightly and proudly declares, "Welcome Stranger," on its door.

I took a plastic red tray, walked the cafeteria line loading up on sliced honey ham and turkey, mashed potatoes, peas, cornbread, chocolate pudding for dessert, and a glass of house red wine. This was the same meal I'd had on Thanksgiving. They must serve it every day in perpetuity. I was famished and devoured the massive meal. Satiated and comfortable, a Thanksgiving fullness and fatigue set in. I thought about Ubering home but didn't want abandon the long march mission. Instead, I ordered a coffee to reenergize and power through the rest of the journey. As I sipped my second cup, a woman asked to join me. She must have been in her 50s, fairly attractive and a hint of sadness in her eyes. She sat down across from me and started eating her apple pie ala mode in silence until halfway through, she paused, looked up and asked me if I was married. When I told her no, she smiled and said, "Smart man." She then went on a long monologue about how she had just left her husband of 30 years. Their entire marriage had been a rollercoaster, through three kids, five grandkids, and at least three separations. "I lost count." She took him back every time and every time she was made the fool. He kept cheating and cheating, but that wasn't the worst of it.

"He was just mean, mean to me, and the few moments he was nice, I clung to them as if I only deserved scraps of kindness, rather than actual kindness."

"Nobody deserves scraps of kindness," I said.

She had finally "stiffened her spine and made up her mind." He wasn't even cheating at that time, or at least, she thought he wasn't. At that decisive moment, "we weren't in a fight, or rather he wasn't yelling at me, which was his favorite hobby. No, he was just sitting there watching TV and in an okay mood."

She finally had "the reckoning" that it was time to go before the inevitable next breakdown in the relationship. The next day when he was at work, she packed her bags and flew to San Francisco.

"Why here?" I asked.

"I loved this city when I visited it as a kid with my family. It always had a certain magic in my memory. Most kids want Disneyworld, but I wanted San Francisco. We came many times because my dad knew I loved it. Once we stayed on a houseboat in Sausalito. One day I am going to have my own houseboat."

"That sounds great. And I agree, it is magical."

I'm not sure if she heard me and it didn't matter. Dialogue wasn't the purpose. I got the sense she hadn't talked to anyone in a while and she just needed a stranger's ear. I wondered if she had even told her kids she was here. Had she cut ties completely, escaped everyone and everything that had been familiar?

"And I don't know anyone here. That's attractive. I have been so afraid of change, so afraid of being alone, that I decided to dive into it and not go halfway. I want to start over fresh with no one around. I was so scared to do this for so long. Such a coward, but now that I've done it, my god, it's not that hard. Being alone isn't that scary. I was so much lonelier with him," she said and then let out a nice laugh, the laugh of liberation.

We chatted a little more and she asked about why I moved here. She listened and then proclaimed, "I love that almost nobody is from here."

"Me, too. It's changing, but hopefully that will stay."

"It will. It's the air and fog here," she assured me. "Don't laugh, but I think there's something from heaven in the fog."

"As good a reason as any to explain this mystical charm of San Francisco."

"And I love this little restaurant. It's a microcosm of the city."

"Good luck with everything," I said standing up. "Get that houseboat."

"I'll probably need to rob a bank for that, but anything's possible."

As I was leaving, I gave her a Cabrillo business card. "I own a movie theatre in the Richmond District. Come by some night. The movie is on the house."

"Very sweet of you."

I put my hand out and said, "My name is—"

She put her hand out, gesticulating stop. "No, no, not now. No names. I need anonymity."

A strange imperative reminiscent of *Last Tango in Paris*. "Sure, not a problem. My card is nameless. Just the name of the theater."

"That kind of name is fine," she said with a smile.

We said our goodbyes and as I paid my bill, I told the cashier to put the emancipated woman's pie and coffee on my tab.

*   *   *

I walked north on Geary enjoying the sounds of heavy traffic and the sight of the elongated #38 Geary busses with rubber accordion waists that twisted, stretched, and compressed as the buses chortled up and down the great artery that was Geary Boulevard. I walked through Japantown, momentarily considering a Kabuki massage. I'd never had one in all my years in San Francisco. I'd heard how amazing they were. I checked my silenced phone for texts and there it was. I took a deep breath and exhaled.

Hey, is all she wrote.

I hated the *hey* initiator text that the millennials seemed so fond of. Puts all the pressure on the receiver to begin earnest communication. Dana had told me to lighten up on that. The first texter was the conversation catalyst. "They get credit for breaking the ice," she'd say.

H: *How's it going?*

N: *Studying. You?*

H: *Walking the city*

N: *Where?*

H: *Near Japantown now*

N: *You're getting good at giving me space*

H: *Ask and you shall receive*

N: *Maybe too good at it*

A Cerebral Offer   233

H: *Miss me?*

N: *Ahhhhhh, let me think about that...YES!*

All the good chemicals rushed around in my head.

H: *I'm so glad*

N: *How about you?*

H: *I'm doing okay*

N: *No, silly, do you miss me?* Frustration Emoji

H: *A little bit*

N: *Ugh!* Angry shouting emoji.

H: *Silly question*

N: *I still need to know it. I want to read it. Damn, Harry!!!!*

H: *I miss you immensely!*

N: Kiss blowing emoji. *Can I come by at 10 before the big meeting?*

H: *Of course. Where?*

N: *Lobby's a bad idea, right? But I just love it there*

H: *I think it's fine*

It felt so good to flirt and play and even better to know that giving her space was working, balancing the power scale a bit more. I couldn't wait to see her and kiss her. Be near her. Feel our bodies and energies entwined. I was drunk on our connection and felt so stupidly happy that I wanted to jump up and click my heels together like a dopey cowboy doing a square dance. I looked around and nobody was looking so like an idiot I did it and walked into the Kabuki giggling alone, a giddy hysterical madman in love.

*　　*　　*

I paid for a one-hour massage. A very young Asian

millennial texting away at blurring thumb speed led me to a room in the rear of the lobby area. She never stopped texting other than to open the door.

"Wait here. Your masseuse, Portia, will be here soon."

I sat down on the massage table in the front of the room. In the back there was a large shower area with a three-legged stool and a big metal contraption whose purpose I couldn't guess.

Then a young, beautiful Asian woman entered. I guessed Southeast Asian, maybe Thailand. "Hello," she said with a bow. I put my hands together and returned her bow.

"I'm Portia."

"Harry."

"Okay, Mr. Harry, we start with steam."

"Sure."

Portia had long silky black hair, an adorable little button nose, the opposite of my Greek proboscis, bold red lipstick, and a short, but shapely body easily discernible in snug white cotton pants and a matching V-neck top with the V dipping very low. She was stunning and she would be touching me all over for the next hour.

But I was only visually aware of her appeal. It had no depth because that space was completely occupied by Nadine.

Portia told me to undress and put on a white robe that she had taken out of a cabinet. I followed orders down to my boxers.

"Everything please," she said calmly, even clinically.

I obliged, a bit embarrassed. I'd had a sex massage in North Beach back in my early San Francisco days, but that was many years ago and the only time. This seemed to be heading in that direction...

She gently wrapped her small soft hand around mine and led me to the back-shower area. She opened the metal contraption and told me to sit down in it. She closed the large doors that covered me so that just my head was popping out. She pressed a button and left the room as steam started pouring into the machine.

About ten minutes later she returned and released me from the steam trap. She led me to a shower and with a handheld nozzle rinsed my sweat-covered body with lukewarm water. Then she filled a bucket with soapy hot water and while I stood, she gave me a sponge bath starting from my head and working her way down, soaping my loins gently while I worried I would get hard. I guess that would have been normal, but I still would have been embarrassed. Fortunately, I stayed south as she sat on the stool and scrubbed my legs and feet.

After rinsing, she briskly towel-dried my whole body and then wrapped a robe around me. I felt like royalty. We walked to the front of the room and she instructed me to take off the robe, put on a flimsy pair of boxer shorts, and lay face down on the table. I then heard the sound of running footsteps before Portia leapt on top of the table, landing on her hands and knees, crouching over me like a frog. She then pressed, pulled and kneaded my body from head to toe.

"Turn over, please," she whispered.

I lay on my back while she hovered over my face, now standing behind me. She slid clenched fists under my neck, rolling them over and over up and down my nape. She continued rubbing and squeezing my shoulders, arms, and legs before slowly sliding a hand beneath my boxer shorts and gently rubbing the one area she hadn't touched. I closed my eyes and instantly enjoyed it.

I started breathing heavily.

"You like this part most," she said.

I enjoyed it a little longer, but then pulled her hand away before it was too late.

"You don't like?"

"No, I like it. It's not that."

"Ok, thank you," she said, unperturbed and calmly bowing before leaving.

Then I finished what she had started.

*　　*　　*

I continued my San Francisco odyssey on foot up Geary, across the Masonic Street overpass. The Copper Penny, a 24-hour breakfast joint was on the right and on the other side of Geary was the 1907, the pub where Jackson had bartended and then had become part of his roman à clef first book. The same pub whose incarnated fictional characters staged an ill-fated mutiny at the Cabrillo, the drama that got all of this going.

I took a right on 8th avenue and walked down Clement Street, a mostly mixed East Asian neighborhood. I was so relaxed from the massage and the Portia-inspired release, that I needed some caffeine to finish the trek. Rather than a Starbucks, I stayed true to the city and went to the Blue Danube Coffee House, an untrendy and ungentrified bohemian spot as I remembered it. I ordered a large black coffee and sat for a moment to have a few sips. A young couple sat next to me, each armed with an iPad, poking away, then switching to the phone intermittently to text, while still chatting, all with supreme millennial speed and rhythm.

"Did you get everything the bank asked for?" the guy said.

"Yes, all the docs are set and transmitted. Did you complete the copyright application?" she asked.

"All set, baby. This app is gonna buy us our own island."

She looked up from her iPad, smiled, and leaned over to kiss the guy.

"I hope so, but if not, I'll settle for a house in Pacific Heights."

Their money chatter continued while I scanned the café. A woman in her 20s sat at a corner table by the window. She had no devices, just a pen and notebook, in which she was writing fast and furiously as if she had a time limit and a word quota to meet. She occasionally paused and looked up, as if to let her thoughts catch up to the speed of her pen.

After downing the rich dark brew, I was back on the road with a fresh hot pork bun from a little market on the corner of 7th and Clement. I cut back across Geary, walking down the residential streets of the Inner Richmond with its small adorable houses of varying bright colors. I always liked this neighborhood and had suggested to Dana we settle there someday.

"The big adventurer making the move from outer to inner Richmond," she joked.

"I'll be ready someday. Give me time for such a major change."

I passed Cabrillo Street and instead took a right on Fulton so I could make the final stretch with Golden Gate Park at my side. Another 34 blocks and I'd be home. When I got back to the Cabrillo, I made my rounds, checked the sales and then went up to the apartment for a nap. I set my alarm for 9pm, enough time to shower before Nadine and the midnight meeting that would change my life forever, for better or worse.

I stripped down to my boxers, got under the blankets, and lay on my back. The caffeine had no effect, but the long trek did. I faded fast into a deep sleep.

13 — A Cerebral Offer

I snoozed the alarm several times before finally relenting to an awakened state. Though I didn't need to, I decided to shave before taking a piping hot shower. I got dressed and bellied up all clean and refreshed at the lobby bar for a glass of pinot.

Our latest bartender, Patrick from South Dakota, was pouring. Our bartenders didn't last that long. It wasn't exactly tipping paradise at the Cabrillo. Patrick decided to change things up and went formal, black bow tie and all. He thought it fit the venue and brought old world charm. I agreed.

"Harry, Joel's been looking for you," Patrick told me.

"Yeah, everything ok?"

"Don't know. He seemed fine."

"I'll find him in a bit. He's probably watching *Monkey Shines* downstairs." It was horror week at the theatre and Joel always insisted on showing it. It had a cult following of about eight people who reliably showed up every year, not exactly a good business strategy.

I scanned the lobby looking for Nadine, but there was no sign of her yet. The crowd was okay for a Tuesday night, but we'd definitely settled back into our rhythm of mediocrity after the surge from Jackson's knockout.

Sandy walked over from the kiosk, which meant she had sold the last tickets for the last show. It was time for her nightly, on-the-house glass of Sauvignon Blanc. She sat next to me triggering instant anxiety.

"Patrick, darling, a glass of Sauvignon blanc, please. New Zealand, preferably."

"Getting country specific now. Pretty fancy," I said, trying to appear relaxed. Sandy had already mentioned meeting my twin in passing yesterday, but I avoided any prolonged discussion by telling her I was busy and ducking into my office.

"I'm aiming for Patrick's job," she said, smiling flirtatiously at him. All of us were aware of Sandy's crush on Patrick. Sandy was probably fifteen years older, but he was the closest in age to her. They both had a certain retro charm, cut from a genteel cloth despite the paltry-waged job. Old money that retained the manners, but not the dollars.

"Sure, we can switch. The kiosk looks cozy," Patrick said, playing along sans flirty eyes.

"Cozy, but lonely."

"How about we switch for a change of pace some nights? Is that okay with you, Harry?" Patrick asked seriously.

"Ummm, I don't know about that. Maybe down the road." I didn't like the idea at all. It was miscasting.

"Harry doesn't like change," Sandy said.

"That's me. Structure and stability," I said with a grin.

"You know, Harry, I've been thinking more and more about seeing your doppelganger near Lombard Street the other day. I think it was Bay Street, actually. I still can't believe it wasn't you."

"I thought you said he had a beard."

"But the eyes. Harry, I felt you."

I shrugged. "What can I say? I have a twin."

Sandy explained it to Patrick, which sparked his immediate recognition. "You know, I read about that in the Chronicle. Man, that was fantastic. I hate those damn speed cameras. Obnoxious mechanical beasts usurping our freedom and invading our privacy." Patrick was animated for the first time since I'd met him. "And, here in San Francisco of all places to have big brother going all 1984 on us. Shame on the city. Shame on the mayor!"

"Wow, Patrick, I haven't seen this side of you," Sandy said.

"Sorry, gets my goat every time."

"You don't even have a car."

"That's irrelevant. It's not about me, it's about freedom, philosophically speaking."

"Anyway," Sandy drawled. "My point wasn't to discuss civil liberties and government encroachment. It was that I saw a guy that looked just like our lovely boss here."

"You know I hate when you call me that, Sandy," I said truthfully, but also hoping to toss a red herring into the conversation. And I hadn't even thought to check newspapers or media coverage of our caper. I was so ensconced in the bubble of my little world gone astray. I wondered if this made national news.

"Well, you write the checks, Harry."

"So Harry has a twin?" Patrick queried, getting us

back where I didn't want to go.

"Patrick, I swore it was Harry, but I don't know. I guess it wasn't."

"How could it be? Why would Harry be repairing speed cameras?" Patrick said, laughing. "And how could he secretly grow a beard. Don't be silly, Sandy."

"Well, maybe he didn't grow it. Maybe it was—"

"Sandy, it wasn't me. Please, you're being ridiculous," I said, calmly, but pointedly.

"Yes, of course, sorry, Harry. I just—"

Patrick cut her off. "Loved the stickers, too. That was my favorite part. Genius."

"I kind of feel bad for Zuckerberg. He's taking a lot of heat lately," Sandy said.

Patrick quickly replied, "He's earned it. Facebook is a propaganda machine now. They have chosen dollars over truth. So much for the Arab Spring glory days."

"To tell you the truth, I didn't even hear about this whole thing. Mark Zuckerberg stickers? Sounds like the Merry Pranksters are back."

Patrick went on a mini-soliloquy about social media and the decline of western civilization. I felt like I maintained a good poker face, surprising myself at how well I could lie.

Sandy interrupted, "There's your friend, Harry," and she pointed to the lobby door.

I nodded nonchalantly.

Sandy whispered, "When the cat's away…"

"You're on a roll tonight, Sandy," I said, shaking my head in a chiding manner. "Patrick get Sandy another one on me. She's earned it."

"That's my boss," she said with a wink.

Nadine walked over and I introduced her to Patrick and Sandy. We made some small talk before escaping to McLellan's and a table for two that allowed for privacy. I updated her on what happened with Sandy and that I thought I played it cool. "I think it'll fade," I said. Nadine was impressed at my ability to lie and wiggle out of jams. None of that really seemed very important right now because from the moment I saw Nadine, everything syncopated into just us.

We ordered two scotches and raised our glasses. I waited for her to make the toast. We stared into each other's eyes as fools in love unabashedly do, until Nadine said, "Here's to being apart less."

"The less the better," I said.

"I mean it. I have really missed you."

"So glad to hear that."

Nadine sighed, "But it's too much, actually. You're starting to piss me off."

"How so?" I asked knowing exactly what she meant, but wanting articulation.

"Goddammit, Harry," she whispered in a faux angry expression, "I'm falling for you. Falling hard."

"Good. Don't stop. Keep going."

Nadine smiled and kissed me. "I don't want to, but I don't think I have a fucking choice."

"Me neither. It's all consuming."

"It scares the shit out of me that I want you so much. That I am craving you, dammit, like an addict.

Physically hurting without you. Fuck."

"I love it. And I love you," I suddenly said, caught up in the moment, immediately wishing I could reel the words back in.

"Oh God, don't say that."

"Sorry, that was unintended, but that's what we're saying, isn't it? Why dance around it?"

"I don't know what the fuck we're saying. But you didn't have to say that right now."

"Ok, I take it back. Judge, please strike those three words from the record." But my attempt at levity didn't alter the clear and sudden shift in her mood and the atmosphere. It was as if someone suddenly turned the lights on in a dark smoky bar.

Nadine took a big sip of scotch followed by a slow, deep breath. "You don't get it, Harry."

"I got carried away. My bad. Let's just—"

"I'm tired of this, Harry. I can't take it anymore."

"What do you mean? Are we breaking up? What the fuck just happened, Nadine? The transitions with you are insane."

She stared at me, blankly. My heart decelerated, perhaps stopping for a few moments, while it plummeted into a deep cavity that I didn't know existed. Then a sly little smile crept up on Nadine's face. "No, we're not Harry. I'm tired of fighting this. Exhausted. I can't anymore."

Nadine launched into a lengthy monologue while I listened to every word she said with rapt attention. She had tried to resist her feelings for me, wrestled with the guilt of cheating and the fear of becoming the jealous, imbalanced woman she had always become with men. She felt the right thing to do now was focus on getting the money, finishing school, and being true to Christine. But she couldn't commit to it because everything circled back to how she felt when we were together. "Our magic," as she called it, was something she would regret for the rest of her life if she didn't follow its natural course.

"Are you ready for me, Harry?"

"I am," I said, feeling like I had whiplash in my chest.

"Ready for all my sudden transitions."

"Bring them on."

Nadine laughed. "You poor thing. I'm all yours now."

She leaned over and we kissed.

"I love you," she said.

"I love you, too."

"Fuck, we actually said it. What the fuck, Harry!"

"Fucking in love. What a mess!"

We finished our scotches quickly, went up to my apartment and made love in just the same passionate way we had before saying those walk-the-plank words. When we finished, I was pulling out and she grabbed my hips and tugged me back in.

"Don't leave me yet. I love it when you're inside me. Not just the orgasm. All of it. Our oneness."

We stayed like that until it was physically impossible anymore. We joked about being Siamese twins connected at the loins, going on daytime TV and being tabloid spectacle. Then we returned to the unbearable heaviness of it all.

"You know, it's going to change," Nadine said, her head resting on my chest and her arms wrapped tightly around me as if she were holding on to keep from falling.

"Sure it will. Eternity is a long ride," I said.

"I wish we didn't start so fast, so intense."

"I don't."

"Maybe we should—"

"Nadine, stop talking."

*   *   *

We arrived in Theatre 2 just in time for the big midnight meeting. The Cabrillo was locked up, and all the staff were home. I did a walk through to make absolutely sure the coast was clear. I had given Jackson a key to the backdoor (the meeting point) so that he could let the others in. Per Jackson's request, I dimmed the lights to movie wattage, but there was no movie playing so it was nearly pitch black, save for the modest little aisle and step lights. I reached out for Nadine's hand as we waited for our vision to adapt to the darkness.

"I can't see a thing," she whispered, as if we were interrupting a movie.

"Me, neither. Just gotta wait a minute or two."

"Harry? Nadine?" Jackson's voice came out of the darkness.

"Yeah," we both said.

"Welcome to our rendezvous."

"Why don't we have the lights on?" I asked. "It's

too dark, man."

"No, no. No lights. We're just a few rows from the front. You'll be fine in a few seconds."

I heard someone else whispering. It must have been Maxy and the Bogdonaviches. Who else? I could now make out silhouettes in the fourth and fifth rows of the front section. Jackson was now waving with a cellphone flashlight in hand. I tugged at Nadine's hand and we headed to the light. As we got there, I scanned the theatre and noticed some shadowy outlines in the very last row. Maybe five or six people.

"Who's in the back?" I asked Jackson as I sat next to him and Nadine next to me.

"The crew," Jackson said.

"No, the last row, not right behind us."

"Secondary crew. Never mind them. They're the B team."

"What the hell is the B team?"

"Too many questions when answers are imminent. Patience, Harry."

"Hi Harry. Hi Nadine," Maxy said from behind us with a distinct tonal change in his voice when he went from my name to hers. That guy had it bad for her. I could empathize. Nadine nodded and half turned around, all very dismissively. I liked that.

Jackson stood up and walked to the front of the theatre. Just then I noticed the podium we used for readings on top of the small stage where the screen was. Jackson climbed the four steps to the stage and stood behind the podium. He switched on a spotlight that shone just on him. He panned the audience slowly with a serious gaze, but a mischievous glint snuck through. His eyes seemed to linger at the mysterious B team in the rear. I turned around again trying to get a look at them, but it was too dark.

"Everything okay, Harry?" Mercy Bogdonavich asked, her face craning over my shoulder.

"Fine, all good," I said, nodding reassuringly to emphasize my lie. "Just wondering about the back-row guys."

"Us, too."

The top of a laptop was visible on the podium. Jackson tapped a few keys and the projector hummed in warm-up stage. A few seconds later the screen was lit up, but in all black. Then burgundy red text appeared on a PowerPoint slide:

Dedicated to the young in whose spirit
the search for truth marches on.

I immediately recognized the quote. It was from the closing credits of Oliver Stone's *JFK*. I was not a big fan of Stone except for *JFK*, which I thought was a masterpiece of American cinema. Like so many others, it struck a jangled nerve with me, perhaps a genetic nerve. I saw it with my old man on New Year's Eve '91. It was a memorable night on many accounts. I was home from school for winter break and heading out for some typical New Year's Eve party with friends. My parents were in the living room, a fire burning while they were chatting. As I was about to leave, I sensed a fight. I had developed an uncanny sixth sense at predicting parental battles just from the atmosphere like animals realizing before humans when a storm or trouble was brewing. It was useful, too, because I would often flee the house before the marital quake struck. This time I stuck around. I wasn't sure why.

Sure enough the phony Rockwellian fireside chatting ratcheted up to both sides screaming over each other. I don't remember a single word they said. It was just the noise of words bouncing off the walls. The reverb of anger. My Mom eventually escaped, yelling over tears all the way into the seclusion of their bedroom. The old man sat catatonically still by the fire.

"You okay?" I asked.

"Sorry," he said as I was about to go downstairs to the garage.

"Whatever."

"It has nothing to do with you."

I laughed. "I didn't think it did. Why would it?" I said proudly, though probably over-compensating.

"Just making sure you know that. Where are you going tonight?"

"Out with friends."

"Enjoy. Forget about our nonsense."

I walked down the stairs and stopped halfway. I wanted to put my fist through the wall. I remember clenching, winding up, and then holding back.

"Hey Dad," I called from the landing.

"Yeah?"

"Want to go to a movie?"

He protested a bit, insisting I go out with friends,

but I could tell he loved the idea. I suggested *JFK* because I knew he wanted to see it. The old man was a zealous JFK fan and had been totally hooked by the whole Camelot mystique in his youth. 1960 was the first election he voted in. He always told me that had JFK lived, history would have detoured from war to peace. "Son, those thousand days were a time when hope and optimism were real, and not a slogan. It all changed after he was shot, especially Vietnam. And it's only gotten worse."

We were riveted by the movie and were both overwhelmed at how convincing the film was on the conspiracy. After, we went to Harvard Square for drinks at midnight, not far from the sandwich shop where my father, the young college student, was eating lunch on November 22, 1963. Everyone in Elsie's was listening to the radio hoping for the best until Kronkite tearfully announced Kennedy's death.

"Son, everyone wept at Elsie's. Not a dry eye there."

*   *   *

"Welcome everyone," Jackson said. "We have a guest speaker. Let's call him Mr. Y," Jackson said with a wry grin, cheekily naming the speaker one letter after the Donald Sutherland character in *JFK*.

"Team, please pay close attention to the presentation. The prelude is as important as the plan, all of which Mr. Y will reveal." Jackson walked down from the dais and pointed to the screening room above. I turned and looked up but couldn't see anyone. I doubted he was using one of the Cabrillo projectionists, but then who was up there and how did they know how to control the lights and screen? Our system was old school, and few could handle the intricate antiquity.

The stage spotlight dimmed, and Mr. Y came out from behind the screen and stood by the podium. He was appropriately hidden in the darkness, more silhouette than person. He could have been a hologram for all we knew. Jackson sat in front of Nadine and me.

"This is all very odd," I whispered to Nadine.

"Very weird. Not at all what I expected."

"What did you expect?"

"I have no idea, just not this."

I whispered to Jackson, "Hey, who's upstairs?"

Jackson raised his hand and dismissively waved away my question without looking at me.

With the JFK quote still on the screen, Mr. Y began, "Congratulations on your successful first project. Mission well accomplished. You got your feet wet at covert operations and built some chemistry, but that was really kid stuff, just a warm up for phase II, which is the real deal."

The silhouette turned to the screen, "Remember youth is not an age, but a mindset. It is only through energy of youth that real change happens. Look at those kids in Florida who took on the NRA monolith and political mire. AOC and the squad in DC. It's the romantic verve of youth that can change the unchangeable. Intractable and acquiescent adults need that jolt to jar their memory of possibilities in order to actually do something, let alone dream anything."

Mr. Y paused, his outline facing us, as if to let those words sink in.

"But we are not here for the guns and bullets of today, but those of many years ago that began the decay of American youth and derailed truth."

The PowerPoint slideshow began with the Zapruder film, the 26.6 seconds in real time, and then replayed in slow motion with text explaining each of the six fired bullets:

1. Missed shot, Kennedy and Connolly seemingly aware of the sound.

2. Alleged magic bullet that struck Kennedy in the neck at the Adam's apple, his hands clinging to the wound, elbows extended, Jackie turning to her husband.

3. Hit Kennedy in the back.

4. Struck Governor Connolly in the back, sitting in front of Kennedy.

5. Another missed shot hits James Tague by the underpass.

6. The kill shot, striking Kennedy in the forehead detonating his brain like dynamite blasting it out of his exploding skull. The infamous "back and to the left" shot.

The slides continued. A diagram of Dealey Plaza from the view of the sixth-floor depository and then a dramatization of the Kennedy limo driving up Houston towards Elm with crosshairs showing what a perfect, clear shot Oswald would have had from the sixth-floor window. Then the same crosshairs showing the disruption of trees, making the shot on Elm nearly impossible from the alleged kill spot. A diagram of the triangulation of fire from the grassy knoll, picket fence, and multiple windows of the Depository. More scenes from *JFK*, including one of my favorites: John Candy's hipster attorney, Dean Andrews, on the witness stand at Garrison's trial of Clay Shaw saying, "The cat's stewing here, the oyster's shucking ya I told him, you got the right ta-ta, but the wrong ho-ho." The autopsy scene where the doctors are examining the wounds, sticking fingers in bullet holes trying to determine if they were exit or entry hits before being interrupted by suits from the CIA, FBI, and military. Then what's left of the brain being weighed. The real footage of Ruby killing Oswald on live national TV. Kennedy's casket being driven to Arlington National Cemetery before transitioning to the fictional image of a giant stack of the 888-page Warren Commission report (with numerical code theories on the number 888 subtitled), sitting mountainously on a table with nine supreme courts justices seated around the table. A giant overhead fan rotating faster and faster until it blows the pages wildly in all directions. All nine justices look bemused at first and then burst out laughing.

Then slides of data: The death toll in all the U.S. led wars after Kennedy's death. The tally of all the weapons and equipment used in Vietnam, Grenada, Iraq I and II, and Afghanistan followed by the total cost of all the wars ($1,258,900,390,000) next to the cost of housing and feeding every person on the planet ($1,908,400,400). A graph of gun ownership and gun production since JFK's death with firearms exceeding U.S. population in 2009. Today there are 357 million guns for our 317 million people.

Back to the image of Kennedy's brain on the scale in Parkland Hospital and ending at the beginning:

***Dedicated to the young in whose spirit
the search for truth marches on.***

There was silence in the theatre for what seemed like several minutes. Nadine looked at me, quizzically. I shrugged, palms up.

Mr. Y broke the silence, "You may wonder why we gave you the JFK conspiracy 101 show. Before we explain the plan, we ask that our team believe in the conspiracy, which means to believe in the truth. Truth needs resuscitation. JFK was killed by forces much larger and much more powerful than a simple lost soul, ne'er-do-well named Lee Harvey Oswald. There is an invisible oligarchy operating the levers from behind a curtain. This theft will expose the Wizards once and for all. If you don't believe this, if you don't have a passion to find out the truth of this great tragedy of Shakespearean proportions, then we ask that you leave the room. You will be paid for phase one, no questions asked. But if you stay and hear the rest of the plan, there is no turning back. You're in for better or worse."

Mr. Y waited a few minutes. Nobody left.

Nadine clutched my hand as details emerged.

"Wonderful. You will be paid handsomely for the most noble of tasks. Noble because it will right the greatest American wrong by exposing the most enormous and intricate deception ever pulled off. It will correct history, bring closure for our country and to the world, and finally eliminate the giant albatross flapping its wings over us for more than half a century. This is the restoration of truth in an era that has mocked and mangled veracity into social media submission. We are at the stage of burlesque and dystopian demagoguery, but we will undo that when the lies are finally irrefutable. The eminent experiment that is America will be back on track"

The PowerPoint began again. A picture of the San Francisco Medical Center (SFMC), a POV camera pans to the entrance of the hospital, down various corridors, to a staircase ascending several floors into a room in front of a very sturdy steel door. The camera takes us inside the room. It looks like a morgue. One of the slots for a cadaver is bolted several times over. The bolts unlock, the iron door opens, and out slides the giant slab of steel made for a dead body, amidst dry ice smoke everywhere. Once that cleared, there is no cadaver, but rather a glass dome covering some spongy material.

"I give you JFK's missing brain."

*   *   *

According to Mr. Y, the "missing" brain was never missing. It has been kept   cryogenically preserved since the assassination. The Wizards have done a masterful job of keeping it hidden, especially when the heat was on during the Garrison trial in the 60s, the congressional investigation in the 70s that determined there "probably" was a conspiracy, and then again in the early 90s after the film created an uproar and conspiracy membership peaked. It has been more or less all quiet on the cerebral front since the film, save for a brief moment that caught Jackson's attention at McClellan's when surprisingly Trump of all people tried to get some docs released to no avail once again on the grounds of the 50+ year mantra of "national security."

Surprisingly, the Wizards couldn't bring themselves to destroy the potentially incriminating evidence because it had become an indispensable artifact of history, the Holy Grail of Kennedy's Camelot, and a long time down the road from now, many generations removed, the Wizards wanted posthumous credit for the amazing feat they had pulled off: an invisible coup d'état in the world's most powerful country with a hapless patsy taking the blame. Dark genius, but genius nonetheless. The brain was their perverse trophy and they wanted history to celebrate them someday.

Underground rumors circulated that they even had an invisible hand in renaming the Washington basketball team. Cheeky secret recognition during their lifetime. Not so unbelievable. At least, it explained the ridiculous choice of that team's name!

*   *   *

The Wizards kept their trophy on the move to keep the conspiracy hounds from picking up the scent. After being transported from Parkland Hospital in Dallas, where the fraudulent autopsy had been performed, JFK's brain was transferred to the National Naval Medical Center (now Walter Reed), where the Wizards were able to guard it closely since it was right under their nose. During the Garrison trial, it began its itinerant life, most recently settling at SFMC, ironically in the Sunset District. Now I knew why Jackson was really back in San Francisco.

A postdoc in forensic sciences was working late one night on an experiment when he happened to stumble onto the brain in the cryogenic storage facility, which had been accidentally left unlocked; there had to be some human error over the decades. The curious postdoc was nosing around at the different cryogenic remains, when the brain piqued his interest. Why would anyone freeze part of a brain? That didn't happen. People froze entire organs, not sections, in the hopes of having them transplanted into a new, younger, and most importantly, a living body.

In addition, a name and ID number was always attached to the frozen brain or any frozen parts, but this one had just the number: 16219213. He plugged the number into the computer and the name Harvey Fitzgerald showed up, but no other details like an address, phone, DOB, etc. All blanks, which was odd. He examined the number more closely. It triggered a vague familiarity, but he couldn't place it. Pondering it more like it were some sort of Sudoku game, he realized that ID was exactly the same number of digits as a date. He played with it more, loving the numerical challenge like any scientist would, until he finally cracked the numerical anagram: 11/22/1963. Google then informed him what had happened that day: Kennedy was assassinated. He didn't know much about the assassination, but it only took a little Wiki research to find out the brain was missing and that its discovery had revelatory consequences.

This discovery also explained the name given to the brain: the middle names of the alleged assassin and the president. It was as if the Wizards had gotten so overconfident that they were teasingly daring someone to figure it out...

Suddenly the postdoc was nervous. He knew he had stumbled onto something incredibly important and even more incredibly dangerous, but he couldn't resist examining the bullet holes to determine where the entry and exit wounds were. He knew very quickly and conclusively that the bullet had entered the front. This was basic forensics. Then the anxiety really kicked in. He put everything back as it were except for deciding to lock the slot. He figured the interested party probably hadn't realized they had left it unlocked. Nothing would seem unusual if it were locked when the next security check happened. No harm, no foul. At least that was his gamble. But if they found out it had been left open, they might investigate and see his name on the access list to the cryogenics lab and storage. He was afraid he'd crack under the pressure of an interrogation. He wiped down all his prints and dashed out, heart aflutter and forehead beaded with sweat.

After a few weeks when it seemed like no one had realized what he had seen, he decided he had to do something. He couldn't sit on this knowledge. He'd been obsessively researching the conspiracy, saw all the documentaries, movies, read the books – *A Rush to Judgment* and *On the Trail of the Assassins*, even the *Warren Commission Report* tome. He knew what his discovery meant. He knew it affirmed what the conspiracy club had been saying forever. Oswald didn't do it. The Warren Commission was a lie. The kill shot was from the grassy knoll and entered JFK from the front, proving true Garrison's back-and-to-the-left theory. His research into the depths of the web's conspiracy wilderness led him to various clandestine groups asking for information on the Holy Grail.

14 — Skyy and Candy

After the presentation, Nadine and I went up the roof of the theatre. It was deep into a cold, starless San Francisco night. We sat huddled close around the fire.

"So we're really going to do this?" Nadine asked.

"Hmmm, I think so. It all seems so meticulously planned and with an insider to boot. I think we're in good hands. I feel a sense of destiny, too."

"Because of your father?"

I nodded.

Nadine squeezed my hand. "Then it's for both of our fathers," she said.

"And beyond our little worlds, can you imagine if this actually solves the mystery? Resurrects truth in an age where truth has been given its last rites."

Nadine nodded. "True truth, such an exotic notion now."

I turned to Nadine and we locked eyes, our gazes unabashedly and unflinchingly one.

She finally broke the oneness. "How long are we going to keep this up?"

"Why not forever?"

Nadine shoved me. "Such a romantic fool."

"That's your fault."

"Our fault," she corrected.

"The crazy thing is I'm more worried about us than the damn crime of the century. I'm more worried about losing you than spending my life in prison."

"Doesn't get more romantic than that," Nadine said with a big smile.

"Or idiotic," I added.

"They overlap like joy and terror. Hey, you know what's crazy?" Nadine asked.

"Everything."

"I've been thinking the same thing as you. More worried about us than prison. We've known each for just a few weeks."

"17 days."

Nadine shook her head. "Damn, you scare me. We scare me." Nadine said, getting up and pacing the roof and then stopping at the edge overlooking Cabrillo Street, just above the theatre's marquee. I came from behind and put my arms around her, and she wrapped her arms around mine, whispering, "We must have serious issues. We're really fucked up, aren't we?"

"Beyond therapy."

Nadine kissed my hands and arms softly and then turned to face me while still in my arms. I ran my fingers through her long black hair while we again locked into each other's eyes. Then we started slow dancing, quietly without any talking. Just the starless night sky above us, and the waves of the Pacific gently tapping the shore in the distance. We must have danced, more like tranced, for ten minutes or more, but time had ceased during one of our moments where the world population was reduced to two.

Eventually Nadine looked up at me. "This is perfect."

I took her hand and said, "Follow me."

I led her to a ladder that rested horizontally at the edge of the roof. When I first bought the theatre, I was on such a high, so incredulous that I owned a theatre and my life would simply be all about movies. As a kid, the sight of the old theatre marquees always excited me. The welcoming entry to the great sanctuary of the cinema. I couldn't fathom that this marquee was part of my theater. The first few months of owning the Cabrillo, I'd climb down onto the marquee and sit there nestled and hidden, listening to the people in line below chatting about whatever as they waited to escape reality for two hours.

"When was the last time you did that?" Nadine asked.

"I don't remember. Been a while. My Cinema Paradiso innocence has taken some blows lately."

"Let's do it," Nadine said enthusiastically. I propped the ladder and we descended. Nadine went first so I could help her make the tricky move from roof's edge to the first rung. Once there, we both sat, backs against the wall, legs extended in the small triangular internal marquee space. Hidden from the world, we kissed for a while.

"You know I think you're overconfident," she said, pulling away from our kiss.

"About what?"

"About us."

"I've never been more sure of anything in my life," I calmly said.

Nadine giggled and shook her head.

"Great," I said. "Now you think it's a joke."

"It is though, isn't it? Love really is a joke. What the hell is it besides a desperate flight from being alone? The biggest joke of the entire human comedy."

"Maybe so. But what's the alternative?"

"Why do we have to cling so much, try and turn connections into something so romantically grandiose? After all, isn't it just a fear of death pushing us to pursue forever?"

"Do we have to go down the existential road now?"

"Instead, we should just enjoy the sex, hang out, and just be. Just be free of trying to sustain this unsustainable thing. We create the pressure."

"You're just afraid of it. Here's what I think. We are experiencing the grandiose, the deeply in love part now. Then we will transition into a real life together."

"You mean kids?" Nadine said, aghast with a wide-eyed and oh-my-god expression.

I laughed. "I don't care. Probably prefer not to. I'm good with quadrupedal kids."

She exhaled. "Me, too. Cats are all I need. Maybe a dog. I just don't have the mommy genes. Never did."

"Settled. Four-legged feline babies."

"Harry, I know you really love me now, but will you love me later when things aren't so grandiose?"

I paused. "That again?"

"Yes, that again," she said, slightly annoyed.

"I welcome it."

"What if I break up with Christine and commit to

you?"

"I'd be the happiest man alive."

"What if I commit to you, but don't break up with Christine."

"Openly?"

"I don't know. Maybe, maybe not. We just see how things go between us and keep it a secret from Christine for now. See how I do this time. I don't want to lose myself. I can't do that again! And I don't want to lose Christine yet."

"Fine," I said. "We play by your rules. Whatever at this point."

Nadine looked away from me, staring into the early morning sky, and said, "Harry, don't give me so much power. That's dangerous."

"Can we go back to five minutes ago when we were dancing?"

"No, we can't. It's always about romance or the goddamn grandiose for you. It's too fucking easy for you." The change in her mood palpably filled the air of our once marquee cocoon. "Just stop being so romantic. Find some balance," she said instructively.

I rolled my eyes, getting annoyed as well. Angry, actually. "Whatever, let's just experience things rather than talking about experiencing things. We're too fuck-ing meta."

"Easy for you to say."

I sighed. "Nadine, relax."

"Don't tell me to relax. I hate that. Do you not understand women? I am entitled to my emotions, my feelings, even when they aren't as you want them. Stop directing traffic."

Nadine was carving out territory, drawing real borders between us for the first time. I thought I should do the same, not giving in too much to lose my self nor pushing away too much to lose her, straddling the damn relationship balance beam.

"I'm tired," I said standing up.

"Me, too. Are you mad?"

Instinctively I wanted to say no, move on from this, avoid conflict, and let it go, but I betrayed my instincts. "Yeah, I am. Frustrated's a better word."

"Good, you should be."

I nodded, unclear why she said that, but not wanting her to clarify. I stood up, reaching down for Nadine's hand. She clasped it and I pulled her up. Our heads peaked above the rear of the marquee. It wasn't a great sunrise, but there was a hint of the sun burning the horizon reddish orange behind the foggy grey of the Pacific. We watched it in silence until the wisp of color faded completely to grey. Down below the day was starting in the neighborhood. A few delivery trucks arrived, unloading at the Chinese grocery story and a Vietnamese bakery. I looked across the street at Madam Francoise's apartment and the unlit neon sign.

"How about we just sleep? I asked.

"I love that idea."

We ascended the ladder back up to the roof and headed to my apartment. Nadine gave me a kiss and said we'd talk later as she turned to leave. I took her hand and led her to my bedroom. There was a time to be in control and a time to pull away. I rarely knew when to do which one, but right now I had a good guess. She didn't resist, and we got in bed, but she sprang up instantly, taking the belt out of the loops of my bathrobe hanging on the back of the bedroom door.

"Let's play differently this time," she said, as she wrapped the cotton belt around my wrists.

*   *   *

After the role-reversal, I fell into a deep sleep, waking at noon to an empty bed. I checked my phone. One text and no calls. I opened the text, disappointed to see it was from Mariana. She wanted to meet later. I showered and walked down the hall to see if Jackson was in. No one answered my knock, so I went downstairs. The first showing of *Manchester by the Sea* was already underway and the lobby was quiet. I went outside, avoiding Sandy and the kiosk, walking across the street to Café Zeitgeist. I ordered a coffee and bagel with cream cheese and sat looking out of the café's front window with a view of the Cabrillo. The dark brew jolted like an antidote. Jackson texted and wanted to meet in North Beach at The Rose, which was one of the old iconic strip clubs at Columbus and Broadway. I thought of commenting on the location, but instead just texted back saying I'd be there. At this moment, my guard was down to everything. It wasn't the time for internal debate and overwrought analysis. My relationship with Nadine had monopolized that and it was draining me along with its relentlessly zigzag dynamic. It was time to surrender to external fates and let them lead. Not in the Jesus-taking-the-wheel bullshit sense, but rather being free and open to life's direction emerging organically as it happened.

I felt young again.

No dikes or dams, just current.

*   *   *

Before Ubering to North Beach that evening, I met with Mariana. She was really angry. Shockingly, Joel had broken up with her. They'd gone out a few more times, had sex twice, and then he stopped calling. He eventually texted that he just wanted to be friends. Now I know why he was looking for me last night.

"Don't ever fix me up with someone, Harry. You're terrible at it," Mariana said.

"I don't understand. He's been obsessed with you forever."

"Well, I guess I didn't live up to the image once he got a taste of my reality."

"Mariana, he's an idiot. That's crazy. You're amazing."

"He said a lot of things, Harry. Got me believing again. That shithead peeled away the nice, well-constructed layers guarding my heart and then once exposed, he stomped on it," she said, getting teary. "He's so cruel. Men are so fucking cruel!"

"I'm sorry, Mariana." I reached out to give her a hug, but she backed away.

"I hate this shit. I should just stick to numbers. The only reliable thing in the world. I hate your gender. Follar hombres!" She yelled before erupting into tears and falling into my arms. I hugged her tightly and she held me as if she'd drown otherwise, her body heaving and quivering.

My relationship with Dana had just ended abruptly; the Cabrillo's existence (and hence mine) was teetering; I had met a woman that made me feel what poets have eternally and valiantly, but unsuccessfully tried to define; and I was part of an underground cabal of criminal activity on the verge of the greatest and most important theft in American history, but Joel breaking up with Mariana was more incredible than any of those things; I would have to get to the bottom of this, but first I had a meeting at a strip club.

Mariana's tears finally slowed and a certain tranquility seemed to settle in.

"Thanks, Harry. Thanks for listening and being there for me," she said pulling away from the hug and wiping her eyes with tissues from my desk.

"Anything for you Mariana. I am so sorry this happened."

"You're a good man. Always been good to me," she said, amidst subsiding sniffles. She looked me in the eyes and for a moment, I wondered if we were having a moment.

I turned towards the door. "Mariana, you'll be fine, right? Sorry, but I have to run."

"I'll be fine, whatever that is. Go ahead."

"You will. I'll check on you tomorrow."

"Can I stay here and work for a while? The Cabrillo always makes me feel peaceful. Might see a movie, too."

"Of course. Mi casa es su casa."

"Wait, is Joel working?" she asked.

"No, he's off."

"Good, he's lucky. I might have punched him in the face if he were here."

*   *   *

With a few minutes to spare, I had Uber drop me off at Café Trieste for an espresso, just a few blocks from The Rose. There were some old men and women chatting in Italian, most likely Sicilians who had come through Ellis Island and kept going and going until they could go no more in America. Amazingly, simple folk still existed in the heart of Twitterized San Francisco, thanks to North Beach. These folk had to be long timers who had moved here decades ago, or even the children of parents who had bought property here long before the Beats arrived and generations before the tech and social media waves of nerdy hipsters. The real San Francisco of Sal Paradise still existed in this little pocket of North Beach.

I sipped my double espresso, enjoyed the sounds of Sicilian dialect instead of English (*Stucazz, proscuitt...*), and scanned the rest of little legendary Café Trieste. There was a millennial sitting at a back corner table writing in a notebook with no phone, no ear plugs, and no iPad noticeable. He was actually unplugged. My guess (or wish) was that he was fighting his own personal revolution against his generation and had probably read the Beats. Maybe even had seen *Kerouac* or read Jackson's novels. I thought of asking him these big questions and confirming the grand assumptions, but I didn't want to know the answers. Demystifying is depressing.

I finished the espresso, walked over to the anachronistic millennial, stood over him as he looked up calmly, coolly, unperturbed by my invasion though he did close his notebook. On the cover of the notebook was "Mountain of Youth by Delmore Jacoby." It had to be novel, or maybe a screenplay. I put my fist out with a smile. He grinned quizzically, stared at me for a bit, and then fist bumped with a return smile. Verbal communication was vastly overrated.

I headed to The Rose passing by the Beat Museum. I remember when it opened in '03 and they had asked me to be on some panel of artists inspired by the Beats. I was embarrassed because I never really felt like an artist. One film did not make one an artist in my view, but I was certainly honored. In fact, sitting on that panel, answering some questions and talking about my inspiration with true fans of the Beats was a far greater honor to me than the Oscars' pomp and circumstance.

Jackson should have been one the panel, too, but he was travelling and writing somewhere, like an honest artist. I crossed the street and there he was—the true Beat turned true criminal, standing in front of The Rose.

"Hey, man, welcome to my new favorite spot in San Francisco," Jackson said, giving me one of his rib rattling hugs.

"Really? Shit, I think stumbled in here or one of the Broadway clubs a few times back in the day. Must have walked by the place hundreds of times though."

"Well, now you are walking into the place."

We got to the door and Jackson greeted the door-man, "Hey, Nate, how's it going? This is my friend, Harry."

Nate and I shook hands. He wasn't a big guy and had an affable smile, not what I expected at the door of The Rose.

Nate said, "Any friend of Jackson's is a friend of mine. And you get the Jackson discount. Plenty of love-ly ladies tonight, boys. Jackson, you picked a good night for your friend."

"Is Skyy working?" Jackson asked.

"She is and she'll be happy to see you, I'm sure."

"Great."

"Enjoy, gentleman. Jackson, fill your buddy in on the protocols, will ya? Spare me the speech."

Jackson nodded and as we entered, Nate gave me a couple of friendly slaps on the back. We walked through a thick purple velvet curtain and entered a large room, stage to the left and tables to the right. There was a bar behind the stage and in the rear, a staircase led upstairs to what appeared to be some private rooms. The real moneymakers for the ladies I presumed.

We sat down in the back at a half-circle, dimpled burgundy vinyl booth. It had a 40s film noir vibe. We slid into the booth and a waitress immediately arrived.

"Hi sweetie," she said to Jackson, leaning over to give him a kiss on the cheek. "And who might this young lad be?"

"Candy, this is Harry."

Candy extended her hand to be kissed and I obliged. She giggled coquettishly. "Finally, a gentleman in this joint. Last guy I did that to looked at me and said, 'How about I kiss your tits instead of your hand.' Some people are so crude. I understand what this place is, but manners, please," she said, winking at me. "The nerve! But not my new friend, Harry." She giggled again. "Jackson, I like him. Chivalry lives."

"He's a good man," Jackson said. "Harry, you'll do well here. They'll all love you."

I smiled, unsure of what to say.

"What are you drinking gentlemen? Shot of tequila tonight?"

"Sure," Jackson said. "Three shots of Tres Generaciones and two pints of Anchor. And can you let the ladies know that we need some privacy for just a bit. Give us about 10 minutes."

"Anything for you two, especially him," Candy said, winking again at me before turning to Jackson. "But you know I can only hold Skyy off for a little while once she sees you."

"Is she upstairs?"

Candy nodded. "You got a little time. I know who she's with. 10 minutes max."

Candy put her tray down, then slid her spaghetti strap slowly over her left shoulder and peeled back the tight spandex shirt setting her ample left breast bouncily free. She tilted her head to the side with a childlike sad face and then took my hand and put it over her boob, rubbing my hand concentrically around her nipple and then over it several times slowly, with surprising sensuality. "Just for you, Harry."

I smiled and looked at Jackson, who seemed a bit disinterested in the Candy show. I looked up at Candy, who then covered up and stood there, smiling at me.

"Harry, give her something for chrissake." Jackson said.

"Oh, yeah, of course. I took $10 out of my wallet. Candy smiled and jutted her cleavage out at me. I put it between her breasts. "Thank you, Harry," she said and was off.

"Damn, she is very sexy," I told Jackson. "So are many of the girls. I always thought this place was a bunch of junkies, tatted up and desperate types."

"It's a mix, just like the outside world. A great microcosm. Plenty of beautiful and interesting women. Candy is really smart. Studying women studies or something at Davis. Don't let the act fool you. She strips, too."

"Women's Studies and stripping?"

"Not as contradictory as you think."

Candy arrived with our drinks and the three of us toasted our tequilas. She wasn't nearly as flirtatious with me this time around. I must have looked disappointed because Jackson said, "Bro, you didn't think she actually liked you, did you? I mean didn't you know that was her schtick? I've seen her do that to dozens of guys, including me the first time I met her."

"No, no, I knew that," I lied.

"No you didn't, but that's ok. They are good at

what they do. Experts at seduction. Just remember they are working and we are customers. But that's not to say you can't get to know them and meet up outside of here for real, sans money. Seen that happen, too."

"Have you done that?"

"No, but Skyy wants to. I told her I just want to keep it in The Rose for now until all the smoke clears in my life. Maybe down the road. Got to see how things play out. Look, you spend time with a stripper you're attracted to, show her you care, be respectful, make a connection, and you can date her. But not in the first few minutes. Just like any other woman."

"Yeah, I guess so. It's been a while since I've been to one of these clubs."

"But that's not your interest here anyway, right? You're still all smitten with Nadine."

"Shouldn't put all your eggs in one basket, right?"

"Really? What the—"

"Never mind. So why'd you ask me here?" I asked.

Ignoring my redirection, Jackson asked, "So you two hit a rocky patch?"

I paused and took a big gulp of Anchor Steam. "Well, I'm still crazy about her, but I'm getting frustrated. She's inconsistent. Can't get her girlfriend out of her mind. I don't know, shit, ahem, trying to reign myself in. I fell too hard, too fast. I'm too fucking crazy about her."

"You sure did, but it wasn't a choice. Time to slow it down now and keep your eye on the prize."

I furrowed my brow and narrowed my gaze. "Kind of the opposite of what you've been telling me all this time. You practically played matchmaker."

"I don't remember it that way."

"There's only one version. Doesn't matter how you remember it."

"Of course it does. We talked about something on a Tuesday is a fact. What we talked about on Tuesday is twisted by memory and perception."

"Not exactly, Jackson. Don't go all alternate facts on me."

"Anyway if and what I said then doesn't apply now."

"Why not?"

"Time and space, Harry. Everything's constant kinesis all the time. Spinning earth in perpetual orbital revolution, magnetic fields out of control, celestial bodies pinballing this way and that, and gravity holding the whole thing from galactic anarchy. Things are changing faster than we can get the words out to define them."

"Man, that's all good poetic and jazzy philosophical bullshit, but what's your point?"

Jackson laughed. "The very serious point is let's have a good fucking time. Get your ya-yas out, followed by a couple of days rest, and then we change the world and solve our financial crisis. Put ole humpty dumpty back together again."

We were silent for a bit while I retraced back to the Kabuki and how I almost paid for it. And now I'm here as if there was some sort of atmospheric collusion nudging towards salacious directions. Or maybe it was all so much simpler and boiled down to testosterone. The subconscious was staging a carnal intervention to overcome conscious frustration with the Nadine rollercoaster.

*   *   *

Jackson explained that The Rose was his getaway after the 100-day penitent celibacy. The libido was one tough hombre, lingering, demanding, and then howling for appeasement. He was proud of his 100-day abstinence, but its curative effects were slowly dissipating and the addiction wouldn't go quietly. His new plan to keep his sexual needs under control was no longer celibacy, nor seeking out casual affairs ("too many potential complications and too time consuming"). So The Rose became his outlet.

"And what about Samira?"

"I don't know, man," Jackson said, seemingly perturbed at the question. "On hold until I am back on my feet. In the meantime, there's Skyy," Jackson said. "She's great, man. Gets me centered and keeps me satisfied." Jackson took a deep breath. "She's amazing."

"For a price, right? Like you said."

"I get a good rate."

"The regular's discount?"

"Something like that."

"So are you really into her or is it just fun?"

Jackson shrugged. "Probably somewhere in between."

"But you just said—"

"Kinesis, Harry. Don't forget. Five minutes ago isn't now."

"Fuck, Jackson, come on. You're all over the place.

I'm relying on you for a lot of shit right now. My whole fucking life, really, my damn freedom, and you're giving me this bullshit, nickel-and-dime-intellectual crap as an excuse to escape contradictions and avoid accountability."

"Harry, take it easy."

"No, man, you're pissing me off. This was about you, Samira and the winery and now you're saying, ahhh, what? It's about some stripper named Skyy?"

"So?"

I rubbed my eyes and then the back of my neck.

"Need a crack?"

"Yeah, crack cocaine to keep up with your twisting bullshit."

"Look, all is good on the plan front. Don't worry. I dig this woman Skyy, that's all. I don't know what's gonna happen with Samira. I mean why should I prove myself with the damn winery? She's holding me ransom. That's not romantic at all."

"But what about the whole Gatsby thing. You said—"

"Yeah, fine. Very well, I contradict myself. Don't be so fucking lawyerly and cross examine my multitudes! This isn't a novel, Harry, it's real life. We're all holding each other ransom on one level or another. Skyy's ransom happens to be more real. She's just making a living. Besides, we have ransom-free moments, too. It's not without romance." Jackson lifted his Anchor to toast. "Look, Harry, when this is all over, you, Nadine, me, and hopefully Samira, maybe Skyy, maybe both, who the fuck knows, will go to see a movie together in your financially viable Cabrillo. Then we'll have dinner on the roof, pop open Dom Perignon, shag, and then get a good night's sleep. The next morning we'll all road trip down to Big Bear Winery and picnic on the vineyard *terroir*. We'll be as free as can be from the money web. You and movies, me and wine, and the women we love, whomever they may be. We'll all grow old together, peacefully and properly enjoying a west coast sunset. How's that sound?"

"Pretty damn perfect," I admitted, despite still being a little pissed off.

"To the western sunset then."

We toasted and just as I put my bottle down, along came Skyy.

"Hi, sweetheart," she said to Jackson and gave him a passionate kiss on the lips. I didn't remember ever seeing that kind of kiss in a strip club before. Didn't even think kissing was allowed. Then again, I didn't know the culture.

Jackson and Skyy were instantly immersed in each other while I was content to be the third wheel, quietly observing this strange world. An older woman, maybe late 40s, with long red hair was on stage dancing. She was a little chubby and better fit the mold of the school of hard knocks stripper. However, she knew how to work the pole. She was an expert at hanging upside down while touching herself. She had the attention of the dozen or so guys scattered in swivel leather seats near the stage. Several of them approached for a close-up, throwing dollar bills for the privilege. One of the few cash businesses left.

Candy interrupted the theatre. "Aren't those two just divine? Such a cute couple." I looked up and noticed Jackson and Skyy had just left the booth and were heading upstairs. "What about us, Harry?" Candy coquettishly asked. She had mastered the game.

"I'm taken," I said, like an idiot.

Candy cracked up and then said, "Story of my life. So a shot to help me get over my unrequited love?" She asked, moving the tray of shots in her hand closer to me.

I laughed. "You're good. Sure, let's do a shot."

"Always the gentleman, Harry."

We did a shot and then Candy took a seat very close to me, her breast pressed against my elbow. "What about you? Deconstuct Harry," she said.

I smiled. "Deconstruct, huh?"

"Yeah, Derrida style," she said, grinning. "Don't assume all strippers are fools. Some of us are, but some of everybody are." Candy's voice had suddenly deepened to an almost husky pitch.

"So, you're into philosophy?"

"Bachelor's in philosophy and women's studies. Half-way through a master's in the latter."

"Really?"

"I know, what's a feminist doing in a strip club? Well, I actually think stripping is not necessarily anti-feminist. It's my choice and I control the interactions. If a customer, man or woman, disrespects me, it's done. And, man, do the male masks come off in this place.

Such rich insights into your gender."

"You're impressive, Candy."

"Yeah, it's a goldmine of experiences that serve the book I'm writing well. I'll turn the fourth wave into a tidal wave." Candy expounded on her story. She lived way out in the East Bay with her bartender/poet boyfriend and made the long commute in for work, but since she worked vampire hours, the commute wasn't unbearable. She was actually a San Francisco native, born in the Western Addition. "Yup, I was born at Kaiser and grew up a few blocks from there in a small apartment at the corner of Divisadero and Turk."

She met her boyfriend in a grad school and they left the city a few years ago, moving further and further out in pursuit of cheap rent.

"We finally had to cross the bridge, but I'm a making good money here. Might be able to find something soon. We miss the city. I am love with my city."

"Me, too, but isn't it feeling unrequited lately? Aren't you frustrated with all the techies and twitters taking it over and forcing folks like you out?"

"Nahhh, not really. I know a lot of long-timers bitch about it, but the way I see it, San Francisco is always changing. This is the current evolution. Who knows what or who is next? Just gotta roll with it and be resourceful. The city's face has changed, but not the soul."

"Well, you're more forgiving and less bitter than me. I miss the Beat and artistic vibe. Not so sure the soul hasn't been compromised."

"It's still there, Harry. Just gotta look more closely.

My boyfriend came here to be a poet. There are still seekers and Beat scions coming west. Hell, the museum is right next door."

"Exactly, the museum."

"That's cute," Candy said, rolling her eyes.

"Well I like your positive spin," I said, thinking how the writer in Café Trieste backed her theory and belied mine.

"Don't be so grumpy Harry. Life can be good."

Then she asked about me and I told her about the theatre, *Kerouac*, the break-up with Dana, Nadine and me, and like a verbal avalanche, it all just tumbled out of me as if I were in a comfortable therapy session with someone I trusted. I did draw the confessional line with the crime, of course.

"Poor Harry has his hands full."

"Kind of."

"My real name is Arlene. My stripper name came from a movie. Can you guess? You should know. The novel was kinda Beat."

I thought about it and couldn't come up with anything.

"Harry, come on! Film lover and Beatnik and you got nothing."

I shrugged, embarrassed.

"One Flew over the Cuckoo's Nest!"

"Of course! Mac's girl Candy."

"Always loved her and she never gets any attention. Such a great role. I mean, she's no Thelma or Louise, but she had control in her own way."

Arlene got up and left saying she had to make the rounds, but would be back.

A young Asian woman was on stage. She was sexy, had the tight body of youth, but surprisingly there wasn't much interest in her. Meanwhile, I saw the red head going upstairs to the private rooms.

"Hey, I love this song," Arlene said, suddenly re-appearing. She snuggled next to me and started singing along in a soothing voice, almost serenading me.

> 'Cause in my head there's a Greyhound station
> Where I send my thoughts to far off destinations
> So they may have a chance of finding a place where
> they're far more suited than here...

"Brava, Arlene," I said, clapping.

She bowed and said, "That song is for you and Nadine. It's great love song if you do a close listen."

"Yeah, a bit tragic."

"Like any great love. Harry, can I give you some advice?"

"Please do."

"From all that you told me, backing off of Nadine is not the right thing to do. You need to go all in. Stop giving her space."

"But—"

"But nothing," Arlene interrupted, replete with index finger over her mouth. "Dive in, Harry. You obviously love her. Go all in like a tidal wave so she knows exactly how you feel. I think she wants that, not space. It might be a litmus test."

"So do the damn opposite. Ugh," I sighed. "I was

sure respecting her space was the right thing to do."

Candy shook her head, eyes closed in disapproval. "She may respect you more if you disrespect it. Stop being so fucking nice. Don't take what we say at face value. Come on, Harry."

"And if it backfires?"

"Well, you come and see Candy and cry on her shoulder," she said, replete with a stripper giggle and a hug.

*　　　*　　　*

I was watching the upstairs comings and goings, curious about the protocols of the secret rooms.

When Candy returned from another check on her rounds, I asked her, "So how much does it cost, the upstairs thing?"

"Depends. There's a menu. $40 for a simple lap dance and then it goes up from there. Up to the lady. I don't do much more than the lap dance, but it's up to the dancer."

"You never go further?"

"Interested?" she said with a wink. I smiled without answering. She continued, "No, not often, but sometimes if I like the guy and he's respectful, I may cross the southern border. Remember, I am in control. Unfortunately, some of my friends here aren't in control, financial need is. If you are interested, I'm sure it's on the house aside from a tip."

"Really? Why?"

"He didn't tell you."

"Tell me what? Who's he?"

One night when Jackson first started coming here, he was sitting at the bar. A guy sitting next to him was chatting with Skyy. He started getting a little too handsy and Skyy was trying to slow him down, but he quickly flipped a switch, cursing at her and getting very aggressive. The bartender went to get the bouncer, but it was too late. The guy lost it and reached back with a closed fist about to punch Skyy in the face. She closed her eyes, bracing herself for the blow that never came. Jackson shot his forearm under the drunk's cocked arm and hooked it as he was punching. His momentum continued, but his arm stayed locked into Jackson's. He lurched forward off the barstool while Jackson pulled back, twisting around and falling with a thud on his back. The drunk tried to get up, but Jackson stuck his foot squarely in his chest, keeping him down like wounded prey. The drunk cursed and struggled to no avail. The bouncer arrived and lifted the drunk up, kneed him in the balls for good measure, and dragged him out.

Jackson was a hero, especially to Skyy, and The Rose gave him VIP status. Upstairs was on the house per Skyy's request, never a cover, and half-price drinks for life, which were usually free anyway since the waitresses rarely charged him.

"Your friend really never told you?"

"No, he's modest."

"He's a good man. He saved Skyy. That monster would have destroyed her face. We love him here. He's always respectful to all of us."

Jackson finally returned and the three of us drank

a bit more with Arlene joining intermittently. When we left, Arlene reminded me to go all in on Nadine. "Remove any doubt she has, Harry." She told me her schedule at The Rose in case I wanted to visit again. I told her to come up to the Cabrillo for a movie on the house.

"I might do that, my new friend," she said, giving me a parting kiss on the lips.

* * *

Jackson and I walked around the corner, lingering in front of the Beat Museum to smoke a cigarette.

"You nervous?" I asked.

"Of course, but it's a nervous confidence if that makes sense. Or maybe a confident nervousness. So Candy is pretty cool, huh?"

I took a deep breath. "She's fascinating. Really enjoyed her."

"Yeah, I figured you would."

"So you've set me up twice now."

"I'm good at it. I should work for Tinder or Match or one of those things."

"And what about your hero status there?" I asked. "That was quite a story."

"Not a big deal."

I nodded. "I disagree and so does everyone in there."

"Look, it's just an escape. A little safe perversion to get through the night. We had our kicks tonight, Jack Ruby style, but in two days, we're going to undo what Ruby did. Money and the truth await. Love not far behind."

"The holy trinity," I said, putting out my cigarette beneath the iconic photo of Kerouac and Cassady, shoulder-to-shoulder, hands in their pockets, Neal's headed tilted to the right, youth and the road ahead alive in their eyes.

"Now get some rest. We need to be on our A game in 48 hours." He said, fist bumping me and disappearing down Kearny Street, apparently not heading back to the Cabrillo with me.

I didn't want to go back right away either, but I was glad to be alone. I walked across the street to the iconic Beat bar, Vesuvio, and went upstairs for a drink. I ordered Dewar's on the rocks and took a seat by the window, which had a great view of North Beach and the legendary intersection of Broadway and Columbus. I watched the late-night vampires crisscrossing the street, heading into City Lights, The Rose, restaurants all about, or just loitering on the streets, anything to avoid going home. I could see many of the faces clearly. I studied their expressions, wondered what words were coming out of those conversing and what thoughts were in the minds of those alone when suddenly at that precise moment of human curiosity, a muse suddenly lit up my mind "like fabulous yellow roman candles..."

I saw Delmore Jacoby writing *Mountain of Youth* in a notebook in Café Trieste, and then putting it in his brown leather satchel, and heading into The Rose after a lonely night of writing. Candy greeted him and they immediately hit it off, falling crazily in love. Images of their life stories leading up to their meeting played vividly in my cinematic mind before shifting scenes to their rollercoaster romance subject to so much judgment by Jacoby's family and friends.

Candy's life came direct from her story, but Delmore Jacoby's life materialized from the mysteries of the subconscious, a wide-awake dream that unraveled so coherently: Old-timey Italians from generations ago chatting and smoking the days away; Neo-Beats penning their stories in cafes. Meanwhile, Candy and Delmore meet a few eccentrics at a City Lights poetry reading, who inform them of a gentrification plan secretly underway to bring get rid of the strip joints, City Lights, The Beat Museum, and transform North Beach into a high rise luxury apartments and chain retail stores. Commericial visigoths sacking Rome; the lovers and eccentrics form a cabal to fight the power, which lures others in from all around San Francisco, including the social media millennials. Old and new San Francisco come together not only to save North Beach, but also the entire city. Under siege, they realize the only way to be really free is for the city to leave the U.S. and form its own country. Not by secession, but actual physical separation from the contiguous 48. They use a secret plan from a radical off-the-grid geologist to sever the city at a fault line just north of Daly City. Weird scenes multiplied inside the *goldmind* and in minutes, the entire surreal plot took its form as if I had already seen the movie and were recalling it from memory.

I urgently asked the bartender for a pen and some paper to begin writing it all down before the long dormant muse disappeared. The bartender tossed a cheap Bic on the bar and pointed to a pile of cocktail napkins. I went through the whole stack and then another on the other end of the bar, asking him for more. He gave me a *what-the-fuck* look, but pulled an unopened box from under the bar and threw it to me. Bard-of-the-bar cliché for sure, but the work was original, a draft of a second screenplay on 1,000 little squares; the one I never thought would exist. I stayed until closing, drinking more scotch with some wait staff, and then Ubered back with my pockets stuffed with the screenplay, *North Beach Exit*.

15 — Thick as Thieves

I semi-woke up late in midst of a dream playing like a movie in my morning mind, conflating the real and the unreal as the good ones do. Nadine and I were walking along Ocean Beach, hand in hand, talking and laughing, a blissful couple free of issues. We came to a jetty and walked carefully across each stone towards its end, where the water turned rough, big waves slamming into the rocks, white foam spraying high. Our footing was precarious on the wet surface, but Nadine was calm, holding my hand firmly as we neared the jetty's slippery end. Without hesitation we dove into the cold Pacific, swimming easily, almost gliding through the wavy high tide, side by side until a sand bar island suddenly appeared. We were the only ones on the tiny patch of land, one so small that it could hold no more than an elevator's worth of people. I could see the Cliff House and the Richmond perfectly in the fogless, sunny blue sky. We lay on the sliver of sand, kissing like *From Here to Eternity*, before falling asleep entwined in each other like climbing plants coiling around a tree.

When I woke up (in the dream), I was alone. There was no sign of Nadine. A long footbridge now connected the shore to the island, which seemed to have drifted further away while I was asleep. It had to be at least half a mile to shore with the bridge rising high above.

The dream turned into gephryrophobic nightmare. The beautiful little island oasis began sinking, water converging wildly on all sides. With my heart pounding and palms sweating, I climbed the bridge's staircase to the walkway. There was no turning back unless I wanted to tread water in the freezing cold Pacific, *Open Water* style, or attempt the impossibly long swim. I spotted surfers near the Cliff House and screamed, hoping I could hitch a ride on a board, but they didn't hear me. I yelled louder, waving my hands like a marooned madman, but it was as if I weren't there.

Climbing the steps of the footbridge, I did my mantras – *mind over matter, just relax, over the golden.* I tried them all, then interchanged them, but nothing worked. My throat shrank and tightened. I thought I would choke on my own breath, my own anxiety. Once at the top, with no other alternative besides jumping, I closed my eyes and ran and ran and ran, primal howls with each treacherous step. I banged into the railings like a pinball, bouncing, falling, getting back up, eyes never opening, until I realized the bridge seemed much longer than it should. I peeked ahead with one eye. It kept getting longer and longer every step I took, a new version of Sisyphus. The bridge now extended up over the Richmond, over the Cabrillo, over my beloved city. I was trapped in my own private phobia. I just kept running until I finally woke up, breathing heavily with beaded sweat across my forehead, wondering if I were in my bed or still on the infinite bridge. I felt the mattress to confirm reality and slowly realized it was a dream. Reality also came with a splitting headache and a parched hangover mouth.

I reached for my phone on the nightstand, but realized it was still in my jacket pocket, probably dead. Searching the jacket pockets, I pulled out handfuls of cocktail napkins along with my phone. After spreading the napkins out on my bed, I plugged my phone in to get some juice so I could call Nadine. I went to the kitchen and drank three tall glasses of water while preparing coffee. A stop in the bathroom for the water to escape and to clean up, and I was back on my bed with a cup of coffee and a cocktail napkin screenplay all out of order. It occurred to me to randomly order them and shoot the film in that sequence, like a Burroughsian cut up, but I dropped that not-so-great notion quickly.

I would put the scenes back in their proper order, but first Nadine. I needed to call Nadine and put Arlene's advice in action.

I turned my phone on, but Nadine had beaten me to the punch. There were five text messages and three voicemails, all of them from her. Reality was as real as ever now. The texts grew increasingly harsher and edgier. Nadine was frantic. She didn't understand why I wouldn't answer. She really needed to see me and I had let her down, by being unreachable.

Harry call me when you get a moment. Sent you several texts.

Me again. I don't understand why you're not calling me back. You always do right away. I love that about you. I'm never the last one to text. You are. Now I'm the last one to text ten fucking times. Are you tired of me already?

Jesus, Harry, I don't like this. It's already 11am. What are you doing? Or should I say who. I don't like

what this is doing to me. If you don't call me soon, I will,
ummm, I don't know what's going to happen. Call me. Is
that too much to fucking ask!

I called her immediately. I wanted to tell her about the dream, Arlene's advice, *North Beach Exit*, everything. I wanted to see her so badly. I missed her. Her frantic need for me, bordering on psychotic and perhaps scary to most, didn't bother me. I welcomed it as passion and desire. To be needed and wanted. It was the perfect segue for me to go all in like Arlene advised.

Nadine picked up immediately.

"Jesus, it's about time!"

"Sorry, I—"

"Look, Harry, if you've changed your mind about us, tell me, don't avoid me. Don't be a fucking coward."

"Jesus, Nadine, take it easy. That's not—"

"Seriously, I can handle it. I don't mean to be going all Glenn Close on you, but it freaks me out. I told you how I get. Now you get it up close and personal. It's not pretty."

"Nadine, relax. I was out with Jackson and my phone died. I was drunk and forgot to turn it on when I got back."

"So you basically forgot about me all night."

"No, not at all. I never forget about you. Ever."

"Where were you?

I paused, then said, "North Beach."

"That's vague."

"We bar hopped, Vesuvio, Joe's, a strip club for a bit. Nothing crazy."

"Meet anybody?"

"Nadine, chill."

"I warned you."

"No, I didn't meet anybody. There's only one wom-an I think about."

"I called Christine last night when I couldn't find you."

"And?"

"And I miss her."

"Did you tell her about us?"

"It was good to hear her voice."

"You didn't answer the question."

"I missed her. That answers the question."

"Nadine, don't let a dead cell phone pull you away from me. We're not breaking up over a fucking battery!"

"Harry, you don't get it. Christine does."

"Get what?"

"The question proves my point."

"Look. I am fucking crazy about you. I will do whatever it takes. This is all probably from the stress of phase two. That's the trigger."

"Maybe," Nadine said, a hint calmness suddenly in her voice.

"Trust me. You'll see. I can get it. If not, I'll get tutored from Christine."

Nadine laughed. "Seriously?"

"100%."

"I like that. Christine helping you. So sweet."

"I like when we find harmony."

"You know, you can make me crazy and calm me

down. I hate when others have that power over me. Steals my freedom."

"We all do. Let me come over and hug you. Right now."

"No, I don't need that now. I need to be alone. I need some freedom."

I hesitated, but then said, "Ok."

Nadine asked me about The Rose. I told her everything except Arlene's advice. We hung up on a good note and decided to keep our distance until after the heist. After that, I would employ my all-in take no prisoners, Arlene strategy.

Five minutes later, as I was organizing the cocktail-napkin script puzzle, my phone rang.

"I want to see you," Nadine said.

"I'm on my way."

"I'm already here."

I rang the buzzer and Nadine came up. We immediately jumped into bed and made love sans any fetish. When we finished, she fell asleep, her head resting on my shoulder. She had this adorable soft purr of a snore. As I lay there, I thought about how Nadine could disappear and not communicate whenever she needed space, but the one time I was out of touch, it was not acceptable. She was defining our rulebook early on and I had to cede control. She could give me kinky control in bed, but out of bed, she was the dom. It all seemed like gravity to the fairy tale. I didn't want weight. I wanted flight. I wanted the movie version we started with. I caressed Nadine's arm draped across my chest, felt her breast gently heave with every breath against my side, and listened to her feminine snore. I tuned into current Nadine's being and tried to tune out the looming issues hovering overhead.

*   *   *

Nadine and I spent the day together. It was our last day before the big day. We watched movies, picnicked in Golden Gate Park, had dinner at McLellan's, and then retreated to the roof at night for wine, fire, and opening the FedEx package that arrived that evening: a thieves Christmas Eve.

The goodies for the great American brain theft had lab coats, glasses that were nothing but glass, wigs, contact lenses that changed our brown eyes hazel or blue, and a putty-like make-up to change the shape of our noses and jawline, and SFMC badges. All the accoutrements for us to be unrecognizable, nondescript medical researchers.

The plan was for Nadine and me to use the entrance for hospital staff. Being a new face would not be a big deal. Postdocs came and went all the time. We were just another pair of exploited young scientists doing research for not that far north of minimum wage. The brain was on the 6th floor, which was either a coincidence or the Wizards cocky cheekiness. Nadine and I would get the brain at exactly 10pm, between security shifts when attention was compromised.

At precisely the same time, the Bogdonaviches, disguised as couriers, would be on the 8th floor waiting for us. We would climb the stairs, pass the cerebral baton, and then the couriers would head to the exit, where there would be a check on samples leaving the building. Since the brain would have no authorization to leave the building, the riskiest part was here. However, Mr. Y and team had made preparations. We not only had to get the brain, but we also had to repack it so that it could make it through the exit checkpoint. While much of JFK's brain had been blasted out of his skull, almost half still remained, about 1.5 pounds.

Nadine and I were tasked with taking the remnants of JFK's brain and placing it in a special stainless steel, cryogenic container that would be hidden in a secret compartment at the bottom of a lab mice cage. The Bogdonaviches should get through easily.

Meanwhile, Jackson and Maxy would be waiting in the parking lot keeping an eye on everything in case the unforeseen took place or they sensed something was up. Once the brain made it to the car and was on the move, Jackson would text Nadine and me, and we would head out the front door and back to the Cabrillo.

Mission accomplished.

*   *   *

The morning of the theft I was puttering around the theatre, nervously doing my walk through, going over numbers, and daydreaming how I would use all the money. Nadine and I texted a few times, sweet nothings and silly emojis reminding each other that we were in love, and that we were going to be together. She also told me to check out the song *Apocalypse* by Cigarettes after Sex. *Harry, this fits us perfectly. Better than Fade into You.*

I was brewing a second pot of coffee in my office

and looking up the song *Apocalypse* on my phone when Dana appeared in the doorway, smiling while I looked at her in bug-eyed surprise.

"Shocked, huh?" she asked.

"That's an understatement."

"May I?" Dana asked, pointing to a chair in front of my desk.

"Sure."

"How are you, Harry? You look good."

"Thanks. I'm okay. You?" I asked, sitting on the edge of my desk.

"Okay, too. Hey, do you mind sitting next to me here? You tower over me on the desk. I feel like I'm in the principal's office."

I sat in the chair next to her.

"Much better, Harry. Level field."

"So let me guess, Dana. You're here to say that I can have the theatre and you don't want any part of it anymore."

Dana laughed. "Not quite, Harry, but you're in the ballpark. I've been thinking about this a lot lately and I feel a little guilty. I cheated on you and ended things, at least officially. I think I have been too aggressive about the theatre. I have an alternate offer, no lawyers, none of that shit. Just you and me being reasonable."

"I love the sound of that."

"I know you love this place. It's your baby. Hell, it's even more than that. It's also your parents, it's your spouse, your whole existence—"

"Might as well throw in siblings, cousins, aunts—"

"Ok, ok, I think we both get the metaphor," Dana said, smiling. "I lost realization of this. It got buried under some residual anger."

"Understandable."

"But it is also true that I put a lot of time and energy into it. I cared about it, too, but not like you. It was a business for me. It's so much more for you."

"Right again."

"So that said, let's forget the other number. I'll take 100K."

"Really? That's just a bit over half of what we already agreed on."

"I know. Less money, better karma. I don't want you to lose the Cabrillo. It's been bothering me ever since the settlement. This should make it easier, right?"

"Very big of you, Dana. Thank you."

"I'm sorry for making this hard on you."

"Never mind. Took two to get us here."

"I'll already revised the settlement letter. It's in the mail. No rush on the payment either."

"Thanks."

We chatted for a while and talked about some good times before hugging goodbye. A warm hug befitting of old friends, not former lovers.

"You'll meet someone special, too, Harry."

"Maybe."

"Just give it time and it will happen when you least expect it."

"I think you might be right, Dana."

"Harry, one more thing. Here you go," she said,

handing me the keys to the apartment and The Cabrillo.

*   *   *

It was D-Day. Nadine and I put on our make-up and disguise, suddenly looking like strangers to each other. We took Lyft over to SFMC, holding hands but not speaking at all the entire ride. I'd like to the think it was due to our focus on the big moment, or maybe the weirdness of the disguises, but I sensed something else was going one. Something about us.

SFMC was on the other side of Golden Gate Park, in the Inner Sunset, southeast of the Cabrillo. The driver cut across the park via 19th avenue and then headed east on Judah, the main artery of the Sunset District. We passed by Judah Café where Jackson, myself, and the other wayward bohemians of our Sunsetter movement caught fire for a brief ripple in time. Their faces flittered across my mind's eye. I felt like gathering them all together again to catch up and celebrate the remembrance of things past.

"So, are you two researchers or doctors or something?" our driver asked, suddenly conversational.

"We're scientists, yes," Nadine said.

"What do you study?"

"Ahhh, well, HIV vaccine."

"Cool. You're doing good work. But is that even a problem anymore? Seems like everyone lives forever with it. Look at Magic. He's had it for what 20 or 30 years?"

"He's been lucky and gets the best treatment."

"Well, regardless, you guys are doing good, noble

work."

"Thank you," we both said.

The chatty driver proceeded to deliver a monologue on his aborted studies in economics at San Francisco State, blaming family and financial pressures for forcing him to quit school and drive Lyft during the day and do restaurant work at night. But he still kept up on the latest economic research, whose "stagnation" bothered him.

"Man, we haven't come up with anything big since the Supply-side theories. I mean, we're so stuck. It's either Supply-side or Keynesian demand-side. And, hell, Supply-side isn't any big innovation. It's just the damn opposite of Keynes."

"Never thought about it that way," I said, wishing we could ride in silence.

"We need a new theory. Obama did 1930s New Deal stuff and this crazy man president is doing Reaganomics again. It's all so old and unoriginal. We need a new Marx, or Smith, anyone to come up with something different that actually works."

He then went on a long monologue about how the U.S. economy has been permanently damaged by a drunk Arthur Laffer drawing a graph on a barroom cocktail napkin and birthing Supply-side economics.

"Can you believe that shit? A scribbling drunk economist has us in debt over 21 trillion dollars."

"Crazy," Nadine humored him.

"Seriously, guys, I know you're scientists, not economists, but you're citizens. Before Laffer, our debt was peanuts. Then Reagan ran with it and now we're fucked. The chickens are coming home to roost soon, and those chickens will speak Mandarin!"

I'd never heard of Arthur Laffer or his graph. Thankfully, we arrived at SFMC and the economics lesson ended. When his Hyundai sped off, Nadine and I looked at each other, gazing the same message to each other, and walked towards the entrance.

We knew the layout very well. We'd studied the map, had done walk-throughs several times, and visualized every step of the way. We took the elevator to the 6th floor. We slid our fake IDs into the slot to go through the secure doors and headed to the checkpoint. Our first real test.

TSA types scanned our badges and looked at a monitor with our fake credentials. Everything seemed fine until a woman unexpectedly asked us, "So what brings you to the 6th floor?"

"Research," Nadine said.

"Of course," her male partner said. "What kind specifically?"

"Ahh, we're working on the Pre-cancer Atlas Project," she calmly answered.

"What's that?" he asked, looking at me.

"Mapping of cancer cells at the cellular and molecular level to see how cancer initiates and progresses with greater precision." I had studied my lines for this cinéma vérité.

"What does that have to do with today? And here?"

Nadine said, "Mice. We're using mice to generate some data for PCA"

"PCA?" the man queried.

"Pre-cancer Atlas," the woman said, proudly. "Come on, Bruce, use your head. She just said that." She looked at Nadine and added, "You have to spell everything out for him."

"Whatever," he said, "You guys are new here, huh? Haven't seen you before."

"Yes, sir. We just came in from NIH. It's a new project," I said.

"We're excited about it. It has great potential," Nadine added. "We're working on some special mice for the project. And if all goes well, they'll come back to DC with us for the next trial."

The man furrowed his brow. "Ok, do you have papers for that?"

Nadine opened her backpack and pulled out our authorization form, which the man immediately read over. "Hmmm, signed by the SFMC President," he said, showing it to his partner.

"Pretty legit looking," she said.

He handed it back. "You guys are clear."

"Thanks," we both said.

Nadine and I walked towards the designated room. We didn't say a word to each other. When we got to the room, I pressed my badge against the sensor and the door opened. Unbeknownst to us there were two guards seated at a desk. Jackson never mentioned that. My heart sank like an elevator whose wires had been suddenly severed.

We're fucked.

We answered the same questions as before. I tried to

remain calm, but I'm not sure I pulled it off. Nadine stumbled over her words as well. This wasn't in the game plan. The more talkative guard insisted this was high security and seemed confused why we hadn't been here before.

"There has to be a first for everything," I said.

"Smart ass attitude will get you kicked out."

"Or even worse than kicked out," the quiet one said, breaking his silence.

Nadine rose to the moment. "Gentlemen, this is a major new initiative that is part of Joe Biden's Moonshot program. Are you familiar with that?"

They both nodded in a way that showed they were not at all familiar with it.

"PCA could be the key to solving cancer and saving millions. We have specialized mice here that we need access to. You'll be seeing a lot of us. This is just day one," she said, pulling out the authorization form and handing it to the guys.

They looked at each other with a capitulatory stare. "Ok, I believe you," he said looking directly at Nadine. "You're suspicious though," he said turning to me.

I smiled and shrugged.

"I'll keep an eye on him," Nadine said, winking at the fool.

The quiet one typed something into his laptop and the talkative one scanned our badges. We went through another door behind them and were thankfully alone in a large room with a variety of animals: mice, rats, rabbits, pigs and monkeys. Nadine and I made sure not to talk since the room was likely bugged. We communicated with our eyes and gestures, cognizant of cameras looming in each corner of the room, just in case the insiders didn't render them dysfunctional as promised.

Nadine seemed calmer and more confident after seizing the day with the unexpected guards. I followed her lead. We counted eight boxes over from the left and Nadine pointed to the one. I took out my key while Nadine went over to the mice cages to get our decoys. I opened little door number 8. It was very cold and smoky with dry-ice-like fumes spilling out. I couldn't see anything, so I reached in, searching with my right hand and feeling a freezing cold box. Even though I had on latex gloves, my fingers instantly stuck to the icy steel, I instinctively recoiled and felt layers of latex and skin peeling off. I silently screamed, staring at my bloody fingers.

"Shit," I whispered.

I put my left hand under my right to try and prevent any blood from dripping on the floor and turning the room into an OJ-like crime scene. Nadine pulled out a first aid kit from her backpack. She used gauze to dry the blood and some antiseptic to clean the fingers. Then she bandaged all five of them, methodically and precisely. This kit wasn't in our package. She had prepared this one on her own. She was on fire while I was a mess.

We looked around, trying to find something to pull this thing out. There was nothing, but I had an idea. I took Nadine's bag, which had a long strap. I gripped the bag and flung the strap towards the rear of the frozen box. After four attempts, I had it resting behind the box and pulled it out slowly and carefully. When it got to the edge,

I stopped. Nadine had found a silver tray that would hold the box. She held it under opening, and I slid the container onto the tray. Nadine put it on a table next to the mouse cage.

It was the moment of truth. I lifted the top panel of the container. After the smoke cleared, we were staring at what looked like a brain.

At least, part of one.

Nadine picked it up using rubber forceps. Sure enough the top right half was missing. *Back and to the left,* echoed in my head. In the area that had been blown out, there was a small hole. I put my finger in it. The hole narrowed as it went to the rear of the brain, confirming that the bullet had entered the front. The entrance of a wound is always larger than the exit. JFK had been shot from the front like every good conspiracy theorist from Oliver Stone all the way to the lonely and mocked blogger whose conspiracy site had only a few hits from his friends and family.

Upon confirmation, we sprang into action. Nadine placed the brain in a plastic bag and into the bottom of the mouse cage, tucked snuggly with bubble wrap so it wouldn't move if shaken. I sealed the sides closed with an invisible calk for extra security.

We exited the animal house and I steeled my nerves for the first hurdle of our exit plan.

"Finished," Nadine said to the two guards, calmly placing the mouse cage on their desk. They inspected the cage and then wrote down the cage's code listed on the bottom. There were eight mice frantically running and bouncing off each like rodent bumper cars in their little prison. They were clearly startled at the sudden change in their sad lives.

The talkative guard pushed the cage towards me and pointed to Nadine's backpack. She gave it to him and he began his search. He opened the front pocket and peered in with a flashlight. He took a long time and shuffled things around. Before he opened the main compartment, he looked up stoically at both of us. We smiled. He pulled out notebooks, books, the first aid kit, thoroughly going through the wrong thing.

"Just nerdy scientist stuff," I said.

He ignored me and continued his probe. When everything was pulled out, I held my breath praying he'd be satisfied.

"All set," he said.

"Hey," the quiet one interjected. "What happened to your hand?"

I smiled sheepishly. "Hazards of the job. We were doing some injections and I messed up. Mice can be pretty uncooperative."

The talkative one nodded, suspicion in his eyes, before saying, "Have a good day. We will see you tomorrow."

"Yeah, see you tomorrow," I said.

While waiting for the elevators, both of us took deep breaths and exchanged looks of relief mixed with the fear that we still weren't in the clear. We went up to the eighth floor for the hand off, but there was no sign of the Bogdonaviches. Nadine checked her phone and then showed it to me. A text from Jackson:

Good news: Cameras disabled without trouble
Bad news: Bogdonaviches out.
Finish the job. Waiting in the parking lot for you.
You got this.

We headed to the final security, where there was a line. Nadine was ahead of me and we watched the scrutiny given to those ahead. It was intense. They were frisking and taking everything apart. Maybe the two guys let them know that we were suspicious, and they started doing this TSA on steroids approach just for us.

But the brain was hidden well. The mouse cage looked like any other except maybe a little extra room at the bottom. The metal base was a bit higher than most to create the extra compartment, but only a discerning eye would pick that up.

It was Nadine's turn. She signed out while they superficially check her bag. She walked ahead and then waited for me. They did the same for me, checking the mouse cage. All seemed fine. I signed out and they handed the cage back to me. The desk phone rang and one of them answered while the other continued checking those next in line.

Nadine and I were walking out, nearly in the clear, when we heard one of them yell, "Hold on, you two."

We turned around.

"Need to check the cage one more time," one said walking towards us.

We stood there as frozen as JFK's brain. As the guy approached, it hit me that they were on to us somehow.

Maybe the guys upstairs checked the locker with JFK's brain that was now empty. Something was up.

The guard put his hands out to take the cage. I put it in his hands while simultaneously kicking him in the balls as hard as I could and taking the cage back as he went down in a heap. Nadine and I sprinted for the exit. I was leading the way like a fullback to Nadine's half-back, blocking people with my free hand. Pandemonium ensued, people screaming, security running behind us, the building alarms going off.

We heard several people screaming, "Stop them! Stop them!" but nobody did. People were either running in fear or paralyzed while watching the drama unfold. We made it to the exit, flew down the stairs, sprinted about 50 feet and saw Jackson's car with Maxy standing at the rear-passenger-side door, holding it open. Nadine jumped in first and I followed. Maxy slammed the door, jumped in front, and Jackson floored it.

"Go, Jackson, go!" All of us yelled.

I looked out the window and saw two guys running after the car, guns aimed.

"Get low!" I screamed and grabbed the top of Nadine's head, pulling her down with me. We heard multiple pops, the back window shattered all over us.

"Holy fuck!" I yelled.

"Oh my fucking god," Nadine encored.

"You guys okay back there?" Jackson asked, driving with his head as low as it could go.

"Yeah, yeah," we said in unison and then Nadine added, "Get us the fuck out of here, Jackson!"

Jackson swerved to the right at full speed, car nearly tipping, heading down 19th avenue and away from SFMC.

Sirens replaced the sound of gunshots. They're after us," Nadine said in a rattled voice.

"We're fine. We're making the switch at Lake Merced," Jackson said.

"Switch to what?" Nadine asked.

"Switching cars. Got a Prius waiting for us. Nobody commits crimes in a Prius. Gonna torch this."

Five minutes later, we were at Merced, sirens fading away. Jackson pulled up next to a black Prius in a parking lot behind what appeared to be an abandoned building. We were the only ones there and now the sirens were no longer even audible. We got out of the SUV and all of us stripped down to skivvies, tossing the clothes, backpacks, disguises, everything except the mouse cage, into the back of the SUV. We put on a new set of clothes waiting for us in the trunk of the Prius. When we finished, we got in the new getaway car, except for Jackson. He pulled out two red gas containers from the Prius, and doused the insides of the SUV, soaking everything we had just worn, carried, or touched. Then he backed away about 10 feet, took out on old fashioned silver flip-top lighter, lit it, and tossed it into the SUV.

The inside lit up like a bonfire and then boom! The gas tank exploded, and it was ablaze with flames flying high in the night sky. Jackson dashed into the Prius and for a few moments, we were transfixed by the soaring flames.

"Damn, Jackson," I said from the backseat. "Straight out of *The Town*."

"Where do you think I got the idea? Saw it during Boston Week at the Cabrillo."

*   *   *

Jackson sped us out of the scene, past San Francisco State and onto 19th Ave, heading north to the Golden Gate along the same path of my recent attempt at facing my phobia. None of this was part of the plan since Nadine and I were supposed to have handed the brain off to the Bogdonaviches and then leave SFMC quietly on our own. Jackson explained that Mercy and Curtis used the excuse of some new progressive Humboldt County law that would solve their marijuana farm issues, but "the truth is they got cold feet."

"Left us high and dry," Nadine said.

"Yeah, what happened to honor among thieves?" Maxy said, turning back to us, craning his rubber neck so that he nearly stretched his head right between us. "But all the better for us."

"How so?" I asked. "Because of the bullets that whistled by us and the pile of shattered glass. Christ!"

Jackson explained that their share would be divided among the four of us. Another 1.5 million dollars each, but it didn't sink in. This was all about the money, but at this moment I couldn't feel the money. All I felt was the insanity of being shot at, the intensity of a life or death escape, and the anxious thrill of actually pulling off the heist. We rode in silence for a spell, each of us trying to process all that happened, until Jackson broke it. "Hey, it wasn't the plan, but we improvised and pulled it off. And what a fucking rush it was!"

"I can barely breathe, Jackson. My heart is pounding out of its ribcage."

"Me, too!" Nadine said.

It was all too much to absorb as I saw the tips of the golden towers looming ahead. Sitting safely in the back under the cover of night, gephyrophobia couldn't gather any momentum. It was buried under the criminal adrenalin overtaking my system. I didn't even have to close my eyes on the cross. Halfway over the bridge, high over the Pacific, two oncoming police cars, lights swirling and sirens roaring, caught our attention, but in seconds they had raced by us without any delay.

Hitting land and no longer in the city felt like a benchmark of safety. Jackson went over the next steps. He was going to drop Nadine and me off at the Larkspur ferry. We would catch the last boat back to the Wharf, maintaining zero communication on the boat as if we didn't know each other, and then going our separate ways home. Maxy and Jackson would change cars again in Larkspur and then head north all the way to Eureka, which was straight up 101, about 300 miles north of San Francisco on the coast along Humboldt Bay, not far from the Oregon border.

There they would meet Mr. Y, or a proxy, and deliver the brain and get the cash. Maxy and Jackson would lay low in Eureka for a spell while Madam X's team released the brain into the media by shipping it to CNN, complete with a DNA analysis confirming it was the real thing and a report of the bullet's entry and exit wounds. The news would hit fast and hard, rocking the American psyche. Once the media drama commenced, Jackson would head back to the city, give Nadine and me our bounty, before disappearing into Big Bear.

We wended across the hills above Sausalito, hit flat land by Mill Valley, before exiting 101 at Larkspur, a sleepy Marin County town (like every other one), and headed east towards Larkspur Landing, where the ferry terminal was. Jackson parked the Prius on a quiet, unlit street about a half-mile walk to the dock. There wasn't a soul in site. Jackson took the mouse cage and put it in the back of a car just in front of where we had parked. The mice weren't moving at all. They were probably traumatized, maybe even dead from the drama. This time it was one of those tiny two-seat Smart cars. Jackson was right about the job being prepared with meticulous precision. Madam X, Mr. Y, and whoever Z didn't miss a beat in their criminal designs.

"Another car that doesn't befit criminal activity," I said as the four of us stood together, probably for the last time ever.

"Exactly," Jackson agreed. "So, here's where we part, fab four. Thank you for a job well done. Lay low and go about your regular business as if nothing happened. And keep an eye out for some serious breaking news."

We four-way fist bumped and then Harry and Maxy jumped into the Smart car. Jackson made a U-turn, pulling up beside us, and rolled down his window, "Remember, split up and no contact until things calm down. You two are on hold, got that?" We both nodded in agreement. Jackson gave us a thumbs-up just before he and Maxy disappeared into the Marin County night.

Nadine and I held hands, looking into each other's eyes, not saying anything. Finally, she said, "I guess we part here."

I took a deep breath. "This won't be easy."

We kissed and then held each other tightly for a long time.

"I'll miss you," she whispered in my ear, before pulling away and walking down the street without looking back.

*   *   *

As I got closer to the terminal, I could see San Quentin just beyond the dock. The irony was not lost. I'd certainly thought about the worst-case scenario many times, but it never gained true or profound traction amidst the feverish rush of Nadine and me, saving the Cabrillo, separating from Dana, and all that was Jackson.

But there it was right in front of my eyes at the end of the road. The same prison that held Neal Cassady for two years on possession of a tiny amount of marijuana some 60 years ago.

Suddenly very alone on dark unfamiliar roads and prison concretely ahead, I was overcome with a sense of dread. Jackson speeding off into the night reminded me of Cassady, the unreliable holy goof, leaving Kerouac alone in Mexico in a time of need. Was that what Jackson had just done? Was this our *On the Road* moment? Or was Nadine about to play that role? Or both…

*   *   *

I bought my ticket for the 10:40 ferry and boarded. There was no sign of Nadine amidst a sparsely crowded boat. Despite the understandable no-contact rule, I desperately wanted to see her face. Make eye contact. The slightest gesture of recognition affirming our togetherness would anchor me from sinking deeper into a consumptive abyss.

I had walked the indoor deck and then went up to search the outdoor deck. I had no phone to text her since the burner was burned.

Where could she have gone? Did she even board?

The ferry left the dock and made its way across the North Bay. I was the only person on the freezing top deck as we passed right along the edge of San Quentin, whose giant imposing beige walls were eerily majestic in the Marin night. Even prisons in San Francisco had an element of beauty to them. We were so close I could make out the shadowy guards in the towers above the walls. If the universe was sending me a message, I didn't need Madam Francoise to decipher it.

I went to the other side of the boat desperately in need of another view. As I stared at the glowing magnificence of the Golden Gate at night, someone lightly grabbed my hand.

"Hey," Nadine whispered.

"So happy to see you," I said, immediately anchored.

"Me, too. I'm gonna miss you so much."

"Too much to handle."

"We have no choice this time. Focus on the Cabrillo, I'll focus on school, and when the dust settles, it will be you and me."

"And Christine?"

Nadine put her index finger to my lips, shaking her head. "Never mind that, Harry." She clutched both my hands tightly, kissed me, and said, "Until next time, my sweet."

Then she disappeared below deck.

16 — Apocalypse

When I disembarked at the Ferry Building, there was no sign of Nadine. *Let go*, I told myself. I had some help in this mission because I suddenly realized that with all the excitement of the evening, I hadn't eaten a thing since breakfast. I was starving and wanted a huge hearty meal, a steak, and some high-end red wine to ease it and me down. I knew a landmark San Francisco spot, John's Grill on Ellis Street, near the Tenderloin, that was open until midnight. I Ubered there and took a seat at the small eight-seat bar. I ordered a medium rare New York strip, fries, and asparagus, jumbo shrimp cocktail to start, and looked over the wine list. I thought of ordering the most expensive bottle they had, a $450 Mondavi Opus One Cab. Why not? I would be obscenely rich soon and had earned a moment of 1%er indulgence, even if it was all by my lonesome, but decided that such an order would make me too memorable on a night I needed to be decidedly unmemorable.

"And I'll have the Oakville Cab."

"Only by the bottle," the grumpy old bartender said.

"I know."

He popped it open and poured me a taste.

"Excellent, sir."

Stoically, he filled my glass. The wine was damn good. At $91, it was a far cry from the Mondavi, but it was still well above my palette's budget. As I drank the first glass down quickly, hoping the noble grape would calm my frayed nerves, I noticed a newsflash on the small bar T.V., surrounded by photos of local luminaries (I recognized Harvey Milk and Lawrence Ferlinghetti). The scroll beneath a replay of the Stanford-Cal football game read, "Breaking News, theft at San Francisco Medical Center."

This was KRON4, a local Bay Area station. I'm sure it wouldn't be long before it went national. I thought of asking the bartender to turn on CNN, but I just wanted to eat my meal in peace, turn off and tune out everything from the last few hours and weeks for just a few moments. While that didn't work (I replayed every step of tonight in my head, slowing the frames down at the wild getaway and the farewell with Nadine), I did enjoy every bite and sip of the meal. Thank you, John, whoever you were.

When I got home, I took a Xanax, jumped into bed, avoided checking the news on any device, and slipped into a deep, dreamless sleep.

*   *   *

I woke up rested and ready to see how much the world knew about last night. I turned on the news, and sure enough, CNN confirmed last night had actually happened. The report had no specificity. They had no idea what was stolen from SFMC, but they knew it had to be something significant. Reporters and "experts" speculated that it was secret experiments on chemical or biological weapons. Others suggested it had to do with Russian hacking of the election with high-tech cyber security research going on undercover at the medical facility to throw the Russians off the digital scent. Others mused about the Mueller Report, AI research, breakthroughs in cancer, the human genome, DNA, and on and on missing the mark by miles, thousands of miles.

The only evidence on us was sketch artist renditions of Nadine and me in disguise, no doubt given by the two guards at the desk. They had the heights all wrong since we had lifts in our shoes and our weights were too much since we had put padding under the lab coats. The make-up, prosthetic putty, and contacts took care of the faces. The renditions were of different people. They had found the torched SUV, but all the forensics were washed away by the bleach Jackson had used. Nothing was left but a pile of ash and blackened metal.

Feeling some relief that so far, the crime had been well-executed and tracks seemingly well-covered. Madam X and Mr. Y were on their game.

I lingered a little longer in bed, thinking about Nadine, before getting up to start my day as a I normally would. I wanted the staff to see me engaging in quotidian habits as if nothing had happened last night. I showered, made a pot of coffee at concessions, grabbed a croissant from Café Zeitgeist across the street, and after breakfast, did my walk through of the Cabrillo. As I was checking on Theatre 2, revelation struck. I knew how I would get through these next anxious and lonely Nadine-free weeks: *North Beach Exit*.

*   *   *

During that time, I continued my daily routine at

the Cabrillo, followed the news reports which soon faded to the background and then into oblivion (aided by the Trump circus which always stole the spotlight), and at night cocooned myself in my apartment working on *North Beach Exit*. It took me a while to sort and make sense of the cocktail napkin eruption and turn it into a semi-cohesive draft of a screenplay. From there with the coffee flowing to keep me going late into the night, I fleshed out the skeleton story adding in new scenes, characters, and plot twists. The long dormant muse proved more than just a one-night fling at Veusvio and carried me through long hours across many nights. I was having my own *On the Road* spontaneous-prose experience that lasted almost as long as Kerouac's 20 days of relentless writing.

There had been no contact from anyone and as much as I wanted to see Nadine or hear from Jackson so that I could disprove my Cassady-Mexico suspicions, I stuck to the plan thanks to the distractive immersion in the screenplay.

Then 15 days after the theft, CNN broke the news of JFK's brain. It was all anyone on the news or in the theatre was talking about. I screened Stone's JFK in both theatres for every showing and sold out every show.

But it didn't take long for alternative facts to rear their poisonous heads. Fox, alt-right outlets, and social media began buzzing in dispute that the brain was really JFK's despite rock hard DNA evidence. Some claimed it was a deep state hoax. Others posed that Oliver Stone was behind the "fake brain." Sure enough, the truth disintegrated amidst the cacophony of too many voices.

*   *   *

And then Jackson arrived.

I was in my office late at night. The Cabrillo was closed up, the staff was gone, and I was steadily working my way through a bottle of burgundy while reading and revising a hard copy of the screenplay when my phone vibrated with a text from Jackson: *Hey man, I'm in back. Don't have the key*.

I let Jackson in and we went up my apartment and sat in the kitchen. I brought a new bottle of burgundy up and he carried up a duffle bag diagonally strapped across his chest.

"You been following the news?" he asked as I poured two glasses and we toasted, no words just an affirmative nod.

"Yeah, it's not going according to the plan, right?"

"No, not really. The truth can no longer set you free in this era."

"Not surprising, I guess. We were a little naïve."

"Not completely," Jackson said and then plopped the duffle bag on the table, unzipping it to reveal stacks and stacks of 100-dollar bills. "Madam X is a woman of her word."

Jackson started piling the packets neatly on the table until he had nine evenly stacked towers rising up about two feet, plus one just over half the height of the others.

"Harry, nine at $500,000 dollars each, one at 300K. You can do the math."

I took a deep breath. "This is scary money."

"Don't let it scare you," Jackson said before going into a long lecture on laundering. I had done some research on this and Jackson affirmed it. I had to start gradually increasing my revenue into the nightly bank deposits at no more than 10-15% more than usual. Banks get suspicious of significant jumps, seeing it as an immediate laundering red flag that they are obligated to report. The recent surge in ticket sales from the brawl served as a nice cover to increase revenue at a higher rate than pre-brawl. To clean up personal spending money or use it to pay some creditors, I could make occasional trips to a casino, get some chips, play for a spell, and then cash in the chips for a check as long as it's under 10K, which requires reporting to the IRS. This was old school money laundering.

"Just be careful, Harry. No foolishly large expenditures. Low on the radar, at least for a while."

"Don't worry about that."

"You got a safe?" Jackson asked.

"Yeah, sure."

"Right after I leave, lock it all up."

Meanwhile, Maxy had fallen in love with the peace and quiet of Eureka. He decided to stay there, avoid the track, and open up a small café in the downtown. As for Jackson, he was heading south to Big Bear to get the winery up and running, and hopefully not alone. He bought Samira an open-ended ticket to LA that could be used anytime in the next 90 days.

"We'll see," he said.

"Good luck, Jacko. And thanks. Thanks for every-thing."

"You, too, Harry. All the best for you and Nadine. I'm pulling for you guys. Now I need to make one more delivery before I head to Big Bear."

I walked Jackson down to the back door. He gave me a big farewell hug and before disappearing into the night, he said, "Come down and see me in a few months."

I went back up to my apartment, took a pillowcase from the closet, and placed the mountain of money into it. I went down to the office, feeling like a thief break-ing into my own business, and took down the framed poster of *On the Waterfront*, which hid the safe. I neatly stacked the loot as far back as I could, closed the door and spun the dial, listening to its ticking spin all the way to silence.

*   *   *

The next day, Sunday afternoon, I was drinking rosé at the bar alone and revising *North Beach Exit* (I did not subscribe to first thought, best thought). I want-ed the noise of the theatre in the background and not the oppressive lonely silence of my apartment. I was soon distracted by chatting with a couple of women that looked like newcomers to the Cabrillo. After they left, I couldn't regain focus.

"Patrick, how about you join me for a glass of whatever you want?"

"Really, Harry?"

"Sure," I insisted.

Patrick poured himself a glass of Syrah and we toasted to Joel. "Look at him, Harry. He went from awkward adolescent to Valentino. Such a transformation."

"Indeed. But at the expense of Mariana," I said.

"Did you see who he's dating now?"

"No."

"He brought her in the other night. The night you weren't here," Joel said, too observationally for my liking.

"How is she?" I asked.

"Don't know, but the outside is a very striking. Black woman with that old style 70s Diana Ross afro. I love that hairstyle. So authentic. She looks like that actress in *The Kids are All Right*. What's her name?"

"Yaya DaCosta," I answered. "She's beautiful. Damn, Joel is on fire."

"He sure is. Such a fool. Pride cometh before the fall."

"Who's a fool, Patrick?" Sandy asked, sneaking up behind me.

"Anybody who's in love," I said.

"You said it, boss. Love is for idiots, right Patrick?" Sandy said. Patrick nodded and then suddenly pretended to be busy cleaning bar paraphernalia.

"So, Sandy. Pretty good Sunday, huh?" I asked.

"Not bad, Harry. *Lost in Paris* is doing better than expected. Appeals to our quirky regulars."

"That covers most of our regulars."

"Indeed. Hey, are you guys following this crazy case at SFMC?"

"I heard something, but not sure what happened," I responded, hoping my insouciance wasn't too phony.

"Stolen mice. Who steals mice?"

"Cats," I parried.

"Harry, that's terrible. And cats don't steal mice, they kill them. You know, I can't help but think it's related to the traffic camera crimes."

I almost choked on my rosé.

"Easy, boss," Sandy said slapping my back.

I cleared my throat after a few coughs. "Just went down the wrong pipe. What's the connection? I don't get it. Pretty disparate things."

"I don't know, but they are both such weird crimes that seemingly have no monetary gain. I am following things very closely. I don't think they are disconnected."

"Good luck, Nancy Drew."

"And you know what I still can't get out of my head?"

Trying to distract Sandy, I gestured towards Patrick.

"Besides him," Sandy said with a wry grin and a flirty eye roll. Patrick pretended not to hear.

"No idea," I said, knowing exactly what she was referring to.

"Your twin who was doing work on a speed camera right before the crime."

"Sandy, I'm not an electrician working for the city. Will you let it go?"

"I know, I know, I am just kidding you, Harry. But you got to admit it was just so weird. Anyway, the story is already getting buried by Trump because he owns the news now. So tired of him and the desperate Democrats getting nowhere. Just want it to be over. I miss Obama so much."

"We all do."

"But I digress. I don't have any evidence on the connection, but my gut is churning. I might solve this case, Harry."

"Good luck. I hope you do. It would be good publicity for the theatre."

"Harry, are you okay?" Patrick asked.

"Yeah, fine. Why?"

"You looked stressed out. I know you have a lot on your plate with the business and all, but this is a different look."

"No, just, ahh, lots on my mind."

Suddenly, my mouth was dry and my heart rate multiplied. I felt exposed. Sandy struck a nerve. I could see both of them staring at me. I really needed to explain this somehow so I launched into a monologue on Dana leaving me and how I was not dealing well with it.

"I knew something was off with you."

"That's too bad, but you'll bounce back," Patrick said. "I'd say you're a pretty eligible bachelor, Harry."

"I second that," Sandy said.

I shrugged. "Thank you guys. Not true, but kind nonetheless."

"It's not easy in the single world," Sandy said, shooting another ignored glance at Patrick.

"Harry, being alone is not so bad. It's liberating,"

Patrick said, walking to the other end of the bar, which was empty.

"But Harry is not alone," Sandy said, patting me on the back.

*   *   *

Another week had passed. Things were getting back to normal on the surface. The news of the theft continued its fade, the police had not been in touch, and it was all quiet on the Sandy-the-sleuth front. Her obsession with Patrick and concern for Dana and I breaking up seemed to take precedence.

Once the script was done, I couldn't hold out anymore and had to see Nadine. The angst of not being able to see her must have catalyzed the eruption of *North Beach Exit*. Now that it was out, I had nowhere to channel my need for Nadine.

After a couple of snifters of 10-year-old Laphroaig, I decided to walk the plank on a Friday evening.

I buzzed her apartment, but no one answered. Undeterred I sat on the stoop and waited like a lonely fool in love. A few hours later, I saw her walking up Cabrillo and not alone.

"Harry," she said "What a surprise."

"Hi Nadine."

There was an awkward pause as Nadine looked at me and then turned to the woman next to her. "Ahhh, Harry, this is Christine."

"Hi Christine. I've heard a lot about you," I said with no ill will.

"Likewise," she responded calmly.

"Do you want to come up?" Nadine asked.

"If that's ok."

Christine said, "You know what, I need some more air. I'll take a short walk and give you guys some time."

"Thanks, babe," Nadine said.

My heart somersaulted at hearing her say "babe." I immediately assumed we were over, but I went upstairs for confirmation for my stupid heart.

I tried to steel myself as we headed upstairs. I didn't want to put on a pathetic display even though I already felt like a puddle of tears could emerge at any second. We sat down in the living area of the small studio. There was a big Persian rug covering most of the floor and the only furniture was an exotically designed, round coffee table surrounded by large colorful puffy pillows scattered on the floor.

Nadine poured us each a glass of wine and we sat on the pillows, not so close to each other. For a few silent awkward moments, we focused on the wine as if it were panacea, instead of broaching the inevitable. I also realized it was the first time we didn't toast before drinking.

"So, ahhh," Nadine finally began, "that was nice of Christine to give us some space."

"Yeah, very big of her," I agreed.

"Did Jackson visit?"

"Sure did."

"It's ridiculous, isn't it. I mean I had less than $100 to my name before he made the delivery."

"It's an obscene amount."

"That it is, but towards a good cause."

"Yeah, that ultimately did nothing."

"Maybe it just needs time to sink into the American consciousness. It's a lot to absorb all at once. Anyway, that is out of our hands. All that matters is that we did it, Harry. That's worth a toast."

We clinked and drank, both of us emptying our glasses. Nadine refilled before initiating again. "Jesus, Harry, are you not going to say anything?"

"Why do I have to?"

"Because you never bullshitted around in our conversations. I loved your directness."

"Well, maybe something has shifted, Nadine. Christ, I mean I just saw you with Christine. Is that not supposed have any impact? Come on, Nadine, snap out of it!"

Nadine smiled. "That's better. That's my Harry."

I was shaking my head. "You're callous."

"I don't think so. You don't even know what's going on. You're making a ton of assumptions."

"Just one actually."

"And that is?"

"Don't make me say it. That's on you," I said, staring into Nadine's eyes. She didn't look away. It was really the first genuine eye contact that we'd made.

"You think we're broken up. Well, I haven't ended things. If I had, you'd know by now."

I rolled my eyes. "Come on, Nadine. Can we not bullshit this anymore? How about a little reality, a little come-to-Jesus moment? I am tired of the games."

"That's rude. I'm not playing games. Never have. Not intentionally."

"Look, all the delays and hesitations have been from you. I've been all in from day one. From the very first moment I saw you. In fact, I came down here tonight to tell you how much I love you and try to get us to go forward and look what I walked into. You and your *babe*."

"I shouldn't have said that in front of you. It's too early, but you're jumping to conclusions, Harry."

"I think the conclusions jumped at me. In my face actually."

Nadine was shaking her head. "You're obsessing on one thing."

"I'm wrong? You're not choosing Christine?"

Nadine looked out the window that overlooked Cabrillo Street before asking, "Did you listen to that song?"

"What song?

"Apocalypse."

"No, I didn't. What does that matter?"

"It does. You'd know if you listened. It explains us."

"I can't believe we're talking about a song. Just tell me what's going on. Though the damn title probably says it all."

"Again, you're assuming—"

"Never mind, Nadine. I get it. I think I should go. Christine will be back soon."

Nadine grabbed my forearm as I stood up and

pulled me back down.

"I want you here when she returns. I want all three of us here," Nadine said, pausing for a healthy sip of the red wine. "Harry, what we have, is magical. Never had anything like it. Not with Christine, not with anyone, and I believe I never will have that again. Not to the level we hit. Our connection doesn't happen twice in a lifetime. Rarely, once. You're my one," Nadine said, tears trickling down her cheeks.

I could feel my eyes pooling up, but I fought them back. "What are you saying, Nadine? Are you not ending it?"

Nadine drank more wine, wiped her cheeks dry, but not for long.

"Those things you call games, were not games, Harry. They are my demons."

"I know. I know. I'm sorry I said that. It was just frustration."

"It's okay. I understand. You've been patient. Very patient. It's actually amazed me."

"I miss you, Nadine. These last few weeks have been torture. Every minute apart I ache for you."

"I don't want to lose you."

"You're not. I am yours."

Nadine took deep breaths with her eyes closed before looking at me wordlessly for a long time. Then she came close and we kissed, my tears sneaking past the defeated defenses. When she pulled away, we looked into each other's eyes for a long time, until Nadine said, "Be with us."

"What does that mean?"

"All three of us."

"Are you just making this up right now?"

"No, Christine and I have been talking about it for weeks. It's the only way forward."

"For you."

Nadine shrugged, conceding that.

"She's agreed?"

"Yes, to try it. Let's just try it, Harry. Let's not be so conventional and boring. We can avoid the plateaus this way and it's the Beat thing to do. Like Jack, Neal, and Carolyn."

"Right, and that ended great," I said rolling my eyes. I took a deep breath, surprised that I had never thought of this possibility. "These things never work out, Nadine. Truth is I don't want to share you. I love you too much to share you."

"If you loved me so much, wouldn't you be willing to share. Willing to do anything?"

"It won't work. Hell, I don't even know Christine and I'm going to be in a relationship with her in our throuple. What a stupid word, too!"

"We've got to let it happen naturally. You two need to get to know each other and the three of us need to get to know each other as well. It'll take time, but I think you will really dig Christine and she will take to you, too. It could be amazing. Don't be so conservative."

"Do you have something stronger than wine?"

Nadine poured us both a glass of Scotch. "You

know, this is a risk for me, too. You two may fall in love and leave me. Harry, the future is always uncertain."

Then Christine appeared.

"Do you two need more time?"

"No, no," Nadine said. "Join us."

Nadine poured Christine a drink and she joined us at the table. There we were, the three of us. Christine was very much the opposite in appearance to Nadine. She had light brown straight hair, parted perfectly in the middle, very 70s hippie style. She was a few inches taller than Nadine, thin, and attractive, but plain.

Nadine raised her glass. "Dare I?" Christine nodded and raised her glass.

"Harry?"

I gripped my glass and downed the rest of the Scotch. Then I stood up and said, "I wish you two the best, but I can't do this."

As I headed to the door, Nadine said, "Harry, just think about it a little more. Give it time. It's too fast to reject this."

*   *   *

When I got back to the theatre, it was 1am, we were closed, and the staff was gone. I walked around the theatre for a while, taking solace in the quiet and soaking in that the Cabrillo was back from the financial abyss.

I went up to projection room, scanned my collection of films, and chose *Cinema Paradiso*. On my way downstairs, I poured myself a pint of Anchor Steam, and then sat in my favorite seat in the empty theatre.

While the previews played, I searched my phone for the song, *Apocalypse*, in the process noticing several text messages and missed calls from her. Ignoring those, I listened to the song, dried my eyes, and then turned off my phone.

The lights dimmed and I watched the movie.

THE END

Ken Janjigian is also the author of *Gone West,* a collection of novellas set in San Francisco, and the novel, *Defending Infinity*. He is an assistant dean at American University focusing on international education and teaches the course, American Film and Culture Studies. Originally from Boston, Ken taught English in Italy before eventually settling in the D.C. area. He also spent several impactful years in San Francisco in the 1990s. To this day, it feels like he never really left the city.